THE GIRL IN THE WATER

J.A. BAKER

Boldwood

First published in 2017. This edition published in Great Britain in 2023 by Boldwood Books Ltd.

Cover Design by Head Design Ltd.

Cover Illustration: Shutterstock

A CIP catalogue record for this book is available from the British Library.

Paperback ISBN 978-1-80549-180-4

Large Print ISBN 978-1-80549-181-1

Hardback ISBN 978-1-80549-179-8

Ebook ISBN 978-1-80549-182-8

Kindle ISBN 978-1-80549-183-5

Audio CD ISBN 978-1-80549-174-3

MP3 CD ISBN 978-1-80549-175-0

Digital audio download ISBN 978-1-80549-178-1

Boldwood Books Ltd
23 Bowerdean Street
London SW6 3TN
www.boldwoodbooks.com

For my husband Richard, my children, and my late parents who nurtured my love of reading from a young age. Those Saturday morning visits to the library as a child have finally paid off. If only you were here to see it...

The river brought them to me. That's the only explanation I have for it. Drawn by the pull of its swirling eddies and rising mists, its allure too strong to ignore, they came my way and never left...

THE ESCAPE

Everywhere hurts as she dips her head and runs. It's like nothing she has ever experienced before. Even childbirth doesn't come close. As if needles are being repeatedly inserted into her joints. Stabbing, jarring, eye watering levels of pain. It doesn't stop her though; she won't let it. The limits of her damaged body will not hold her back. She pounds the pavement with exhausted legs, feet burning, chest wheezing as she weaves her way out of a dimly lit, tree-lined avenue. Legs pumping until her muscles feel fit to burst, she turns the corner, the anticipation of seeing her family once again searing over her skin, like pinpricks of electricity. The thought of falling onto the warmth of her husband's oversized chest, of putting up with the constant battling of her teenage offspring, inhaling the familiar smell of her lovely old kitchen: they all loom large in her mind, forcing her on. A sob rattles through her chest. She takes a ragged breath and suppresses it then stops abruptly, frustration gripping her as she is faced with another long road, almost identical to the one she's just left behind. Where are all the people, for God's sake? What kind of ghost town is this? Where is the help she so desperately needs?

Her gaze drops to the pavement and tears cascade down her face, hot and unstoppable as she attempts to work out where she actually is. She could hazard a guess but her brain is like cotton wool, refusing to function as it usually would, deprived of nourishment and arrested by fear. Hysteria begins to claw its way up her gut and into her throat. What if she's being followed? She visualises a dark, sinister figure lurking in the shadows, waiting for her to trip over or get lost or simply collapse from sheer exhaustion, her body folding in on itself from the shock and horror of it all. Her mind goes into overdrive. So many hiding places. A body slotted away down an alley just waiting to pounce. Full of intent and hatred, and laced with a special kind of madness. She starts to run again, picking up her pace at the thought of it. She has to keep on until she is sure she is safe. And until she sees somebody, she doesn't feel safe. Not in these dimly lit streets. Darkness can swallow people, eat them alive. The filthy, soaking-wet slippers on her feet slap at the puddles on the pavement, sending sprays of dirty water up over her legs. It doesn't matter. There was a time she would have stopped, cleaned herself up. Not now. Everything is different now.

She slows down and winces, screwing her eyes up against the wave of pain that works its way up her shins, continuing up through her ribcage and landing with a ferocious slam into her skull. She reaches up to touch the wound on her head, fingers trailing over a blood-encrusted gash the size of her fist. Folds of torn, wet skin shift softly under her touch. She retches and presses the heel of her hands into her mouth to stem the vomit that rises.

She looks up again at the road that stretches off into the distance. Terraced houses on either side fence her in, their windows veiled in darkness. At the end of the street, she can see the corner of a huge, Victorian-style, sandstone building, ancient and imposing like a mausoleum. An old hotel perhaps? Or a theatre? Maybe a museum of some sort. It has that kind of look about it: antiquated, formidable. She stares at it, uses it as her focal point, telling herself if she can reach it, everything will be all right.

In the distance, she hears the rumble of an engine, its low purr increasing as it edges closer. A beam of white light dips and rises as it turns the corner and slowly moves towards her. Summoning what little strength she has left, she jumps up and down, waving her hands above her head, shouting to the driver for help, screaming for him to stop. Her heart pounds in her chest. This is it. This is the part she has waited for, for so long. The part where she collapses into the safety of a warm, dry car with a kind-hearted person who expedites her home. The vehicle slows down and a dark-skinned man with slicked-back, silver hair leans over the passenger seat and stares at her with a perplexed expression before shaking his head and moving on, the car lurching as he hits the accelerator with exaggerated force. A lump lodges in her throat and more tears spill down her face: a fountain of despair. She is bewildered at his lack of compassion. Pissed off and bloody furious, actually. What kind of person would ignore somebody in their hour of need? And right now, she is very much in need.

She breathes hard and stares down at her hands, black and bloody, then at her trousers, filthy, creased and torn and she can only imagine what her face must look like. This looks like a fairly nice area, a leafy suburb land. The kind of area where people aren't used to seeing scruffy-looking strangers staggering around the streets late at night pleading for lifts. What did he think she was going to do though? Rob him? Beg for money? She runs faster, too scared and too angry to stop now. A row of doors pass her by in a blur. She briefly considers knocking, pleading with the residents to help her, but is frightened of what lies behind them. Experience has taught her that things are rarely what they seem. Even leafy suburbs have their dark secrets. Nobody can be trusted. Absolutely no-one. Probably a good thing she didn't actually get in that car. She'll find her own way home. She needs to get to a place with lots of people, somewhere with crowds. Safety in numbers.

The building remains tantalisingly distant as she slows down to catch her breath. She hasn't eaten for so long, she can't actually remember when it was. A couple of days? Three or four? Probably even longer. She has lost track of time and has no idea what day it is. Her legs buckle as she bends over and rests her hands on her thighs. She stands up and pushes on again, the searing, throbbing pain in her head becoming unbearable. She can't stop though. Too risky. Just a few more minutes and she will be there.

She hears the yell before she sees them.

'Christ almighty! What's the hurry?' A group of women in their mid-twenties step out from behind a high privet, staggering on stiletto heels, reeling backward as she ploughs into them, scattering them like nine pins. They stop and stare open mouthed when they see her up close, see how filthy her face is, how her hands and arms are smeared and streaked with blood, and the size of the huge, weeping gash on the side of her head as she crumples at their feet, sobbing hysterically.

'Sorry. Oh God, I'm sorry. I just need... can you?' She reaches her arm up before snatching it away and curling up into a tight little ball, the cold of the concrete a welcome sensation on her burning skin.

'Fuckin' hell! Did your husband do this to you? I'd 'ave his balls on a skewer if any fella ever tried to do that to me.'

Water seeps through her mud splattered clothes as she unfurls and slumps awkwardly on the pavement, making no attempt to get back up. She is tired.

So very, very tired. She murmurs, her voice hoarse, her lips cracked and sore as she tries to speak. The gang of women crouch down beside her, their long hair hanging over her face. It is soft and warm and smells of apples and honey. Even in the grey, dying light, their faces glow with carefully applied make up, their lips shimmering with soft tones of peach and pink lip gloss. She weeps some more at the incongruity of it.

'Sorry love. You'll 'ave to speak up. Hang on a minute,' One of them stands up and punches a number into her phone.

'You calling an ambulance?' one asks the other, who nods and cups her hand over the mouthpiece before turning away to speak.

'Okay, what were you saying? If you give us your husband's address, I know someone who can sort him out.'

She shakes her head and stares up at the sea of faces hovering over her. 'Where am I?'

There is a short burst of laughter followed by a stony silence.

'Christ. He must 'ave given you a right good pasting if you don't even know where you are.' A tall girl with kind eyes and a full painted mouth takes her hand and stares into her face solemnly. 'You're in

York, sweetheart. Just stay still now. An ambulance is on its way.' She looks up at her friend who nods to confirm.

'York? Why am I in York?' she mutters but nobody is listening as the whirr of a siren pierces the distant night air and they all turn to look.

1

FEBRUARY 2014 – THREE MONTHS EARLIER

Even in the midst of the chaos, I can hear it. With the removal men shifting wardrobes, sideboards and tables and chairs off the van, even above the shouting and grunting as they heave the bulky pieces of furniture around, staggering with them across the gravelled drive and into the house, even with me yelling at them to be careful with Martyn's mahogany desk, and even with the dog running round in circles and yelping at everyone and everything, I can hear it. It rushes by the back of the house: an unstoppable surge. A roaring, frothing wall of water that will continue to flow in spite of what day it is, what state the economy is in or what war is occurring in the Middle East and being talked about repeatedly on the news.

The river makes its way over undulating ground, carving its way out to the sea while we fret over other things. Some important, some minutiae. It understands none of these man-made problems. The river rolls on regardless, forcing itself through the earth, constant and relentless. I don't expect anyone else to comprehend it, to understand my draw to this part of the world, the nagging desire to hear the rush of the current. Why would they? But this is where I need to be, near to where it happened, back to where it all began.

'Where do you want this one then?'

An overweight, sweaty man is standing in the doorway, blocking out the light behind him. An unsightly sheen sits on his skin and perspiration runs down his temples as he stares down at a large, unmarked box, one of the few I haven't written on with my black marker pen. I did most of them but this one somehow slipped my attention. His chest rumbles as he struggles to catch his breath. I look around at the empty hallway and the rooms leading off from it and am mystified as to what to say to him. This place is completely alien to me. It's not my home. I left my home this morning. This is where I live now and I don't even know where any of my things should go.

'Over there,' I say a little too sharply and point to

an alcove in the dining area. It seems like as good a place as any. He draws a deep breath and lifts the box up, its weight causing him to stagger awkwardly as he makes his way past me into the large, empty room, lunging forward as he puts it down at his feet. I want to shout after him to be careful, that it probably contains all my crockery and we'll need it to eat off pretty soon but I can't seem to summon up the energy. It's been a long day and I'm exhausted. It's highly likely that tonight's bed will be no more than a mattress on the floor with a crumpled bed sheet slung over it but that's fine with me. I can handle that. I can't remember ever feeling so exhausted. Right now, I could sleep where I stand.

I watch from the large, bare living room as the removal men drag the last of the furniture out of the van. A battered old rocking chair, the one I used to use to nurse Tom on the nights he refused to sleep. I say nurse; it was more of a ferocious jiggling movement accompanied by a stream of sleep deprived tears. There's an ugly chest of drawers that I have kept for no other reason than it belonged to my mother and finally, a small, mahogany box that contains every major event of my life. Very telling, really. Such a small container for all that's gone before. I had intended to transport it myself to keep it safe but in all the disorder and confusion, it somehow ended up being put in the van, probably manhandled by a dozen or more clammy removal men. No matter. What's done is done. I march outside and grab it off the bulky male who is carrying it across the driveway. He mutters something under his breath as I turn away. I'm too tired to answer him. I don't trust my tongue to stay polite so I stay silent instead. I'll be glad to see the back of today.

Martyn is standing, staring out of the kitchen window when I get back into the house. Beyond the river, in the distance, there is a view of the North Yorkshire hills and he is staring at it intently, looking at the shadowy shape they etch into the grey sky beyond. He's been quiet all day, loitering in the background, keeping out of the way. I can't say I blame him. It's been an ordeal and I doubt I've handled it well. Who does? Isn't moving house right up there with death of a loved one and divorce when measuring levels of stress? Put like that, I think I've acted like a bloody saint.

'I hope to God we've done the right thing moving here, Phoebe,' he whispers hoarsely, a light rattle evident in his chest.

Typical Martyn: full of doubts and worries. I move towards him and place my hand on his shoulder reassuringly. 'I'm certain. Look around you; this is a dream home. Give it six months and it'll feel as if we've lived here all our lives.'

'I'll take your word for that.' His voice is flat, monotone, his spine rigid as I try to manipulate some flexibility back into his posture.

'Trust me,' I say, hoping to appease him. I want everything to be perfect, unscathed by what has happened.

He shrugs his shoulders resignedly then smiles as he turns and nods towards the hallway. 'Have they gone, the removal guys?' He taps his walking cane on the floor and hobbles over to the table where he slumps down into a wooden chair, suddenly fatigued by it all. I stare at his face. He is looking old; the skin around his eyes baggy, his forehead lined, the shine on his irises dulled by years of constant pain. The past few years haven't been kind.

'Just unloading the last few boxes,' I say and listen to the sharp, metallic grate as they roll down the shutter at the back of the van. 'I'll head back out and speak with them.' I kiss the back of his neck and walk outside, keen to catch them and take the remainder of our things before they come back in the house. I really don't think I can take any more of this moving palaver. I am bone tired and my tolerance levels have been eroded to the point of non-existence and rightly or wrongly, I don't think I can stand to have them back in here. I need to look around properly, see our new house for what it really is. Not the kind of cursory look when you first step foot in a house you are considering buying, but a proper look, a chance to decide what should go where, a chance to become immersed in its ambience and get used to the sheer size of it without the hindrance of half a dozen dirty men hanging around, cracking silly jokes and generally getting in the way. Besides, Martyn needs some quiet time now. He's starting to get twitchy and fractious and may even need a nap. It's long overdue.

I stand at the gate and watch as they lock the rear of the lorry up, hitch up their pants and clamber into the front seats. I see them watching me and feel my face burn. I've been mean. Not exactly mean but definitely curt. No need for it really but right now, I'm running on empty and in desperate need of a break.

I'm flooded with relief as the engine splutters into life and the large, green truck rumbles its way through the village and disappears out of sight. This whole experience has been way more draining and stressful than I ever expected it to be. I sigh quietly. At least it's over with and I can at last sit down with a cup of tea. That is of course, if I can find the kettle.

As I head back inside, I can hear Tillie yelping and running around frantically. Poor old girl. She will be ready for a walk, her ageing bladder full to bursting. I look at my watch and widen my eyes at the rapid passing of time. Where has the day gone? She will also need feeding. I usually set my watch by Tillie's toilet breaks and stomach demands. She is my dog now and mine alone. Her physical needs are beyond Martyn's capabilities. I don't mind. On my bad days, Tillie is my reason for getting up out of bed and getting on with my day. As soon as I get sorted, I'll take her over the fields and into the other end of the village. We can do a bit of exploring and call into the corner shop to buy something for tea. Maybe Martyn will come along. Or maybe not. I suppress a deep, mournful sigh. Most likely it will be definitely not. He can sleep in my absence.

I mentally go through what we need. I know that I've got some bits of food sorted for when we get up in the morning: boxes of cereal, teabags, biscuits. Nothing substantial, but enough to get by. I'm not sure how Martyn feels but I have no appetite at the moment. With all the to-ing and fro-ing, food has been the furthest thing from my mind. Hopefully, the walk will help me to work up a hunger. I perk up at the thought of going for a long stroll, of facing the chill of the late winter air, fighting off the bite of the bracing, north-easterly wind that whips up the from the river in sharp, stinging blasts. I'll get some cheese and bread to make sandwiches for supper. We can eat together and discuss the house, decide on where to put our furniture. I stare at the forty-foot living room, stacked high with containers, and blink back unexpected tears. I'm more exhausted than I even realised. I shut my eyes against them and steady myself. I will take a walk, reacquaint myself with the sights and when I return, everything will look brighter.

'I think I'll hang around here and sort out some boxes in the study if it's all right with you?'

I nod and smile at Martyn's comment. Like he was ever going to come with me anyway. It's a game we play: pretending we have a normal life, pretending he is normal. It's what keeps us together. It's what keeps us sane.

Martyn is picking his way through the mountain of containers stacked up in the living room as I clip Tillie onto her lead and put my shoes on. The boxes stand so high, we can't even see out of the huge bay window. It's going to take us forever and a day to unpack so I guess the sooner we start, the better. I rummage in my pocket to check I've got some doggy snacks and poop bags. I feel the familiar oily sensation of plastic between my fingers and delve further down to the bottom to check for snacks. They are there, dry and crumbly and probably months old but it's better than nothing and right now, chances of finding dog snacks amongst this lot is practically zero.

'No problem,' I say. 'Is there anything you want bringing back?'

He shakes his head and looks around. 'A team of servants to help us with this lot?'

He's right. I laugh and roll my eyes. Even a team of servants would have the Devil's own job unpacking this lot. What were we thinking when we bought it all? At the last count, we had eight tea sets, five large cutlery sets and four teapots. And for some bizarre reason, we also have two large coffee machines and two bread makers, neither of which actually work. Too much stuff. Far too much.

I exhale noisily and shake my head as Martyn shuffles further into the pile of cardboard boxes, the rustle of his movements the only indication he is still present as he disappears out of sight, swallowed by our wall of belongings.

* * *

A mist is rising from the ground, grey and opaque, concealing the grass beneath my feet as it climbs its way up, wrapping itself around my ankles. I make my way over the field towards the far end of the village. Icy clouds swirl around me in ghostly wisps like a vapour trail, almost enveloping Tillie completely. She jumps up and down, aware I have treats in my pocket. Her legs may not be as good as they once were but her sense of smell is as acute now as it was when she was a pup. I reach in, snap one in half and hold it in my fingers. She takes it from me, crunching on it greedily before we continue on, the fog slowly thickening to a real pea souper by the time we get there.

You could call it quaint I suppose; the local shop is a throwback to the 1960s. Barely touched by the passing decades, the exterior boasts a peeling facade and a window littered with faded posters and handwritten cards selling fridge freezers and washing machines along with a section of desperate pleas to find missing pets. I stare down at the dusty windowsill, my eyes drawn to the array of dead flies laid frozen, their spindly, black legs pointing skyward.

A bell above the door tinkles lightly as I go in, announcing my arrival in the gloom of the place. The noise echoes around the empty aisles, eerie and anachronistic, reminding me of my childhood. A memory jars me. *This shop: a group of friends stuffing items in their pockets they hadn't paid for, them goading me, shouting at me because I point blank refused to steal at their behest. Her face behind them, grinning, drinking in my misery.* I force the memory down, squash it like an annoying insect and look around, trying to take it all in. Such a stark contrast to the shops I usually frequent and yet so familiar. Stirrings in the furthest recesses of my mind threaten to swamp me as I make my way up and down the narrow aisles. *A shopping list scrunched up in my tiny hand, fear eating at me at the thought of what might lay in store for me when I get home. The arguments, the endless accusatory looks...*

I blank them out and focus on what I need. The shelves are covered with patterned oilskin cloths that remind me of the tablecloths my grandma used to own. They have a sad-looking handful of working-class vegetables sprawled over them. Cauliflowers, turnips and a handful of mangy looking carrots stare up at me. I imagine they still sell powdered custard and packets of Angel Delight as well. Maybe even some Arctic Roll ice cream. I suppress a smile and wander through the rest of the narrow, towering aisles. The whole shop has a certain smell to it. Not exactly musty but neither is it fresh. It's exactly as I remember it, just smaller and older. I don't mind. I would rather shop here than push a trolley round some slick, overpriced supermarket that's full of plastic produce. Especially a supermarket that employs staff who are forced to wear badges with smiley faces on them that proclaim how delighted they are to serve you. This is real life, how shops should be. Full of real produce, served by real people. I clear my throat and begin to fill up my basket. It's as if I've never been away.

'Looking for anything in particular?'

The voice seems to emerge from thin air. A middle-aged woman with short, blonde hair and a blotchy complexion rises up from behind the counter. I find myself staring at her reddened skin, at the tell-tale patches of rosacea that have been left undiagnosed, untouched by the range of readily available creams and potions that could cure it with ease. She groans as she straightens her knees and dusts down her legs with gnarled hands that proclaim a hard life full of solid graft. Her nails, I notice, are bitten to the quick.

'We're a bit low on fruit and veg at the minute. Delivery man can't make it till the morning but you can 'ave what we've got at a lower price. And if it's eggs you're after we only sell fresh. Straight from the farm over the back, they are. We all do our bit round here to support each other.'

I smile as she places a tissue over her finger, runs it around the inside of her nostril, sniffs, and then pushes it back into her pocket. She steps out from behind the till and follows me down each aisle as I load my basket up with eggs, some bacon, a tub of butter, a slab of cheese and half a dozen bread buns, her eyes never leaving me. I've read somewhere that you can analyse somebody's entire life just by looking at their groceries. Perhaps that's what she's trying to do with me: work me out, get inside my head. I wish her well with that one. Her proximity begins to unnerve me as I lean over to reach the back of the fridge and she leans forward too, chatting all the while about how I'm her final customer and how she is just about to close up for the evening.

'Just something for a quick snack, eh?' she says as she steps back behind the counter and rings each item in the till before putting them in a bag. I nod and hand her the correct money. 'Not seen you in here before. You staying at one of the holiday cabins down the road, are ya?'

I slip my purse back in my bag and shake my head. 'We've just moved in further down the village. Today, actually. Just getting something for our tea.'

I can feel the sudden curiosity in her demeanour. I'm the new kid in town. A person of interest. I imagine people moving into the village is about as exciting as it gets round here.

'The Peterson place over by the edge of the woods?' she says, trying to keep her voice low key. She looks around surreptitiously and I want to laugh at her attempts at being discreet. This is the quietest shop I've ever been in. Walls really must have ears.

'Bit further afield,' I reply as I sling my bag over my shoulder and hoist one of the carrier bags off the counter.

'Oh, right. Not the Peterson place. So which way you headed then?'

For some reason, I am reticent to tell her everything. Being cautious is part of who I am now, an inclination I can't seem to shake. It's a form of self-preservation. Besides which, in a village this size, she is bound to find out anyway, 'Back over that way,' I say, nodding my head to indicate the route behind her.

She narrows her eyes, trying to work it out. I'll bet she knows every house, every villager, everything that goes on around here. If I need to know anything about anything, she'll be the lady to come to. It takes her a while to work it out. When she does, her eyes light up with sudden recognition.

'The big old barn conversion next to the green?'

I tell her that's the one. She raises her eyebrows, gives me a look and purses her lips.

'Nice big place that one is. Heard it's got right good views out back as well,' she says haughtily.

'It certainly has,' I reply, placing the bag on the floor. My hands are tired and already it's slipping out of my grasp, 'We overlook the river.'

'And t' footpath too,' she sniffs as if to emphasise her point.

I nod, already used to this reaction. Many thought me mad when I first said I was considering moving into a house that had a public right of way cut straight across its garden. The solicitor advised me to take out insurance to cover against any injuries incurred by people passing through. I politely declined. Even Martyn had his reservations about it but I stood my ground. Properties in this area that overlook the river don't come on the market that often so it seemed like the right thing to do, the obvious thing. It was now or never. Truth be told, the house isn't that important to me and nothing like the property we moved from. Our big old semi is a far cry from this place. It's a bold move for us and I do realise how fortunate I am to be able to live in such a grand old place. And it is grand; the kind of property estate agents brag about having on their books, the kind of house most people only ever dream about living in. But that's not why I bought it. You see, it's the river I really want to be near. The river is what brought me back. Having to put up with a damn silly footpath is worth it just to be back where I really belong.

'That's why it took so long to sell, you know. 'Cos of the path. Nobody wants a load of strangers traipsing through their garden, do they?'

Her face suddenly colours up, aware of her blunder. I shrug my shoulders and smile. She seems nice enough, this lady. I'm not about to defend my position, get all bristly and territorial and make her feel uncomfortable. I'm new around here and need all the friends I can get.

'Guess I'm not like other folk then. It really doesn't bother me. In fact, once the weather picks up, I'm looking forward to seeing them all.' The lies trip off my tongue with ease. Years of practise.

Her relief is palpable. She continues, her voice lighter, contrived. 'Supposed to be a cracker of a summer this year as well. So it'll get used plenty.'

'I hope so,' I say and pick the bag back up, trying to keep an air of friendliness in my voice. Exhaustion is threatening to engulf me and I've yet to make it back home: dog, bags and all.

'You in that big old place on your own then? Or you got family living with you?'

I stop and my breath catches in my chest. This is the bit I hate. The explanations. Having to tell people about Martyn's injury and subsequent lapse into depression, about how he relies on me for everything, about how I pray day in and day out that he'll miraculously get better and not need me to be his main and only carer. I feel a small veil of darkness descend at the reality of it all. Some days, it's like a long and endless route. Then other days... well, there are other days when I feel glad to be alive. Still, at least he didn't find the move too traumatic. In actual fact, he has probably handled the whole thing better than me. I've been a bag of nerves, pre-empting everything, creating problems that aren't actually there, whereas Martyn sailed through the whole procedure with aplomb, not complaining about the drive here, not minding at all when he had to wait in the car while I shifted small items into the new house. I wouldn't want him to risk further injury by carrying anything. When I think about it, he's been marvellous throughout. Not once did his temper get the better of him. Not once.

A small tic takes hold in the corner of my eye. I flick at my lashes to bat it away and wiggle my jaw to relieve myself of a headache I feel coming on.

I pretend I haven't heard her question and begin to walk towards the door. It's easier that way. I haven't the energy or the inclination to go through it all.

'I'll see you around then?' she says to my back, her small, bright eyes boring into me.

I turn and give her a generous smile. 'Absolutely,' I reply, before heading outside to collect Tillie, who is sitting waiting patiently for me. Such a good girl, she is.

'Come on, my lovely. Let's head home,' I say quietly. I lean down and unhook her lead from the railing that is now damp from the mist. 'We'll get sorted in that new kitchen of ours and make some supper.'

I look up to see a crop of blonde hair and a ruddy face watching me through the door, the expression serious and her gaze immovable as she scrutinises my every move. All the while, a voice in my head screams, *she knows...*

2

I got lost on the way back. Silly really when you consider how well I used to know the place. It was the fog, you see. Somehow, I took a wrong turn and ended up on what appeared to be the other side of the river. Except it wasn't the other side at all. In my confusion and rising sense of panic, I had followed it round an oxbow and could see the house from where I was standing. A large, Tudor-style barn in the distance, hovering high above the mist in a world of its own, untouched by the elements. The whole detour unnerved me slightly, but somehow I managed to find my way back and now stumble in the front door; exhausted, damp and dishevelled. I drop the bags at my feet and heave a sigh of relief as I wipe the back of my hand across my face and push my sodden hair back out of my eyes. Droplets of water drip from my eyelashes and chin onto the tiled floor in tiny splashes like baby tears. I try to kick off my shoes but they're so filthy and damp, I end up slumping down on the floor to remove them and am in a complete sweat by the time I've managed to practically tear them off my feet. They sit next to me, a heap of mangled fabric and mud.

Martyn is standing in front of me and he is livid. He had been worried, he says. What if I'd fallen and drowned in the river? Been overpowered and dragged away by the current. What then, eh? I smile at him and haul myself upright. I drag the bags into the kitchen and begin to unpack the shopping, doing my best to make light of the whole situation. I try to dismiss his concerns and tell him it was a silly mistake on my part but the air is thick with his anger. My hands tremble as I fill the kettle and get out a couple of teabags. Mugs. I need to find some mugs. Hunger gnaws at my stomach, now empty after such a long walk, and I feel a growing sense of unease at Martyn's deteriorating mood. I do my best to draw him out of it but he remains resolute in his stance. Sometimes I think he even enjoys it.

'Don't ever do this again, Phoebe. Are you listening to me? You having an accident is the last thing we need right now. Jesus. As if our life isn't difficult enough...'

I turn to face him and nod, hoping he can see my concerned expression, the way my cheeks colour up when I'm anxious, how a spasm takes hold in the corner of my eye when he speaks to me like that. Today had all been going so well and then I go and ruin it with my stupid sense of direction. He continues to stare at me, his eyes unblinking as he follows my movements around the kitchen. I dart about, trying to radiate a sense of lightness, give the impression I am unperturbed by his mood. That's the only way to deal with it: to show him that I am busy and that I refuse to get dragged into a completely avoidable row. I hum quietly as I open a box and get lucky. Two cups are sitting at the top of it. I fish them out and continue through the process of making tea, taking as long as possible, waiting for the moment to pass. My tactics work. By the time I've finished, he has calmed down and I feel myself relax. I even manage a nervous smile as I stir in his milk and look his way.

I understand his plight. Of course I do. He feels emasculated by his disability and his reliance on me for everything. I'm almost certain I would be just as angry if I was him so I completely get it. That's why I let things go. Acceptance is easier than resentment and anger. So is forgiveness. And I have that by the shed load. That's just how it is.

My pulse begins to settle as I place Martyn's cup in front of him. Steam billows out of it. Earl Grey. A particular favourite of his. He sits at the island in the centre of the kitchen, his shoulders dipped as he carefully sips at the steaming liquid, pale and tinged with a grey hue compared to my ordinary breakfast tea. I have no idea how he does it. It's like drinking perfume. I drag a chair over and join him and we sit in companionable silence, drinking and staring out at the hills in the distance.

It wasn't always like this. There was a time when he was able bodied, less prone to flare-ups, able to face the world with a smile and not perceive everything as a threat or see it as a sign of imminent danger. Perhaps we'll have those days again, although I very much doubt it. It's just a silly pipe dream I have. I know deep down it won't ever happen but I keep it, store it in my head, use it as a little teaser, something to keep me going through the dark times. And God knows we have plenty of those.

'Some ramblers came by while you were out,' he says, his eyes refusing to meet mine.

He keeps his gaze fixed on the misty, darkening countryside beyond. He is always ashamed of his outbursts. He's not by nature a violent or cruel man. They're fuelled by his lack of mobility and lack of contact with the outside world. I nod at his words and quietly sip my tea, unsure what it is he wants to hear, so I play it safe and say nothing. I don't want to lose it, this piece of tranquillity. Times like these are rare, fleeting. So I snatch at it greedily and savour the moment.

'I suppose we'll see quite a few of those now, won't we?' he continues, the colour starting to seep back into his cheeks.

'I suppose we will,' I reply quietly hoping it was all just a blip and is now behind us. Perhaps seeing the odd walker will help him now we've moved here, provide him with a crumb of comfort in his tiny, insular world. I watch him for a while, see how his eyes crease up at the corners as he speaks, and admire how tenacious he is in the face of such adversity, how he battles on against all odds without question.

I clear my throat and stand up. 'I need to go and make the bed up.' I grimace at the thought. I have no idea where the sheets and duvets are so the sooner I start the whole arduous process, the better. It might take me minutes, it might take hours. Depends if I get lucky with opening the right container. I'm almost certain I labelled them but am almost at the point where I can no longer think straight.

'Do you need any help?'

My eyes well up at his suggestion. Oh, if only he could. If only. I shake my head and tell him I will be fine. He gives me a weak, helpless smile and my heart melts.

My small box is exactly where I left it. I pick it up and head upstairs to the main bedroom. Every bone in my body aches as I carry it carefully and place it on the floor at my feet. I flinch at the thought of all those grisly removal men manhandling it and give it a quick rub to remove all traces of them. I consider opening it, just having a quick rummage. I do that sometimes: lay everything out, check it's all intact, read it carefully. Remind myself of everything I've been through. Tell myself I'm a survivor. But not tonight. It's late, I'm tired and we need a bed.

I stride across the room and plonk myself in the middle of it all. The detritus that is currently our life. Luckily, most of the larger boxes are marked and it only takes me two attempts to locate the quilts and pillows. I fling them over the mattress that is laid haphazardly on the floor. The frame is yet to be assembled. All in good time. I briefly wonder if I should make up the spare bed for Martyn or if he'll sleep with me. It all depends on whether or not his back and leg are giving him more grief than usual. Sometimes, we go to sleep together and when I wake up the following morning, he's taken himself off. Too much pain, too many demons. More often than not, by the time I get up, he is downstairs, wandering. I have no idea what time he gets up. I've learnt to not ask. It's like tearing at an exposed vein, asking him about his thoughts, trying to get him to let me inside his head. Sometimes certain things are best left unsaid.

It hasn't always been like this. We were happy once. We had a life. A real life, not like now, where I do what I can to get us by and Martyn wanders around all hang dog and soaked in simmering anger and self-pity. We used to do things together: go shopping, go on holiday, have friends around. Now we simply exist. But I'm hoping that by moving here to this house, this oversized and overpriced house, will change all that. Here, I can give life another go, be comfortable with my surroundings and be able to cope with what goes on in my own head. Martyn seems to forget he's not the only one with a past. We all have our own demons to cope with.

Excitement surges through my veins at the

thought of it. Being back in my own part of the country, near the water and with the rolling hills of North Yorkshire so close, you feel you can reach out and almost touch them. Village life is who I am. City living never really suited me. This is where I really belong and if I am being honest, always have. Just the thought of being so close to the river as it rushes past my house each and every day. I close my eyes and let out a shuddering breath. It will soon feel as if I've never been away.

I decide to leave the other bed for tonight. Making one up is enough and I simply don't have the energy to attempt another one. Martyn can either come and sleep with me or find somewhere else to lay his head. Not that there is anywhere else that will be more comfortable. The old wooden kitchen chairs we have out for convenience are hardly conducive to sleeping and the breakfast stools around the island aren't even comfortable for sitting. I grab a handful of towels and my bag of toiletries and head into the bathroom.

Martyn's medication plops out into the sink as I empty the bag to look for the soap. It topples over and lands face up, rattling around the sink, an echoing reminder of our daily struggle. My heart begins to pump rapidly as I try to recall whether or not he has taken today's dose. In all the mayhem, he may well have missed it. That would explain his agitation earlier. I pick it up, open the packet, push his tablet out of the blister pack and trudge downstairs.

He is sitting, staring out of the kitchen window, his shoulders hunched, his eyes glazed over, our exchange of pleasantries a few minutes earlier now just a dim and distant memory. A sliver of ice darts down my spine. I know that look. I know it all too well. I start to sing softly as I fill the kettle, hoping it will make this whole thing marginally less difficult. I have a lot of strategies I employ regularly to deal with my husband. And sometimes they work, and sometimes they don't.

'You want another cup of tea, love?'

His silence is loaded with a slow, festering anger, the air heavy with his fury. I'm able to sense it now but not always able to stop it. If only. As surreptitiously as I can, I open the small capsule and empty its powdery contents into the cup. It's easier to do it this way. He is too far gone now to reason with and if I try to force it on him, there's no telling what he will do. He still hasn't responded to my question but then I didn't really expect him to. I was only trying to fill an awkward silence, to halt his declining temper before it erupts into something unmanageable, something quite ugly.

I stir the hot water into his cup and dip a teabag in it before adding the milk. As unobtrusively as I can, I sit down next to him and slide the mug towards him. More silence ensues. An interminable, protracted air of nothingness where I can hear my own blood as it courses through my system, hot and thick with fear and trepidation. He takes a sip and then another, his expression unreadable. I try to relax, to subliminally urge him to do the same. Then turns to face me and the look in his eyes makes my throat close up.

'What?' he whispers at me, his nostrils flaring as he fixes his eyes on the cup. 'What's this for? More bloody tea, Phoebe? I didn't say I wanted any more, did I?'

And before I have a chance to stop him, Martyn picks up the cup and hurls it against the wall, the shattering of porcelain an explosion in the heavy silence of the room. A stream of amber liquid runs down the white walls and covers the floor, pooling in the spaces between the tiles, turning the cream grouting a murky shade of orange. Had I not seen it with my own eyes, I wouldn't have thought it possible for a small vessel of liquid to disperse with such force and cover such a wide area. A couple of drips of scalding hot tea hit my cheek and ferociously burn at my skin. I dab the side of my face with a tissue as carefully and furtively as I can, but obviously not sneakily enough as Martyn sees me and is on his feet, his hands balled into fists at his sides. I watch him through narrowed eyes as he rocks from side to side, his tall, lean body quivering with unspent anger.

'For God's sake, leave your bloody face alone! There's nothing wrong with you. Not everything is always about you, you know!' He is standing close by, roaring over the top of my head.

With shaking hands, I drop the tissue and am up, out of the chair to get away from him, begging him, shouting at him to leave me alone, to calm down. In my haste to escape, I step on a fragment of the shattered cup and hop about in pain. I inadvertently let out a yelp and clamp a hand over my mouth. Any reactions from me will only aggravate him all the more. I've learnt that particular lesson the hard way. A muffled sob escapes as tears sting at my eyes. It's not just the pain, though. Dealing with Martyn isn't easy at the best of times. And today, I am utterly exhausted. I know however, from past experience, he mustn't see the tears. Martyn hates weak people. And usually I'm not, I'm really not, but it's been a trying time and such a long day.

I sniff and swallow hard. I have to keep it together. I have to be the strong one around here, the tough one. Without me, Martyn is incapable of functioning. Without me, he is nothing. As quickly as I can, I limp out of the kitchen and upstairs into the bathroom where I examine my bleeding foot and carefully pick out a small but sharp ceramic splinter, dabbing at the sore spot with a wad of toilet paper. I half expect him to follow me and listen out for the creak of the stairs as he makes his way up. I can hear him below, pacing the floor, up and down, up and down. I visualise his furrowed brow and raging expression. My skin prickles as I brace myself for the sound of his foot-steps coming to get me, hobbling up the stairs, his unabated rage fuelling him. But then suddenly, all the noise downstairs stops.

I sit perfectly still and pray that he has finally calmed down. The sound of my breathing rattles around the room. I let out a tentative sigh and run trembling fingers through my hair. I find myself becoming grateful for the smallest of mercies these days. With any luck, his temper has now dissipated and normality has returned. That's the thing with his rages: they are explosive, unpredictable, but over within minutes. I say a quiet prayer of thanks to who-ever may be listening for my reprieve and stand up, slowly putting weight on my injured foot. I won't try to give Martyn his medication now. It can wait till the morning. He's always better first thing. More ap-proachable, less volatile. I stand for a little while until the tears stop flowing and my heart stops jumping around my throat, then stagger into the bedroom, over to the mattress and drop onto it with a thump, my eyes so heavy, I can barely keep them open. I drag the duvet up over my head and feel a heavy blanket of welcome sleep begin to descend.

3

'I said it would sell sometime this year, didn't I?'

'You've said it for the last three years, Mike. It had to happen eventually.'

Anna moves away from the window and makes an attempt at tidying up, a pointless activity when Mike and the kids are all in the house. She gathers up a pile of magazines and slots them into the paper rack, picks up the rug to give it a shake, then moves back to the window, her curiosity too piqued to look away. What kind of people have the money to buy a house that size anyway?

'Looks like they've got plenty of stuff to fill that big old place.' Her stomach tightens as she watches furniture get carried inside. Item after item after item.

She has counted at least four Chesterfield sofas being dragged off the van and an oak sideboard so big, it would fill her entire kitchen. She always said it would take a lottery winner to be able to afford that house and judging by the gear being hauled off the removal truck, it looks like that's what they have got living opposite them. Some people seem to have it all.

A clatter from upstairs disturbs her viewing. Anna grits her teeth and races up there, hollering all kinds of threats to Mason and Callum who stare at her with boyish innocence. The bedroom is littered with games and leads trailing from Xboxes and Play-Stations, the floor covered with magazines and balled up socks where they have pelted each other from their beds. With only a year age difference between them, it's more like having twins. Neither of them takes the lead when it comes to keeping the place clean. Being the elder of the two at thirteen, Anna wishes Callum would exert a more positive influence over his younger brother, be the sensible one, but most days, they both seem to be as bad as each other.

Anna rolls her eyes and stares at the mess. She should tidy it but simply can't face the thought of it. It's so cluttered with clothes and gadgets and books and general detritus, she wouldn't know where to start. Her heart isn't in it. Maybe tomorrow. Or next weekend. She gives the boys one last warning look from under her lashes then closes the door and leaves them to it. She is more intrigued by the goings on over the road and finding out who their new neighbour is than sorting out her errant children. She does that on a daily basis and now it's worse since they're off for half term. The last two days have been hell. Their behaviour, although sometimes mildly entertaining, is really beginning to grind on her.

'It's all solid mahogany and oak furniture by the looks of it. I'm pretty certain I saw a solid walnut bookcase get carried in. No plastic or cheap veneer stuff over there. Must have some money to have bought all that lot.'

Mike rustles his paper and stares at her over the top of his glasses, his eyes narrow with exasperation.

'Well, obviously. Otherwise they wouldn't be able to afford a house that size, would they?' His laugh is a loud bark, laced with sarcasm and, thinks Anna, perhaps just a touch of jealousy. Mike works hard but even if they saved for a hundred years, the old barn conversion would never have been within their reaches. The previous owners spent most of their time abroad and Anna never really got to know them. She sighs. A house that size and it standing empty for so long. Such a waste. Until now, that is.

Anna ignores him and focuses her gaze on the house as a car pulls up onto the gravelled drive, its tyres crunching seductively. Such wealth and luxury. She hopes the new owners appreciate what they have. She knows she would. It parks up with a low grind behind the hedge that surrounds the front of the house and now Anna can't see a damn thing, save for the bobbing head of a woman that she guesses is in her mid to late forties, as she goes backwards and forwards from the car to the house. How annoying.

'This must be them,' she says with a squeak. Her stomach flips and she has no idea why.

'Why do you presume it's more than one person? Might just be a single person moving here for a bit of peace and quiet, away from prying eyes.'

The jibe isn't lost on her and Anna steps back slightly from the glass, her face suddenly warm. Her voice is quiet as she tries to get a good view from behind the curtain. 'Well for once, you might be right. There's a middle-aged lady carrying stuff in from the car but I can't see anybody else with her.'

Mike coughs and rustles his paper with satisfaction as Anna keeps a close eye on the removal men over the road. How much more furniture can one family have? The car, however, is actually quite small. Nothing too flashy. She expected a Mercedes or maybe even a Jaguar. They're the sort of cars rich people drive, aren't they? Not like her battered old Toyota Yaris that is covered in scratches and has seen better days.

She sighs and moves off into the kitchen. It's too cold and damp outside to do any gardening and the river is too high to go walking. Bloody rain. This recent prolonged spate of wet weather has put paid to many of their planned walks with the boys and now they're stuck in the house, bored and driving her mad. They've badgered her to go down to the river on their own but she doesn't trust them to stay away from the edge even when they're with her. There's no way she's about to let them go down there unsupervised. It's really fast flowing at the moment and the river path is slippery and unstable. The very thought of them wandering close to it... She shuts her eyes and swallows hard. As much as they annoy her, she doesn't want them injured. Or worse. Christ, the very thought... Anna opens the cupboard door and stares in at the contents.

'I'm going to bake something and take it over in the morning. I want our new neighbour to know that we're friendly.' She stares up at bags of flour and sugar. They do it all the time in America. She's seen it in films. Happy housewives turning up on the doorstep with a basket full of fresh baked bread and homemade cookies. She's not quite sure she's up to doing both but a baking a cake is easy enough. No harm in being friendly, is there?

'Bloody nosey more like,' Mike says and rolls his eyes behind his paper.

Turning her back to grab a handful of cake tins, Anna makes a point of ignoring his comment. She's won't rise to it. Sometimes, it's easier when he's at work. She leans up and drags a bag of flour down from the top shelf, enjoying the heft of it. On a bad day, bustling around in the kitchen is what keeps her going. And cooking for a new neighbour might be a bit twee but she suddenly feels energised. Useful. A productive member of the family as opposed to somebody who empties the laundry basket and washes their dirty pots every day.

She grabs the sieve and thinks back to when they first moved in here. It took her two days just to find the coffee and teabags and a further week to work out where most of the boys' clothes were. But it wasn't just that. There was such a strong feeling of isolation. She still feels it sometimes when the house is empty, when the boys are out and Mike works the occasional night shift. It's an odd sensation, the first night in a new house, not knowing where everything should go, living in an unfamiliar area surrounded by complete strangers.

And then there's the darkness. Nights round here are unlike any other she has experienced anywhere. The evenings are so intense, so very dark. No streetlights, no light pollution from neighbouring towns, just a huge mantle of inky blackness that weighs down on you, oppressive and relentless. Add to that there is the roar of the river in the distance, interspersed with the occasional hooting owl and crying fox. Anyone new to the area would be right to feel cut off from the rest of the world. That was exactly how Anna felt. Not desperate, not even frightened, but most definitely lonely. Village life can take some getting used to, especially this place with its proximity to the river and lack of youngsters. Tranquil and picturesque in summer, the same place takes on a slightly sinister air once the nights begin to draw in. It's completely bloody amazing to open the curtains every morning to see the rolling hills and beauty of the river as it carves its way through the earth but moving house is a lonely, exhausting process and she doesn't envy her new neighbour one little bit. The thought of it makes her shiver. She wouldn't do it again for a pension.

She opens the bag of flour and leans over to turn the oven on. She'll make a chocolate sponge. Everybody likes chocolate. And she'll hand it over with a smile. It's the very least she can do.

All afternoon is spent in the kitchen slapping Mason and Callum's hands away as they attempt to spoon out large dollops of cake mixture whenever her back is turned. She moves deftly around the kitchen feeling buoyed up as it becomes filled with an appealing sugary, buttery aroma and realises that she is actually really looking forward to meeting this new villager, a woman who looks closer in age to her than Jocelyn next door, who's in her sixties, and Doris, who lives the other side and is an octogenarian. It will be so nice to have somebody younger to chat to. Jocelyn always has a litany of ailments to reel off whenever Anna sees her, whether it's her knees or her hip replacement or more recently her prolapse, and Doris is currently undergoing assessments for dementia. She's fed up with having to feign concern and sympathy every time she bumps into them. It's wearing, and more than that, it's boring. A fresh face around the place is just what is needed. As it is, the entire village is in danger of slipping into a coma. It needs shaking back to life.

The timer sounds on the oven, its tinny, ear-shattering, singular chord echoing throughout the kitchen and filtering into the living room. Anna looks up and shakes her head as she hears the boys' footsteps thundering down the stairs once again. They've been in and out all afternoon, hoping for leftovers. Walking stomachs is what they are. Together, they troop into the kitchen, eyes fixated on the kitchen surface like a pair of ravenous, salivating wild dogs. A strand of greasy hair falls over one of Mason's eyes as he watches his mother. Anna looks up at him. Why is getting a wash such an anathema to her children? They weren't brought up to be so dirty. She budges him aside with her hip and empties the cake onto a wire tray. His arm shoots out as he attempts to grab at it, his hunger the only thing that matters.

'Don't even think about it. This one is for the new people over the road. There's another one cooking that'll be ready in half an hour. You'll have to wait.'

She throws the oven gloves to one side and starts to gather up dirty pots, staring outside as she vigorously rubs at the worktop. That's another thing about living here. The fog. Almost a permanent feature regardless of what season it is, it rises from the river, causing a noticeable drop in temperature. With smoky tentacles that veil the sun and drape themselves over the landscape, it coats everything with a dewy residue. Sometimes, Anna finds it oppressive, slightly threatening even. But not today. Today, nothing will dent her happiness.

'Bit small, isn't it?' Mason's hand hovers over it, his eyes shining with anticipation.

'I've only seen a woman my age go in and out. How many cakes can one person eat?'

Callum is leaning back against the sink, his pale skin exposed above his hipster jeans. Anna pushes him to one side and turns the tap on.

'Nah. She's not on her own.' His voice is a small growl, halfway between that of the boy he currently is and the man he will soon become.

'And how do you know that then, smarty pants?' Bubbles froth up as she fills the sink and empties a baking bowl and a handful of cutlery in there. They hit the bottom with an almighty clatter. She winces and thinks of the scrapes that lot will make on the bottom of her prized Butler sink.

'I heard her talking to someone while I was walking past earlier.'

Anna turns to face him, her expression dark and

formidable. 'And where did you go to? Not down to the river, I hope?'

He tuts and narrows his eyes in annoyance. 'God, Mother. How many times? No, I've not been down to the river. I'm not completely stupid, you know. Just thought I would have a wander, see if anyone's about.'

'And were they?' She rubs at the rim of the baking tin, her hands red from the heat of the steaming water.

'Around here? In the back end of beyond? You're having a laugh, aren't you?'

Anna shakes her head and smiles. That comment is well worn. Since moving here, all they have done is complain about being bored. Their village may not be the busiest place but they're only a stone's throw from the bus stop and there are a handful of kids who live locally that they both know. She is about to launch into her 'when I was a child we made our own entertainment' spiel but is interrupted.

'Anyway I did hear that woman talking to somebody in her house as I walked past,' he says as he flicks his hair out of his eyes, blinks rapidly and then pulls it back over again, straightening it with a repeated tugging motion, 'and she's definitely not there on her own, that new person. She was shouting at somebody. Didn't seem like she was that happy. In fact, she sounded like a bit of an old bag if you ask me.'

'Callum!' Anna pushes past him and gives him one of her well-practised stares. He shrugs his shoulders and slopes away, suddenly disinterested.

She feels nothing but sympathy for this woman. She and Mike had a furious row the day they moved in here. Funny thing is, she can remember how upset she was and the awful, hurtful words they said to each other but for the life of her, she can't remember what the argument was about. Just goes to show what a waste of time and energy it all is.

She places the cake in a tin and sets it aside for the morning. She'll take it over then. Give them time to settle and see what the morning brings. Tomorrow, as they say, is another day.

4

I consider ignoring it. Visitors are absolutely the last thing I need this morning after Martyn's meltdown last night, but the knocking is so loud, so insistent, I feel as if I have no choice but to open the door. I take a sharp intake of breath when I first catch sight of her, feeling winded and unable to speak. It's her face, you see. It stops me in my tracks, makes my blood run like sand. I blink and look away to give myself some time to deal with her presence, to steady my breathing and stop my heart battering around my ribcage like a loose boulder, then look back again. Who is she? This woman on my doorstep: this woman with *her* face and expectant smile. I want to shut the door on her, make the memories go away but know I should make an effort and be nice. Not an easy task when I'm weighed down with the number of chores I have to do today. I simply cannot spend another day in here with piles of towering crates and no clothes or towels to hand. I have masses of unpacking to do and yet here she is, standing, watching me, waiting. I give an embarrassed smile and my face burns at my predicament. I am still in my dressing gown after sleeping late and feel half naked. Martyn is still pretty fractious after last night's carry on and I need some time alone with him to make sure he is settled. He's had his medication and we now need some time for it to kick in. I just need a few minutes to contain him. He's upstairs right now, pacing, and won't react well to strangers being in the house.

My head buzzes as I watch her intently. I want to ignore her, to tell her to go away, but can't seem to tear my eyes away. The likeness is striking. My mind races as I try to make sense of why she is here, standing on my doorstep looking so much like her. I feel the familiar tugs of paranoia and ignore its desperate clutches. Suzie's face was a lot younger, obviously, and this lady before me is nearer my age, but she has the same oval-shaped face, the same features. The same radiant smile. Even her hair is the same as Suzie's was: light brown with a slight kink to it. The kink that Suzie hated and tried to straighten out which resulted in so many tantrums. She is exactly how Suzie would look if she were alive today. I know I shouldn't but I can't seem to stop staring. Despite knowing Martyn can make an appearance at any given moment, I am transfixed, my feet rooted to the spot.

She hands me a brightly coloured tin and offers me her hand to shake. 'Welcome to Cogglestone, our lovely little village. I'm Anna. I live at Pineleigh over the road: number eighteen? We moved in two years ago and I remember the whole palaver as if it were yesterday. It's so stressful, isn't it? I thought some cake might help.'

I listen to her gabble on and watch her mouth move, but I don't seem able to take in anything she is saying or give any kind of response. My mind has shifted a gear and is currently in overdrive. All I can hear is Suzie's voice. It fills my head: her desperate, blood-curdling howls as she screamed for me to help her. I can see her now as if it were yesterday: her eyes wide with terror as the water gradually rose around her and she disappeared under it, tiny bubbles of breath rising to the surface as she gasped her last.

Temples thrumming, I swallow hard and blot the image from my mind then shake this lady's hand. My palm is clammy and I am struggling to keep the tremor out of my fingers as I clasp them around hers. Her palm is cool, her fingers slender and small. I try to remember what she said her name was. Anna. I think that's it. Yes, I'm almost certain she is called Anna. Not Suzie. Definitely not Suzie. And she lives over the road. At number eighteen. I am overcome with wooziness and hang onto the door handle to steady myself. Jesus. What are the chances? And she lives there? This woman, the *very image* of her, standing right in front of me. She hands me the tin and waits. I stare for what feels like an age before realising she is waiting to be invited in. Please no. Not now. Not when she looks so much like her. I can't do it. Maybe another time when I'm more prepared. But not today, not now. I just can't.

'Thank you but I really must get on. So much to do,' I find myself saying and without stopping to think, I shut the door in her face. The noise it makes as I slam it closed reverberates around the empty hallway, an echoing reminder of what I have just done. A buzzing sensation fills my head. I lean back on the wall, cold and firm against my clammy body, and take a deep breath. God almighty, is this what I've become? I briefly consider re-opening it but something stops me. I just don't think I can continue looking at her without my legs giving way. I stand up straight then lean back against the doorframe, its sharpness and icy edge causing me to wince. I just need a minute to sort myself out.

I close my eyes and attempt to stem my breathing, which is raspy and irregular. This is silly. I must get myself right so I can sort Martyn out and then get started on unpacking and tidying this house. I simply cannot let myself get sucked into thinking about Suzie or things from the past. Thoughts like that will only drag me down to places I'd rather not revisit. I could do it with ease. Oh dear God, how effortless it would be to let myself go down that route, to sit and wallow in self-pity, allow the toxic memories to corrode my brain. But it's not going to happen. I am stronger than that. Besides, I have things to do today. I am busy.

Overhead, I hear Martyn clumping about. He's not brilliant this morning and in his condition, the slightest upset can have a detrimental effect on his well-being. He has a delicate constitution and it doesn't take a lot to alter his equilibrium. I will probably need to give him some painkillers to get him through the day. They might make him drowsy, more manageable. I perk up a little at the thought of an amenable Martyn. I'll get more done that way.

Outside, I see a shadow as Anna the neighbour passes by the window and heads back over the road. The pounding in my temple has reduced to a small tap. I bring my hand up and rub at my forehead. I don't know what came over me. She caught me off guard, you see, and I'm not a fan of unpleasant surprises. I will apologise for my behaviour another time, when I'm feeling more in control, less out of sorts. Right now, I have a husband to see to, boxes to unpack, a house to sort out and tidy.

Surprisingly, it doesn't take too long. Within a couple of hours, I have actually managed to empty over ten boxes and get the contents stacked into the correct cupboards. I stop and look around. The dressers and cabinets are polished and full. Everything is where it should be. It's a remarkably good feeling, knowing I've broken the back of the work. And Martyn has been a pussycat, settled and happy, pottering about the house, his mood lighter than last night. If the weather perks up, we may even have a wander in the garden later, work out what we can plant and where. I hum softly as I stand and admire the room. Clean, tidy and ready to live in.

An unfamiliar sound slices through the stillness of the room, killing the moment. I trace it to the dining room where my phone was placed yesterday and welcome the quiver of excitement I get when I realise what it is. I use it so rarely, I'm not sure I will ever become accustomed to its ringtone. I need a new one, something lighter that is less of an assault on my ears, but I haven't the energy or the inclination to work out how to do it.

I push my hair back off my face and answer it without looking at the screen. I already know who it is.

'Hi Mum, how's it going?'

My soul lightens as Tom speaks. I never realise how much I'm missing him until I hear the sound of his voice.

'I'm absolutely fine, darling. How are you and how is Mya?'

'We're great Mum, just fine and dandy. How did the move go? Not too stressful I hope?'

I laugh lightly and brush aside the memory of last night. All water under the bridge now.

'No, not at all. It was a bit of a breeze, actually. The removal men were a filthy lot but then that's the nature of their job, isn't it?'

I hear Tom sigh and can picture him rolling his eyes at my words. He thinks I'm an insufferable snob. I'm not. Of course I'm not. I just don't want to live like a hippy, surrounded by joss sticks and raffia matting the way he does.

'Anyway, I just thought I'd call and check everything was running smoothly. I didn't want to bother you yesterday. I knew you'd be up to your eyes in it.' His voice is clipped, his tone distant.

I've annoyed him now. He will go off and probably have a moan to Mya about how his mum is so old fashioned and more concerned with people's manners and decorum than is considered healthy. It's not true. I just like things to be right. Life is difficult enough without making it harder by being disorganised and messy. There's nothing wrong with wanting order in one's life, is there?

'Everything is perfect, darling. How's life in the Big Apple?'

I try to draw him back in so I can hear his voice for just a little while longer. Tom left for America shortly after his father's accident and I haven't seen him since. That was two years ago. Such a long time to go without seeing my only child. Unexpectedly, I feel a lump rise in my throat and have to fight back a sob. I fix my gaze on a copse of trees on the hills far in the distance to stop the tears escaping. Once I let them flow, they'll never stop.

'Yeah, yeah it's great, Mum. We're moving to a

new apartment soon. It's a lot bigger and in a better area. Work's good too. I got a bit of a promotion and now I have more of a say when we're marketing the company.'

I feel myself begin to shut down. He has a life there now and will probably never come home. Is this what I had planned for him? When he was a child, I had visions of him being a doctor like his father, not working for some IT company on the other side of the Atlantic. I have never even met his girlfriend. I always ask after her and try to show interest in her life but in actual fact, I know nothing about her: where she went to school, what her family are like, what *she* is like. It's as if I've been drawn out of the equation without even realising it.

'That's great, sweetheart, just great. I'm really pleased for you. If you're happy then I'm happy.'

I hope I sound convincing enough in my affirmation of his happiness despite wanting to sink to the floor to cry like a baby. I listen to him chatter on about work and his life far away from me.

'Mya and I have googled the new house. It looks amazing, Mum. Once we've got sorted in our own place, we'll have to think about coming to visit.'

Have to think about. His words cut through me. Not even a firm commitment to come and see his own mother. The tears threaten to spill over and the sour taste of bile begins to build in my gut. I will soon have to end this conversation before it becomes apparent I'm unravelling. A residual tiredness from yesterday gnaws at me, lowering my resilience.

'That will be lovely, darling. I look forward to it. Anyway, it's been lovely talking but I must dash as...'

There is a brief interlude before Tom speaks again. 'Is everything all right, Mum? You sound a bit... well a bit off, if I'm honest.'

I close my eyes and tighten my lips as I exhale. Hot air rushes out of me, slightly acrid with fear and resentment. He has my mood sussed. At least we still have some common ground. He is able to detect the nuances of my moods, to predict and pre-empt the workings of my mind, which is quite something when I barely understand it myself. I clear my throat and try to laugh.

'Oh, gosh no, not at all, sweetheart. Just a bit tired from the move. I think it must all be catching up with me. You know how it is.' *That and coping with your father,* I want to add, but remain tight lipped. Martyn is my problem and mine alone. He may be Tom's father but there is no love lost between the two of them and any mention of Martyn will ruin everything. I speak to my son rarely. I'm not about to spoil our time together.

I hope I've sounded convincing enough. I cough again to conceal a sob as tears begin to roll. Why, when I look forward to speaking to him so much, do I always end up feeling utterly miserable?

'Yeah, course. It's still early morning here so we're off out to work soon anyway. I just wanted to check you're okay with the move and everything that's gone on. You've had a tough time lately with Dad and your friend and everything. I just wanted to make sure you're managing.'

I feel a wave of dizziness at his words. *Managing*. My son wants to know if his own mother is able to cope with her lot in life. I close my eyes to steady myself. Am I managing? Who is to say? I never speak to anybody about it. There is little point. Talking can't change anything, make any of it any better. So I just wade through life, trying to make of it what I can. I smile and nod as Tom talks some more about his work and plans for the future, none of which includes me. Afraid he will sense my troubled state, I gabble on, say anything to keep him on the line for as long as I can before he tells me he really must go and so we bid our goodbyes, me with great reluctance and a huge lump in my throat, Tom with a dismissive farewell.

I turn my phone off and throw it across the table. It bounces across the wooden top, skidding off onto the floor with a crash. Tom's mention of his father was minimal. That's hardly surprising, really. Although Tom's decision to go into IT rather than medicine was disappointing for me, it completely infuriated Martyn. He said it was a waste of a damn good brain and told him it was a short-sighted move. Chasing the dollar was only ever going to be a short-term investment, he had said, whereas a degree in medicine was an insurance policy for life.

Right on cue, Martyn limps into the room. I watch his face for any signs of a mood which I have no energy to manage, but instead, he smiles and with an awkward gait, slumps down in the chair next to me. I am overwhelmed with relief, almost giddy with it.

'What's in there?' he asks and points to the brightly coloured tin sitting on the kitchen top next to the fridge. I feel a sharp breath catch in my chest as I remember the lady at the door. I was rude to her. She had caught me at a bad time and I reacted badly. I must make it up to her. Getting off on the wrong foot at our first meeting isn't a particularly auspicious start to a friendship.

'Cake,' I say quietly, hoping he doesn't detect the edge to my voice. Suzie's face has once again embedded itself in my head and refuses to go away.

'Shall I get us some?' he asks, his tone soft and warm. It takes me by surprise. I hear it so rarely, it makes me misty eyed.

'I'll do it,' I say, jumping to my feet. If I can keep myself busy, Suzie's face will disappear from my mind, retreat back into the farthest part of my brain where it belongs.

The tin opens with a soft, metallic thump. It's a Cath Kidston design. I know they're not cheap so I carefully place the lid to one side and lift out a beautifully decorated chocolate cake. I am swamped with guilt at my behaviour towards Anna – yes, I'm certain that's what she said her name was – as I cut into it and put each slice on a plate. I will apologise when I take her tin back. My behaviour was unacceptable. It was just the uncanny resemblance and her untimely appearance on my doorstep that threw me, you see. But I guess that's something I am going to have to get used to. We live so close, I can hardly avoid her. I am just going to have to come to terms with it and forget about Suzie, about how our last words were in raised in anger.

She had been showing off as usual, dancing about

on the riverbank, making sure she had the attention of all the others around us while I was left to clear up the mess everyone had so thoughtlessly discarded. And although she was wearing red and white striped hot pants – the fashion item of the day back then – she had insisted on stripping down to her bra and knickers in another of her bids for attention as she headed down to the water and jumped in. All the boys had flocked around her, and a few of the girls too, like flies around excrement. I had watched meekly from a clearing in the trees as they all splashed and cavorted around without a care in the world, too self-conscious myself to strip off and join them, my envy and resentment growing by the minute. Of course, there was no need for me to feel that way because after a while, as was always the case, they all tired of her. I could hear her barking orders at them all about where they should stand, what they should play, what the rules should be. Then, with a certain amount of inner satisfaction, I watched as one by one, they all trudged their way out of the river and back onto dry land where they made feeble excuses about having to get back for their tea, before gathering up their belongings and leaving.

'Phoebe. For God's sake! What the hell do you think you're doing?'

The boom of Martyn's voice and a crack of porcelain as it hits the floor, drags me back to the present. I look down to see my plate in pieces at my feet and my hands covered in clumps of deep brown icing. It is smeared everywhere: over my fingers, up my arms, on my clothes. Martyn is looking at me aghast, as if I have just committed some kind of terrible atrocity. I refuse to rise to it. I will handle the situation in as dignified a manner as I possibly can. Give him no opportunity to gloat or cause yet another argument.

'It's only cake,' I mutter feebly, 'it'll soon clear up.' I stand up and survey the damage.

'You do know what you were doing, don't you?'

I ignore him, disregard the scorn and sarcasm in his voice and instead, march past him, grab a roll of kitchen paper and rub it over my arms and clothing then kneel down and slowly wipe the floor clean.

'You were off in your own little world there. Muttering and swearing and shoving your hands in the cake, smearing it around the plate like a toddler. What was all that about then, eh?' He leans down to try and catch my eye. 'Having another of your little "moments" as we like to call them, were we?'

I pay no attention to him and continue cleaning the tiles until I can almost see my face in them. I listen to him in the background making derogatory remarks about me, laughing softly, pointing to bits I've missed with his cane. And then silence. I continue wiping, determined to eradicate all traces.

When I finally get up again, my knees cracking as I do, Martyn has gone. Lost interest and wandered off, leaving me to ponder over what happened. I hate losing control like that. It's embarrassing, unseemly and something I thought I'd managed to get under control. I have to stop thinking about that day by the river and focus on the here and now before I get dragged down to a place I don't want to go to.

I walk over to the patio doors, fling them open and breathe in the cold, clean air. I make a small promise to myself there and then. No more visits to the past. No more Suzie.

5

Anna's face burns with humiliation as she scurries away from the house, her feet crunching over the gravel driveway as she stumbles over the road and back home. By the time she gets in the front door and slams it behind her, she is close to tears. Stupid, really. It's nothing to get all worked up about. It was only a bloody cake after all. And besides which, her timing was all wrong. That poor woman was obviously up to her eyes in it, unpacking and shifting and rearranging things. Moving house is nightmarish.

Anna looks around and thinks back. Despite its many flaws – and God knows there are many: beams riddled with holes from a woodworm infestation and windows that have seen better days – she really does love her house. But the memory of moving in will never leave her. That awful, horrible day, fraught with worry and anxiety, waiting for money to change hands, traipsing backward and forwards transporting things, realising most of your furniture doesn't even fit. Awful. And anyway, it's her own daft fault. She should have left her welcome visit for a couple of days before bothering her with piddly little cakes. Mike was right. She was just being bloody nosy, hoping she might get invited in for a look around. It's a fabulous house and truth be told, she is more than just a teensy bit jealous. Anna's house is a three-bedroom, Victorian building with dark corners and sloping floors. This new lady's home is a show home: huge, immaculate and expensively furnished. Everything hers isn't.

By the time Anna has emptied the tumble drier and set up the ironing board, she has convinced herself that her new neighbour didn't mean any harm, although there was something in her expression that made Anna feel a bit uneasy. A hard, unblinking stare that put her on edge, made her skin prickle. Or maybe she is just reading too much into it after having the door closed on her. She shrugs idly and tells herself to never give up. If there's one thing she is determined to be, it is friendly and neighbourly. There is no way she is about to let this embarrassing situation get to her or stop her. She is nothing if not tenacious. She'll just give her some time to settle in and call round again when the poor woman is unpacked and settled and not feeling under so much pressure. Bad timing. That's all it was. Just bad timing.

Mike marches into the kitchen and eyes up the steaming iron. 'You haven't forgotten, have you?'

She stares at him, willing her brain to register his words. Nothing comes.

'New flooring? You wanted me there to check it's the right colour? Said you wanted a second opinion?'

Anna slaps the flat of her hand against her forehead and closes her eyes in annoyance. She has nagged him about it for days, complaining that everything has to wait till weekends because he is always at bloody work. How can she have not remembered when it has been in her mind all week?

'Right. Of course.' She unplugs the iron and folds the board up, dragging it behind the fridge. She stares in the mirror and frowns at her reflection, 'Just give me five minutes to run a comb through my hair and I'll be right with you.'

As if it's not bad enough having a new neighbour with a house big enough to fit ten of her own in, she also looked like the kind of person who wakes up looking perfectly groomed. Not pretty – well, certainly not conventionally pretty for sure – but flawlessly put together. Expensive looking. Like she buys her make up from the most exclusive shops and gets her hair done at the best salons.

In the bedroom, Anna brushes her flyaway hair, sprays perfume around her in a fine mist and applies a slick of lipstick. Not brilliant but better than plain and pale faced. She slips her feet into a pair of leather boots and stares in the mirror. An image of a middle-aged, underfed woman stares back at her. How did she get this old and this thin when in her head, she is still eighteen years old? Anna clicks her tongue and hurries back downstairs. She's only going shopping for floor tiles for God's sake, not parading down a bloody catwalk.

She checks her handbag and listens as Mike hollers upstairs, issuing stern instructions to the boys about how to behave in their absence. He comes back carrying jackets for them both. Anna waits as he hands hers over and slings his own over his shoulders then snatches up the car keys from the fruit bowl.

'Ready?' he asks.

'No arguing over colours or designs,' she says smiling. 'You did promise to be nice.'

'As long you buy me lunch afterwards.'

She follows him out to the car. 'It's a deal.'

6

Upstairs, Callum and Mason listen out for the familiar slam of the door and stop everything they're doing.

'The parents have left the building,' Mason croons, a crooked smile forming as he clambers up to the window and watches their dad's silver Vectra pull off the drive.

'What's the plan then?' Callum swings his legs off his unmade bed and hitches his trousers up past his exposed hipbone. He kicks his way through the mass of machinery and games that cover the bedroom floor and leans into the wardrobe to retrieve a pair of multicoloured baseball boots.

'I'll give Sammo a ring. Tell him we're out and

about. His old man'll drop him off at ours. Sammo's always good for a laugh.'

Callum sucks his teeth then nods in approval. 'Nice one. What about AJ? Shall I message him d'ya think?'

'Aw man, no party without the one and only AJ. Course you should.'

They each tap away at their phones, letting out small guffaws at the replies before stuffing them in their back pockets and heading downstairs.

'Sammo reckons he'll be here in less than ten. His dad was heading this way anyhow.' Mason is standing in front of the open fridge staring in, his face bathed in the glow of the yellow light. He lunges his hand in and grabs at a wedge of cheese.

'She'll notice, you know.' Callum watches as his brother cuts off a hunk of cheddar and presses it between two slices of bread. Mason shrugs nonchalantly and sinks his teeth into it, flecks of doughy residue stuck between his teeth.

'Gotta eat, haven't I?'

His younger brother shrugs and turns away. 'Your funeral, mate. You know what she's like.'

Mason continues to munch noisily. Callum watches him and then grabs at a milk carton, swilling it back greedily, rivulets of milk running down his chin and neck in small white streams. He pushes it back inside and marches past. 'Gonna head off outside. Don't forget to lock up.'

'I'm right behind you man. Wait up.'

Together, they stroll outside and hang around, waiting for the others to turn up. The cold bites at them, a wave of icy wind buffeting them as they dance about outside the front gate.

'Fuck, it's freezing!' Mason hops from one foot to another and hugs his hands under his armpits for warmth, their denim jackets and hoodies no barrier against the bracing north-easterly wind as they wait for their mates to arrive.

'Is that them?' Callum cranes his neck and stares off down towards the end of the village at two willowy figures who are heading their way.

'Yo Sammo!' One of the shapes raises a hand as Callum's voice reaches them.

'Must have both got a lift,' mutters Mason as he shoves his hands deep in his pocket to warm them up.

'No shit Sherlock,' Callum replies and they both laugh. It's a phrase they both use regularly and it never fails to elicit a cackle.

'So what's the plan then?' AJ and Sammo run the last few metres, their long legs gazelle-like in their dark, skin-tight jeans. Callum and Mason shrug listlessly.

'Dunno. No plan really. Just hang around, have a few laughs.'

If there's one thing they both know, it's that sticking to the rule of no friends in the house when their parents are out, is absolute. Their mother can sniff out lies and traces of uninvited guests at fifty paces and they know from bitter experience that trying to pull a fast one just isn't worth it.

'How about heading off down there?' AJ nods over in the direction of the river. They all stare at one another, waiting for someone to make a decision. Mason nods and flicks at his hair.

'Yeah. Sound.' He stares at his brother. The river might be high but it's easier than trying to cover their tracks if they go in the house. She would find out. She always finds out.

The four lads slope off over the green and down towards the bushes. They spend a good few hours by the river, skimming stones and making mud slides. AJ even tries to build a makeshift bridge over the water using logs and sticks and all manner of debris he can find in the dense undergrowth until eventually, boredom sets in. Callum rubs at his hands and sniffs loudly. Even with keeping moving and using the shrubbery as protection from the wind, there is no denying it is freezing.

'What now?' Mason asks, the tip of his nose red from the cold.

AJ shrugs listlessly. 'Dunno.'

'What about hanging around that unused garden again? Was a right laugh last time.' Sammo is pointing towards the back of Phoebe's house, his finger wobbling about as they all gaze at the summerhouse they had used as a hang out when the place was empty.

'Nah. No can do,' Callum says, a flicker of apprehension in his belly. 'Someone moved in yesterday so it's out of bounds now.'

Sammo smiles and Callum feels the flicker turn up a notch. That's the only problem with his mate. He might be a good laugh but sometimes he takes things too far. It's a double-edged sword really. His antics are hilarious but they come at a price. And this place is too close to home for Callum and his brother to be involved in anything too raucous. Their mum would kill them if they upset a new neighbour. She's really hot on stuff like that, making a good impression and everything.

'What difference does that make? Just adds to the fun.' A glint is evident in Sammo's eye. Callum flinches slightly and looks over at Mason who is staring at the floor.

'No way, Sammo. The other owners were in Spain while it was empty. This new one can see us from her kitchen window.'

'Like I said,' Sammo repeated, his voice crackling with menace, 'all part of the fun.'

AJ smiles while Callum and Mason exchange a worried glance. It's okay for them. None of this is near where they live. Sammo always makes sure of that. His dad would kill him if he did anything bad near his house. Sammo and his old man are pretty close since his mum died but his dad rules their house with a rod of iron. Mason finds himself wishing he hadn't bothered letting his brother get in touch with him. This is obviously one of Sammo's nutter days where anything goes. He has times like that, as if he is almost bordering on lunacy. Mason's mam reckons it's since his mother passed away, some kind of rebellion or kick back at being abandoned. Mason just reckons it's because he is some kind of thrill seeker with no inhibitions. A right loony. He remembers the time Sammo once climbed up on the school roof and abseiled down by tying the assembly hall curtains to some external pipe work. By the time he had reached the bottom, the fire brigade were there along with his dad who grounded him for like, forever. Such a nutcase. The only reason he wasn't excluded from school was because he gets straight A's and is heading for A*'s in all his exams.

'No way,' Mason pipes up, 'Like my bro just told you, the place is out of bounds. You can't break into stuff when it's not empty any more. The last time was a good laugh 'cos there was nobody living there and we could doss around in there not bothering anyone but a woman and her husband moved in yesterday so it's a no go. Let's go back down by the river, yeah? Or we can grab some skateboards and go over by the path where it's wider.'

AJ and Sammo look at each other and smirk.

'Didn't know you two were such a pair of nancy-boys. What's up? Scared of getting caught by Mummy and Daddy?'

The words hang in the air, sour and acrid as all four lads stare at one another.

'Do whatever you want, Sammo. You too, AJ,' Mason croaks, resentment and annoyance evident in his tone, 'but count me out. If you wanna act like a complete prick, that's up to you but I'm off.' He stares at Callum who nods and starts to wander back in the direction of their house.

'Yeah, go on you pair of soft twats. Run and cuddle in to Mummy's apron.'

They ignore the jibes and head off home, looking back only once to see their mates disappear behind the shrubbery that leads onto the path at the back of the garden.

'Not worth the fucking hassle,' Callum says as they unlock the door and let themselves in.

7

It has been a morning of ups and downs. So much to deal with, so many oscillating moods. Neighbours banging on the door, memories resurfacing unbidden. And now this. My hands rest on the oak unit as I stare out at the far end of the garden. As far as I can tell, there are just two of them, wandering along the public footpath, wearing hoodies and low-slung jeans to complete the picture. I guess this is to be expected. As the lady in the shop so kindly pointed out, I will have a load of strangers traipsing through my garden. I just didn't expect it so soon. And I definitely didn't expect teenagers. This is a rugged area, a path that forms part of a well-known local walk. I presumed it would be used by ramblers, people who were serious about their love of the countryside, not gangs of youngsters skulking around, looking for trouble. I move back as one of them looks up at the house and feel a slight jab of fear as they start to walk up my garden towards the old summerhouse: the same summerhouse that had a broken lock when I initially viewed the property. Everything suddenly begins to slot into place. The sheer arrogance of these two wasters, it would appear, knows no bounds. I do know this place had been vacant for some time before I bought it so maybe they presume it is still empty? Well, it's going come as a terrible shock when they find out their silly plan has been rumbled. Of course, there is another reason I need to get rid of them. Martyn. If he comes in and spots some suspicious-looking teenagers hanging around his garden, he will have a fit. Best thing to do is to scatter them before the whole thing escalates. Which it will. It's been that kind of day.

I shrug on my coat and pull on a pair of old wellies then step outside. The stillness hits me as I stride over the back step and look around. Wherever there is a group of young lads, there is noise. Except at the minute, there isn't. It is completely silent. The distant roar of the river greets me as I make my way over to the sage-green summerhouse with its fading paint and dirty windows, but it is the only sound for miles. No voices, nobody there at all. I tentatively creep around the side of it, expecting to be greeted by a wave of surprised faces and perhaps even a fog of cigarette smoke. Nothing.

They are here somewhere. They have to be. There's nowhere else for them to go. They are here in my garden and I will find them. I turn and start to make my way back up towards the house and that's when it happens. It doesn't hurt too much. Not really. But as the clod of mud hits the side of my face, a red mist descends and I find myself marching over in the direction from where it came, my anger rising by the second. I find them huddled down the side of the old coal bunker, a pair of spotty, teenage miscreants. They look up at me and slowly creep out from their hiding place, two acne-ridden, gangly youths caught in the act, a supercilious smirk on their faces that riles me even more.

'What the hell do you two think you are doing?' I am absolutely incensed by their lack of guilt and in no doubt that it shows in my face. I briefly close my eyes to try to disguise my rage, and do my best to look authoritative.

'Just having a laugh, grandma. Lighten up, will ya,' the smaller one says and they both fall about laughing, clutching their sides in an exaggerated manner like a pair of overgrown toddlers. Such immaturity from boys who, less than a century ago, would have been put to work in all manner of hazardous conditions. That's what's missing in this day and age. Discipline and a healthy helping of fear.

I observe them carefully. They are kids, no more than twelve or thirteen years old. I keep my gaze steady, watching their every move as very slowly, I begin to back up towards the house. The smaller one nudges the other and they start to follow me, thinking it's all a big game, and completely unaware of what they are about to be faced with. I have no doubt that they'll cave in when they see a six-foot tall man standing in wait for them. Six feet four inches to be precise, with hands like shovels. Compared to Martyn, these two delinquents are mere babies. I continue backing up, taking it carefully, watching my step so as to not fall. I am almost at the door when I hear Martyn behind me, feel his hot breath on my neck. I hear the sharp grating sound as he grabs something from the kitchen. My stomach plummets. I run inside to try to stop him, to wrestle it from his grasp, but it is too late. He's too far gone to do anything and I'm left with no option other than to watch, fear pulsing through me as I see him step out towards the boys, his hand thrust forward, primed and ready. I look down, already aware of what I will see. He is brandishing a knife, a large, jagged, bread knife, its blade glinting as it meets the glare of the low sun.

'Shit!' The boys stagger backwards and slide over, one of them falling on his rear end in the mud. He scrambles to get up but Martyn is faster and I stare open mouthed as my husband kneels over him, the serrated blade just centimetres from the young lad's face, so close that the boy's hot rapid breath mists up the steel of the knife.

'Jesus! All right. It was only a bit of a laugh! Christ almighty, we're really sorry!'

His friend is rooted to the spot, his eyes wide with fright. A small spot of saliva trickles down the corner of his mouth and he snaps it shut and rubs at his chin with the tattered sleeve of his dark-blue sweatshirt. Martyn looks at them both and speaks slowly, enunciating every word.

'Leave. Us. Alone. Don't ever come here again. Get out of my garden and tell nobody about this, you understand? Nobody. You never speak of this again. Not even to each other. And if I catch you hanging round here any more, I will take this knife to your throat and slice it in two. Is that clear?'

The smaller of the two looks over at me, fear

oozing from every pore. 'Jesus! Yes, it's clear! Fuck, we were only kidding, missus.'

Martyn continues, untroubled by their fear. Unstoppable. 'Nobody. Understand?' His voice is barely audible, deeply sinister and wholly intimidating.

'Nobody. We promise! Don't we, AJ?'

The other boy nods and as I look, I see a small wet patch begin to form on his crotch, a dark spread of terror for all the world to see. I wince, my own initial anger now diminishing, aware that yet again, Martyn has taken it too far. His anger has won and gotten the better of him. And yet at the same time I feel... What is it I feel? Apart from my own rage beginning to slowly dissipate, somehow I now feel vindicated. These boys with their stupid antics could have seriously hurt me. What's to say they would have stopped at hurling mud? What next? Small stones, shards of glass? Boys of this age don't always understand the consequences of their actions. They need to be taught what can happen if you let yourself be led by your friends. And now they have been given a salutary lesson on how to behave around other people. And hopefully, it will stay with them for many years to come.

I push Martyn back in the house and watch as the youngsters scramble up awkwardly. One of them turns to face me, his face wet and streaked with tears.

'We're sorry, missus. Please don't...' His eyes drop to my hand and I look down to see that I am now holding the knife. I don't remember taking it or Martyn handing it to me but it is there, cold and heavy, my fingers curled around its smooth, solid handle.

'Remember,' I say coolly, 'not a word to anyone and that way you won't get arrested for trespassing.'

He nods violently, a river of snot and tears running down his face. He catches up with his friend and together, they dart out of the garden, onto the path and round back into the village. They gallop away at an almighty pace and keep on running until they are two small specks disappearing into the distance. I stand and watch, hoping they keep to their promise to stay silent because if they don't, we are well and truly done for. Then I slowly pad back into the kitchen and heave a sigh of relief.

Back in the house, I rummage in my bag and find a couple of headache pills. My temples pound as I throw them in my mouth and hold my head under the tap to rinse them down. I turn to see Martyn watching me. I want to shout at him that it was all too much but am not sure if he has calmed down enough for me to reprimand him or whether or not he will turn his mood on me. I am too tired to take any chances so remain silent and wait for the incessant drumming in my head to ease up. This isn't the way I planned to spend my day. I so wanted us to be happy in this place and already, he has tainted it. Will this nightmare ever end?

We continue watching each other, a curtain of silence separating us until at last, he speaks.

'I was only trying to protect you. They could have seriously hurt you.'

I am taciturn. Always the best way. When in doubt, say absolutely nothing. My eyes travel down to his walking stick. It's laid on the ground at his feet. He must have dropped it in his haste to get out there and 'help' me. I bend over and pick it up, feeling the familiar curve of its handle under my palm.

'Here. Don't try to walk for too long without it. You'll only damage yourself and suffer in the morning.'

He nods and takes it. Behind him, the knife sits on the oak dresser where I have placed it. I will get it later when he isn't around and this time, I'll hide it away at the back of a cupboard. Somewhere he can't reach.

I stay still, not wanting to distract him, to tip the

balance. Because that's what it's all about. Balance and a certain amount of delicacy. Knowing when to speak and knowing when to say and do absolutely nothing at all.

'I might go for a nap if it's okay with you? I didn't sleep too well last night,' he says. This is his way of calming down, escaping from a situation he has created and doesn't know how to solve. I tell him I think it's a good idea and wait till he is out of the room and heading upstairs before I take the knife and hide it away.

And so it continues. Just when I thought we could start afresh, Martyn goes and does it again. I close my eyes and breathe deeply, my nostrils flaring as I inhale a lungful of cold air. This simply isn't fair. And although I'm no saint, I don't believe for one minute that I deserve this.

I stare around the kitchen, my eyes eventually landing on something bright and eye catching. Anna's cake tin. I should really take it back. And while I'm there, I can apologise, start again, be friendly. God knows this day needs some improvement.

I am still in my wellies. I pull them off and slip into my favourite loafers, slip my arms into my coat, then reach up and grab the tin. Before I have chance to change my mind, I charge out of the house and lock up.

I stand at the end of the drive and cast my eyes along the village, still impressed by its beauty, even after all these years. To one side, a sweeping village green, manicured and lush, with the river beyond, and to the other side, an array of houses, all different in style, each boasting their own unique charm. Cottages, large villas, small villas, bungalows, houses restored to their former glory and then those newly built in keeping with the village 'look' so only a trained eye would spot the difference between them. Fields huddle the perimeter of the village green and continue for as far as the eye can see. I breathe deeply. Seeing this is so far removed from the red-brick houses and countless buildings I used to live near that I'm not sure I'll ever lose an appreciation of it. I count along and stop at the Victorian-style villa even though there is really no need for me to. I could find my way to it blindfolded. There is a scribble of wrought iron running around its perimeter and two hanging baskets sitting either side of the front door. Not much has changed. The front lawn has been paved over and the fence replaces the hedge that used to house sparrows, blue tits and blackbirds but apart from that, everything is pretty much how I remember. I march over and knock at the door with the phrase *no time like the present* rattling around in my head.

My heart leaps up my chest when I first see him. It takes a few seconds to realise that this is a different boy from the one lurking around in the garden earlier. He is the same height with the same type of greasy-looking, lank hair that hangs in front of his eyes. Admittedly, when it comes to teenagers, I am guilty of thinking that they all look the same, with their low-slung, tight jeans and floppy hairstyles. I am so relieved, I almost laugh out loud. I hold out the tin and smile.

'I just wanted to give this back to your mum.'

He doesn't respond but continues to stare at me, a glazed expression on his face. My heart pounds and I begin to worry that I'm mistaken and it actually is one of the other boys. I'm about to make my retreat when at last he speaks.

'Oh right, yeah. Sorry, she's not in at the moment. I'll let her know when she gets back.' He watches me carefully and bites his lip, obviously unsure how to respond. 'Er, do you wanna come in and wait? Not sure how long she'll be, though. She's out with Dad looking at floor tiles.'

I shake my head and smile at him. He seems quite

sweet. And nervous. Especially compared to those two earlier. *Rapscallions* my mother would have called them. I can think of far worse names for boys of that ilk, most of them too disgusting to say out loud.

'Tell her thank you and that the cake was delicious. I'm sorry she caught me unawares earlier. I was just a bit snowed under with unpacking and everything.'

The boy twists his lip slightly to indicate his confusion and nods. 'Yeah, no problem. I'll let her know.'

There is a distinct chill in the air as I leave Anna's house. Despite that, it's bright, the sun hanging lazily over the horizon, a reminder of spring close by. I feel a slight stab of disappointment at not getting to see the inside of the house and find myself wondering if Anna is the type of person to go for the minimalist look, knock walls down and tear the very heart and soul out of the house, or if she has decided to retain its inner charm. I really hope it's the latter but remind myself that it is no longer any of my business.

I decide to have a stroll through the village. Martyn is sleeping; for a few brief minutes, I am free from his demands, able to do as I please. I head past the village green where I stop to stare at the line of undulating hills opposite. The copse of trees is still the same: a small, huddled shape in the distance, like an old man stooping. That pleases me immensely, the thought that nature has held fast in my absence. I let out an audible sigh. It really is quite breath-taking. I feel a stab of pity when I think of Martyn. Stuck inside, day in, day out. Such a miserable state of affairs when you consider what an active, intelligent man he used to be and now life is simply passing him by.

The road narrows as I walk past the row of houses until it's no more than a lane running through a series of fields to the next village. With just one postbox, it could hardly even be described as a village. More of a hamlet. I continue on down the lane, a different place entirely without fog: pretty, not at all sinister. On a whim, I stop and lean back against a fence that is rotten and leaning so badly, I worry it might collapse under my weight. Delving deep into my pocket, I rummage around until my fingers land on it, cool and inviting. I lift out a battered cigarette packet and flip it open. Three in there, along with a lighter. My secret stash. It's been so long and I shouldn't really. Before I have a chance to talk myself out of it, I put one between my lips, light it up and take a long, dizzying drag. Shrouded in a haze of bliss, I rapidly inhale again and look up, my eyes drawn to the cornflower blue of the sky. The sun emits a trickle of warmth as I inhale once more. I blow a long line of smoke out and watch as it curls around and disappears into the air around me, leaving a lingering, white haze in its wake. Three puffs. Enough to keep me going. For now.

After five minutes or so of picking my way through puddles and flattened slabs of cow pats, I decide to turn around and walk back home. I think of Tillie and how she would have loved this and then remember how it would have taken twice as long while she stopped to sniff every blade of grass and pee on anything that didn't move. It's quiet, nobody about. No teenagers with parents trailing behind or worse still, the police in tow, ready to file a complaint. A low, constant drone fills my head at the thought of it. With any luck, they will be too frightened to say anything. Who would believe them anyway? Our word against theirs is what it would come down to. Anxiety flutters around my brain, tapping at my temples with a relentless, rhythmic force. I do my best to ignore it and stare off into the distance as I pick up my pace. I suddenly feel exposed, as if all the eyes of the village are upon me, scrutinising my every move, knowing about the events of this morning. Knowing about Martyn. Knowing about me. Before I can stop myself, I'm almost running, hurrying along, needing to get back in to the safety of the house.

When I return, it is silent. Martyn will probably be fast asleep by now. I switch on the radio, make some tea and enjoy the solitude, resting back into the comfort of the sofa, surrounded by the sound of classical music in the background. I love times like this but am acutely aware that they're as rare as hen's teeth, so I always make the most of them while I can. A little piece of heaven is what it is. I take my time, determined to enjoy it. Somehow I manage to clear my head of everything – Martyn, Suzie, the awful carry on earlier – and close my eyes against the rising tide of misery that permanently threatens to engulf me. My tea is almost cold by the time I finish it but that's fine. I feel better than I have in a while. I put my cup down beside me with a light clink. And then, as is always the case with good things, my peace and quiet comes to an abrupt end.

8

I wish she had been in when I called earlier as I would much rather be sat at her kitchen table than have her sitting at mine as she is now. I like to plan before I have visitors, you see. Especially after that awful debacle with those boys earlier. That particularly unpleasant incident has upset the stability of the house, put me on edge around Martyn. I had my peace and quiet, my little bit of utopia, managed to settle my nerves and now I'm now on tenterhooks again, listening out for him above us. That's the thing. I don't know how he'll respond if he wakes and comes down to find a stranger sitting here with me. He really isn't good with uninvited guests. They make him nervous which in turn makes him unpredictable. And as this morning's carry on clearly shows, an unpredictable Martyn is a dangerous one. I wanted to be able to pre-empt her visits, prepare my husband, get him in the right frame of mind. But here she is, pretty, bubbly, charming. Sitting opposite me. In my house.

I try to look away from her face. Ignore the way her hair bounces around as she talks, not stare at her slightly upturned nose. God, it's like having Suzie sat here with me. Except of course, it couldn't possibly be. Suzie isn't here and hasn't been for a long, long time. She died thirty-eight years ago, and I need to keep reminding myself of that fact, which is so very hard to do when it feels like only yesterday.

I try to banish all thoughts of her and listen to this lady, this vision of the past as she tells me all about her life, about her sons and husband, her life in the village, even about the death of her sister a few years back. About how much she misses her. Her mouth moves in slow motion, her eyes shimmering with unshed tears and the more she talks, the more I want her to stop. I have a vision of slapping my hand over her mouth to stop all sound coming out and feel a small shriek begin to build inside my head. I have

to exercise all my self-restraint to prevent it from escaping. A pain travels down my neck as I twist to
listen to a creak above me. I quickly finish my tea in
the hope she'll take the hint and finish hers. Instead,
she continues to chat about things: her hobbies, her
house – just things, nothing of any substance. But the
resemblance, it's making me lose focus, setting my
nerves alight.

I give myself a stern talking to. The way she looks
is something I am going to have to become accustomed to. I have only just moved in and Anna and her
family aren't going anywhere. Avoiding her simply
isn't possible. I listen out for more sounds of movement, the tell-tale noises that will tell me Martyn is
up and about, but it has gone quiet up there. I rotate
my frozen shoulders and try to relax and join in with
the conversation. After all, this is what I wanted, isn't
it? More contact with people, to be able to make new
friends, perhaps even get out of the house a bit more
and leave Martyn to potter around here on his own.
How fantastic would that be? How bloody amazing.
To be free of him. To be me.

'So as I say, it's lovely having somebody closer in
age to chat to. It was beginning to seem like a retire-
ment home around here.'

I snap back into the conversation, my attention

constantly being diverted by the worry of Martyn wandering above us or yanked back to that day by the river all those years ago. She seems nice, this Anna. I'm being rude and have to make more of an effort. It's tiring being permanently on edge. I let out a stifled yawn and stretch my neck to release the tension. Tillie patters around behind us, oblivious to everything and everyone. She is fixated on the birds that are swooping and diving outside the window. Great tits and thrushes fight for the scraps of bread I threw out earlier, their tiny wings flapping ferociously as they lodge small chunks of dough between their beaks and dart off into the trees. I envy them: their freedom and ability to flit off whenever the fancy takes them.

'Maybe we can get together for coffee sometime on a regular basis, swap recipes and stuff? I enjoy a bit of gardening too, although our tiny patch is nothing compared to yours. You are so lucky. This is a fabulous house.'

I ruminate over what she is saying. *Lucky* isn't a word I would ever use to describe my life. I am anything but.

She eyes her watch and makes a move to get up. Just in time. I hear a slight creak above us. I freeze and look up. The hairs on the back of my neck prickle in alarm. She doesn't seem to hear it, thank God. It stops once more and I exhale more loudly than I intended to. She scrapes her chair across the tiles, stands up and leans on the back of it.

'This is an amazing place you have here, Phoebe. One of my boys was out the back and said they thought they heard you talking with somebody on the day you moved in.'

And so it begins. I quickly consider my options. Should I lie to her? Is that really the best way to begin a friendship? I think she lives too close by to do that. I'm just not sure Martyn is up to a stream of visitors quite yet. Or if he will ever be. I steel myself for what I'm about to say.

'Yes, that would my husband, Martyn.'

I leave it at that, hoping it's enough for her. Of course it isn't. It never is. People are naturally curious. Too curious sometimes. And that's when things usually take a turn for the worse. Some people just can't leave it be.

'Oh, he must be out, is he?'

Her eyes shine with girlish innocence. I want to scream at her that apart from the journey here, he hasn't been out for two years. But I don't. Of course I don't. It isn't her fault we live like prisoners. So instead, I speak softly, remaining calm and composed, my unflustered, steady demeanour belying the torment that lies within.

'He's upstairs, napping. Martyn rarely leaves the house. He's disabled, you see.'

This usually stops people in their tracks, makes them acutely embarrassed, injects an awkward silence into the conversation. Not with Anna. If anything, it seems to fuel her interest. She sits back down, leans towards me and cups my hand in hers.

'Oh Phoebe, that must be so difficult for you! I had an inkling when I first saw you. I have a sense about these things, you see. Grandma Radley, my mum's mum, used to read tea leaves and I think I must have got it from that side of the family.' I am seconds from telling her to shut up and that she knows nothing about such nonsense. Bloody tea leaves? She continues on, her eyes suddenly shimmering with excitement. 'Has he always been disabled or is it a recent thing?'

My head begins to throb and I have to clear my throat to speak. It is thick with trepidation. I don't want him coming down here. I don't want her hurt.

'It's a recent thing. A couple of years ago, actually. We were cliff walking at Whitby and Martyn slipped and fell. He broke his hip and collarbone and suffered a fractured skull. He was very ill for quite a long time afterwards. He has a limp and sometimes suffers headaches but unfortunately, the psychological impact has been the hardest to deal with. It's been quite devastating for him.'

I try to still my trembling fingers which remain cupped in Anna's warm palm.

'Oh, I'll bet it has! Poor man. Does he suffer from nightmares? Probably PTSD.'

I am inexplicably maddened by her words. Suddenly, she's an expert. Everybody is. Except they don't have to live with it, whereas I do. I've lived with it for over two years now and it feels like an age.

'He's developed agoraphobia and suffers from depression and a personality disorder. He also needs a cane to help him walk but his mental state is far worse than his physical one, I'm afraid.'

I close my eyes, suddenly overcome with dizziness and exhaustion. This is the first time I've spoken openly to anyone about Martyn and his issues. Since the accident, we've just got on with our lives, tried to ignore our predicament and just make the best of what we have. There are many times I've been in danger of becoming agoraphobic myself. I've been so reluctant to get out and meet people, to talk about our lives and our problems. I wonder if this is what I need. Maybe this will be the catalyst that will, at long last, turn our lives around.

'Oh you poor, poor dears!' Anna stands up again, leaving go of my hand, which is now clammy and trembling and she starts counting off things with her fingers. 'Well first off, we must meet him and assure him we're here to help him out then with a bit of gentle persuasion, we might be able to get him to amble around your lovely garden. It might help if he gets to meet the walkers that pass through here. I know a bit about phobias with my studies with the Open University. I mean, I'm no expert but...'

'No,' I half shout, not meaning to but too worried to disguise the anxiety I feel at her suggestion, 'he won't respond well to interventions from strangers.' I suddenly feel I'm losing my grip and try to steady my breathing. My heart begins to vibrate wildly, climbing its way up my neck at her words.

She looks at me, her eyes glassy and wide. 'But we're neighbours, not strangers.'

My mind is in a complete whirl. I stare up at the clock on the kitchen wall. 'I'm really sorry but I need to go and wake Martyn so if you'll excuse me...'

I make my way into the hallway towards the front door, hoping she'll follow me. Anna remains in the kitchen, her voice filtering through to me as she speaks. So accepting. So innocent. So terribly, terribly naïve.

'I can stay and give you a hand if you like? I'm studying for a diploma in psychology and as I said earlier, I know a thing or two about mental health issues.'

I am running out of options and now need her to leave. If Martyn wakes and finds her here, there's no telling what he will do. A million things go through my head about how I should never have moved here, how I should have accepted the stronger medication the doctor offered at our old surgery, how I could once again just push this woman out of the door and slam it shut behind her.

'But if you're sure you can manage, then I guess I'll be off. I've been out all morning and have things to catch up on.'

She is beside me in an instant and I am delirious with a mixture of guilt and relief. Here she is, baking for me, being friendly, offering to help and here I am, working out ways in which I can shove her out of the door.

'Look, I'm so sorry to appear rude, Suzie. It's just Martyn wakes up in such a grump and I need to calm him down before we do anything. Maybe I can call around and see you another time when we're both feeling a bit more relaxed?'

She stares at me for a few seconds, puzzled, then gives me a small smile. 'Of course. That's probably a good idea. It's Anna, by the way,' she whispers as she touches my shoulder lightly, 'not Suzie.'

And with that, she is gone, her hair bouncing in the breeze as she makes her way back home.

9

THIRTY-EIGHT YEARS EARLIER

I watched as the others splashed about in the puddles, too excited and full of themselves to notice me lurking in the background. That had always been the way: Suzie leading the pack, full of spirit and energy while I hung about like an unwanted puppy.

Mother had made Suzie take me along while she stayed at home and put up with our father. Besides his drunken, boorish behaviour and bouts of indescribable rage, she also had to cope with his health, which had been failing for some time. Poor Mother was at her wits end as to how to manage it all. Summer holidays were the bane of her life, trying to keep us entertained and out of her hair while having to put up with our father. Suzie couldn't see it of course, but I could. I used to watch as our mum struggled to help him in and out of his chair when he was deep in the drink, the sheer effort of it draining all the colour out of her face. I was too little to help but I willed her on and wished there was a better way. An easier way. Which eventually, after he died, there was. Unfortunately, it wasn't the easy way for me. But that's another story.

'Come on, don't be such a spoilsport Phoebe!'

Suzie stood in front of me, damp and full of excitement, her eyes glistening like tiny, azure marbles set deep in her flawless face.

'I don't want to get wet,' I said sullenly. I tried to not whine but couldn't help it. I was tired and bored and wanted to go home. Even watching Mother try to cope with Father's demands and dance around the conflict caused by his alcoholism was infinitely better than watching Suzie act like she was something she wasn't when her friends were around. It drove me mad to hear her false laughter and see how she manipulated everyone around her. Of course, they were all too blind to see it, too transfixed by her beauty and confidence. *Thirteen going on thirty* our aunt used to say.

'Oh, come on. Let your hair down for once, why don't you? It's such good fun. Everyone's having a whale of a time!' she shouted as she spun around, moving closer to me with every step. The pavement glistened and sparkled under her feet like a sheet of glass embedded with diamonds.

'It's only rain, Suzie! Why make such a fuss over a bit of rain? And why dance around like an idiot?'

She didn't hear me. She was deaf to my pleas, too caught up in the moment. I continued to watch as they played games, leaping over huge puddles, some of them landing smack in the centre, sending dirty water spraying up into the air. I failed to see the allure. And Suzie was old enough to know better. This was a pastime for seven year olds. As far as I could see, it was just plain silly. Then in what seemed like an instant, the rain stopped and a split appeared in the clouds overhead, revealing a perfect blue sky. A whoop of excitement went up as the rest of Suzie's gang clapped and cheered. Such childish behaviour. I was irritated beyond reason.

'Let's head down to the river!' one of them yelled, 'It'll be really fast after the downpour. We can go swimming.'

My skin prickled as I saw the look of delight on Suzie's face. 'We're not allowed to go down by the river when it's been raining. It's slippery and gets flooded. The path might even be under water by now,' I said, hoping my words might sway her.

She would go. Of course she would. Like Suzie ever took any notice of anything anyone ever said, least of all me, her younger sister. And if Suzie went, I would have to go too, trailing behind like a bad smell. Making friends had never been my forte, unlike Suzie who seemed to attract people as easily as breathing.

She laughed and placed her hands on her hips defiantly. 'Exactly how old are you? Aren't you supposed to be the naughty younger one and I'm the older, sensible sister?' She turned around and marched ahead. 'Why don't you try having some fun for once in your life, Phoebe, instead of being a boring, stuck up, old fart?'

I was incensed. Not just by her words but also by my powerlessness. Arguing was futile. If I went home alone, Mother would worry where Suzie was and I would be turned right around to go and find her. Head down, I traipsed along behind them all, hoping against hope the river would be full of fishermen who would chase us away.

It wasn't, of course. They all steered clear of that particular stretch of the riverbank when the schools were off. They didn't want to be bothered by gangs of noisy kids splashing about and disturbing their peace. We had the river to ourselves. Or rather, they did. I had no intentions of joining in with their stupid behaviour. Strangely enough, Suzie wasn't the first to strip down her underwear. She was beaten to it by Tamsin Cartwright, who paraded around like a circus animal, her pale, almost translucent skin covered in huge, ragged freckles. I wanted to yell at her cover up her stupid, pulpy body and stop embarrassing herself but found myself without a voice. The only noise I could make was the rustle of leaves and snapping of twigs underfoot as I shuffled about aimlessly under the shady canopy of the trees. I briefly considered going home and hiding out in the garden shed until Suzie came back. And of course, if I had, it wouldn't have happened. My not being there would have changed the whole complexion of the day's events. But what is done is done. There's no changing the past now, is there?

10

MARCH 2014 – FOUR WEEKS LATER

The day stretches out in front of her, filling Anna with a deep inertia. She sighs and bites at a piece of loose nail. She can either sit around all day doing nothing or she can fill her time with any number of chores that she has been putting off for God knows how long. Boring stuff, jobs that she hates doing: washing curtains, steam cleaning rugs. They all need doing. Or she can throw herself into her next OU assignment. Five chapters to get through and a 2000-word essay. Her heart sinks at the thought of it. She isn't in the right frame of mind today. Reading about comparisons and contrasts of how social order is made and remade will be enough to make her want to curl up into a tight ball and sleep through to the end of next week.

She sighs loudly, pulls the blinds apart and stares out at the back garden at the post-winter mess. A mass of debris greets her gaze: leaves scattered everywhere, a mud-splattered patio, snaking ivy that has somehow managed to curl its way up the side of the shed and is now on its way over to next door's garden. Hardly surprising, really. Winter has dragged its feet this year and the rain has been pretty torrential. Even the last few weeks have been awful despite it being March – dark and stormy and downright bloody depressing – but today, it's warm enough to venture outside and be part of the elements as opposed to being beaten down by them. She continues to stare outside at the general mess and especially the state of the lawn. It might be warmish but from here, it looks as if a year's worth of weeds have attempted to take over the flower beds. Everything is knotted and tangled, a sprawling invasion of chickweed, nettles and groundsel. She reaches for her boots and then stops, deciding that the garden in its current state is not a job for the fainthearted. Next week is when she will get to grips with it. Or perhaps next month. Definitely an all-day task for when she's feeling more energetic, more positive.

The spare room, however, definitely needs doing. Not a particularly pleasant job but she can sort it in anticipation of Toby coming to see them. Her heart leaps halfway up her chest at the thought of seeing her brother again. Since the death of their sister Bridget a few years back, she puts as much effort as she can into preparing for his visits. She feels the loss more since giving up her job at the school and Toby moving down to Lincoln. She tried her hand helping out at the corner shop for a while to keep her mind ticking over and actually loved it, but found it too difficult to keep on top of the housework and with no parents handy to help out with childcare, it all became too much. And now there is a definite void in her life. No work routine, no older sister to go to for advice or even just for a general natter. Just a big, gaping hole where her life used to be.

Dragging herself upstairs, she spends the remainder of the morning de-cluttering the spare room, bagging up old toys and clothes and turning the mattress so she can put clean bed sheets on. It's while she is on a footstool dragging all manner of junk off the top of the wardrobe that Anna sees her. From this height, she can just about see into Phoebe's front window over the top of the hedge that runs round the perimeter of the front of her house. Not a clear view but it's enough. A pulse hammers at Anna's temple and her chest constricts as she watches her neighbour. The room is dark and gloomy looking, full of shadows and tight corners, but even in the murkiness, Anna can see that Phoebe is rocking back and forth on the edge of the sofa, head dipped, arms wrapped around her body like a straitjacket. Anna levers herself up onto her tiptoes, her arms clasped tightly around the edge of the wardrobe for balance. It's too great a distance to see Phoebe's face clearly but even from this far off, it's patently obvious that she is completely and utterly distraught.

Anna stands stock still, feeling slightly sick, unsure of what to do. Her head swims. She shouldn't by rights be seeing this, but now she has, she can't possibly just ignore it, can she? Knowing what that poor woman has to go through with her husband every day, that would be cruel and downright mean, possibly even dangerous. What if she tries something awful? Attempts the unspeakable? Phoebe's disabled husband is hardly in any position to help her. Plus, she is new to the area. Anna is the only one round here who knows her predicament. She should call over again. No cakes this time. Phoebe doesn't seem like the kind of person who likes to sit around chatting and putting the world to rights, not a coffee morning type of woman at all. But she does need a friend right now. And she is obviously really upset.

Guilt tugs at her. She absolutely should do something. She just isn't sure what that something is. Anna continues to stare over, feeling more than slightly voyeuristic. It's one thing to watch somebody carry out boring, everyday tasks when they're unaware you're watching but a whole different league when you are able to see someone at their weakest: vulnerable and distressed and clearly not coping with their lot in life. Anna climbs down and wipes her palms on the sides of her trousers. Clammy with embarrassment and shame.

She gathers up the bags of rubbish and dirty bed linen and backs out of the room, closing the door behind her to stop the boys going in there and ruining what she has just spent a good few hours sorting and putting right. Those two barely leave the house in adverse weather and spend most of their time squabbling and complaining about how bored they are while making no attempt to do anything about it. Sometimes, during the winter months, it feels as if the walls are closing in on them all and it makes her jittery and anxious. Spring has arrived just in time to alleviate the growing sense of claustrophobia that settles on her in October with a heavy thud.

She is on her way downstairs to load up the car with bags for the local charity shop when Callum hurls himself through the front door, nearly knocking her over in the process, a whirlwind of excitement fuelled by uncontrolled teenage hormones charging though his system.

'For God's sake Callum, slow down, will you!'

She dumps the bags at the bottom of the stairs and rummages in the key box for her car keys. He runs around her, looking sweaty and agitated, an excited sparkle dancing in his eyes.

'Mountain Rescue are all over the place! There's a huge van parked up next to the village green!'

He rushes past her and throws himself onto the couch with a thump, then kneels up to stare out of the window, his chin resting on his mud-stained hands. Anna feels a flutter of apprehension in her stomach as she closes the box and walks over to him.

'Mountain Rescue? What are they here for?'

He glances at her briefly then looks back outside. 'Dunno but it looks serious. There's a load of people there too and a police car. Didn't see any policemen, though.' He is barely able to disguise his disappointment at his last statement.

He points over to the roadside where a handful of people are knotted together, talking. Their dark clothes are in stark contrast to the surrounding countryside and emerging foliage. Buds are starting to appear on trees and bushes, slowly and tentatively, as if they're waiting for a late frost before quickly disappearing again, shrinking away from the biting cold. Behind the throng of people is a huge van with the Mountain Rescue logo on the side. A middle-aged man steps out of it and heads over the road towards them. He is wearing a body warmer and a pair of khaki trousers that are tucked into his pale-green, thick, woollen socks. On his feet is a pair of well-worn hiking boots. He is carrying a clipboard and has a very serious look on his face as he merges into the crowd who greet him with a series of reserved, clipped nods.

'They've been here for ages, knocking on doors speaking to people further down the village near the river,' gasps Callum, barely able to conceal his excitement at the prospect of something out of the ordinary happening near his home. 'They might come knocking here if we're lucky.' He turns to face his mother and lowers his voice, 'I mean they might come here and ask us some stuff, y'know.' His face develops a sudden rosy glow as he takes note of her perturbed expression, 'I mean, I don't want anything really *bad* to have happened or anything like that...'

His voice tails off and he returns his gaze to the window, the initial lustre of his excitement now tarnished by his mother's frosty glare.

Anna has a sensation somewhere down in the pit of her stomach that she can't shake. It isn't fear or God forbid, any kind of teenage type exhilaration at the thought of what may be going on out there. She doesn't know what it is. It's only as she heads outside to the roadside and begins to load the car up with bags of goods bound for the charity shop that she realises what it is she actually feels: dread. She has the strongest sensation that something terrible has, or is about to, happen.

Unlocking the car, she gazes over at Phoebe's house. It looks the same as always. Why wouldn't it? It's a quiet, old place with a quiet, dignified family who, if she is going to be perfectly frank, are bordering on aloof. People who keep themselves to themselves and appear to all intents and purposes completely normal. Except Anna knows the heartache that lurks within those walls. She has seen their distress first hand. And she wants to help in some small way. She really does, but she has absolutely no idea where to start.

She stares down at the pile of bags and wonders if she should leave them till another time and instead call over to see her neighbour to offer some support. She is all too aware that the time isn't right. Would Phoebe want to be seen weeping and helpless? Probably not. But then, perhaps there will never be a good time. Sometimes you just have to do it: bulldoze your way in and do what is required.

Anna stalls and considers her options, then picks the bags up, shoves them in the boot of her car and slams it shut wearily. Her conscience may punish her for it later but right now, she has to focus on Toby's visit. Phoebe will be close by every day; her brother's time with her is brief.

A slight breeze suddenly hits the back of her neck. She stands completely still, sensing somebody close by.

'Afternoon. Lovely village you have here.'

The soft voice doesn't fit the large frame of man who is stood so near to her, she can see the pores on his nose and a few stray hairs on his eyebrows that jut out at divergent angles. He smiles and steps to one side to let her past.

'Hi there. Sorry, didn't mean to startle you.'

'No problem,' she says and smiles back at him, swallowing hard. What is it with situations like this when something major is going on? Why does it make her feel as if she has carried out some terrible crime? Mike would blame her Catholic upbringing. *Ridden with guilt for simply existing*, he would say. 'I was just loading up the car. I've been having a bit of a sort out ready for my brother coming to stay.'

She feels her face flush up and stops talking, aware that she is rambling. This man is a perfect stranger. He doesn't need to know any of what she has just told him. She suddenly feels clumsy. Stupid and out of place. As surreptitiously as she can, Anna wipes her palms down the sides of her trousers and offers him her hand to shake.

'You've probably spotted that there's something going on,' he says quietly, staring over his shoulder at the crowd of people gathered on the village green behind them. 'I feel like apologising actually for ruining the peace and quiet. Lovely little place here, isn't it? Tremendous views.'

Anna is immobile, suddenly not sure how to react. Should she wait for him to offer information or should she just go ahead and ask? She looks down at a piece of paper that is hanging limply from his hand. An A4 printed sheet. Anna stares at it, willing him to tell her what is going on right outside her doorstep.

'Ah right, yes sorry I should explain.' He holds up the paper and straightens it out for Anna to read. 'Not quite with it today, I'm afraid.'

He waits while Anna reads it, her head swaying slightly as she scans the text. She stares at the picture on it and reads it again, her head beginning to throb slightly. This is awful. Worse than she first imagined. Much worse.

'So as I was saying, I'm not quite firing on all four cylinders. Nancy is a close friend of mine and we're all really concerned. Not like her at all this. Totally out of character.' His lip quivers softly as he speaks.

'I'm so sorry,' she whispers and without thinking, Anna reaches out and touches his arm.

He stops for a second, lowers his eyes and takes a series of small, erratic breaths before continuing. 'If it's not too much trouble, we're asking local people if they have seen her and wouldn't mind putting these signs in their windows.'

'Of course,' she murmurs then falls silent. What is there to say? Except how sorry she is and how the hell did all this happen right outside her house? She nods mutely and takes the poster, studying the woman's face, desperate to summon up any memories from yesterday. Her mind remains stubbornly blank. It was an unremarkable day. She ironed, watched the telly, made the beds. A day full of nothing.

'We're over the far end of the green if you do remember anything,' he says quietly, 'That's her car.' He points over to a small, red vehicle next to the growing mass of people. Anna nods and gives a half smile before heading back inside. Suddenly, she doesn't feel like driving into town to get rid of her charity bags. Truth be told, she doesn't feel like doing anything much at all.

11

I wake up groggy, like I've been drugged. My eyes feel as if I've been in a sandstorm and I ache everywhere. Shafts of light filtering through the blinds are arranged in tiny parallel slivers on the bed beside me as I try to adjust my vision to the early-morning glow. The house is silent save for Tillie's snuffling as she turns over on the rug outside my door. I hear her claws scraping against the carpet as she rolls about and am able to visualise her laid on her back, paws facing up over, tongue lolling sideways out of her mouth, eyes darting around for any signs of movement nearby. I close my eyes and mull over the events of the last twenty-four hours. They are too painful and horrible to even think about. I shiver and slink back down under the duvet, hoping to block it all out. Yesterday was not a good day.

Martyn didn't sleep in our bed last night, which is just as well under the circumstances. I roll over into the still taut sheets on his side, enjoying the feel of the cool sensation on my skin. My face burns as images from last night force themselves into my mind. I press my balled-up fists into my eyes and try to blot it all out. Outside, I hear the sharp trill of birdsong. Spring has finally arrived and the birds have now found their voices. Robins, terns, finches. I welcome them all. At the minute, I welcome anything that will take my mind off yesterday's terrible affair.

I uncurl myself and reluctantly drag the covers back to sit up, a slight chill brushing over my skin. My back clicks painfully as I reach over for my dressing gown and slip my feet into my moccasins. Keeping my head down is today's plan. Staying out of Martyn's way and trying to make it through the day is about all I'll be able to manage.

I drag the blinds to one side and stare out at the sky. It's a pale-blue colour, warm-looking and spring-like, but that's no indication as to the temperature outside. This is the UK after all, not the Mediterranean.

I shiver and shuffle off to the bathroom where I

listen to the wood pigeons as the sound of their cooing filters through the extractor fan like a surround sound system. It puts me in mind of a store I visited in Yorkshire many years back where murals of the countryside covered every wall in the ladies toilets and the background music was chattering birdsong. It was so absurd and out of place, I've never been able to forget it. I let my mind wander back there, allow myself to be coated in the warmth and happiness of the memory.

I had been shopping that day, looking for a birthday present for Tom. I enjoyed the challenge of finding that all-elusive gift that would surprise him and bring a huge smile to his face. In the end I had settled on a mini helicopter from a shop that sold gadgets for men. It was a small piece of machinery but could fly at a fair old height and I just knew, after much searching, that it would perfect. As it turned out, I didn't even get a chance to give it to him because shortly afterwards, Martyn had his accident and our lives were altered irrevocably.

The warm glow and happiness leaves me and a murky veil of fury begins to descend. I drag my fingers through my knot of morning hair. If I'm not careful, the downward spiralling mood will shroud me and keep me within its clutches for the rest of the day.

That's how it goes sometimes. Especially this morning. And today is a very dark day indeed. The darkest for some time, and given our lifestyle and circumstances, that's saying something.

I stand up and rub at my eyes. Firstly, I'll walk Tillie and after that... well, I will wait to see what the day brings. All plans are on hold for the present. But as I have told myself many times before, this too will pass.

I shower and dress and sit for a while in the quiet of the living room, going over yesterday's events time and time and time again until my head throbs and my stomach is a tight ball and I can think no more. I blow my nose and wipe away the tears, then head into the hallway, grab my coat and clip Tillie on her lead. Just a short walk today. Only far enough for her to stretch her legs and relieve herself and then back here. I don't feel like seeing anyone today. And Martyn had best make himself scarce too. I am not in the mood for any more of his antics. I have just about had enough.

We walk down to the river from the garden and along the footpath. It's silent, nobody else around. I stand and watch the ripples, mesmerised by the way the morning sunlight bounces over them, swirling and disappearing only to be replaced by more. Suzie face appears in the water. She is always there, flitting around, dancing on the periphery of my thoughts. I think of her constantly: that day down by the river, how perfect her skin looked and how the sunlight bounced off her hair, her dying screams as she sank beneath the surface of the water. Fighting back yet more tears, I lean down to stroke Tillie, then straighten up and head off through a clearing in the bushes. That's when I see them, knocking on doors, asking questions, looking for *her*. My pulse quickens and a hot, angry glow spreads over my skin. I can't think of any way I can escape from this. I suddenly feel helpless. Trapped.

'Come on, Tillie,' I murmur as I reach down to run my fingers through her short, stubby ruff. Sticky buds are tucked under the fur and I gently drag them out one by one as we continue walking past the group of people gathered by the roadside. 'Let's get back and get a late breakfast, eh?'

I walk just a little too quickly; Tillie's tiny legs struggling to keep up as I march home at a lick. I hurry inside and lock the door behind me, my head swimming as I bend down to take Tillie's lead off.

Martyn is nowhere to be seen. Probably still in bed, his memory erased, his conscience clear. I take a couple of seconds, try work out what to do for the best, then I go from room to room angling the blinds so it's almost impossible for anyone to see inside. They would have to cross the gravel drive, their feet crunching over the stones, and stand to one side to peer in. It would be in such an obtrusive and calculated manner, it would be obvious to anyone watching exactly what they were doing. Today is a day to hide. I am not in the mood to see anyone and certainly not up to a barrage of questions from strangers.

I quietly pad upstairs and see that Martyn is indeed still asleep in the spare room. He is laid on top of the covers and the curtains are wide open, light flooding into all four corners of the room. Unless you knew otherwise, you would think the place was unoccupied. I stare at him, at his lined face and greying tousled hair, the way his eyes flicker occasionally as he sleeps, and I feel sickened by the very sight of him. It's all I can do to stop myself from striding over and slapping him hard across his stupid face. I close the door and head downstairs, my heart beating a rapid, uncomfortable rhythm as the thought of what happened yesterday jumps into my head. I quash it, blank it out. I have no choice. It's the only way I'm going to be able to keep going, to make it through the day.

Breakfast consists of toast and coffee whilst reading the papers online. I have to act normal. I absolutely must. My routine is all I have. The toast sticks in my throat and I have to force it down, swallowing rapidly and taking long slurps of my cappuccino to aid its journey. Tillie sits patiently at my feet, waiting for any crumbs. I finish eating and continue to read, the words blurring as I stare at the iPad. None of it makes any sense to me. Usually a keen observer of the political pages, today I have no interest. I push it across the table and sit in silence. No movements from upstairs. Nothing happening anywhere.

My skin suddenly prickles as I hear a light but definite rap at the door. I flinch and creep towards the living room, blood surging through my ears, making me light headed and slightly nauseous. They are here. I know exactly what this will be about. From the hallway, I can see that a stranger is standing outside: a large, male outline. Probably somebody involved in the search, possibly even a police officer. My stomach wants to heave. I swallow and head towards the kitchen, fear blinding me. Tillie starts to run around in circles at my feet. Gently, I pick her up and put her in the utility room with her crate of toys. Thank God she isn't a barker. I shut her in and tiptoe back into the kitchen where I sit to one side, away from the window. I'm tempted to close the blinds completely. But then what if they decide to walk round the back? They can easily access the garden via the walkway.

Another thought occurs to me. What if they continue to knock and wake Martyn? I can't let that happen but then I can't answer the door to them either. I simply can't do it. The problem is, of course, they probably saw me walk past them and come in the house. They know I'm here. My breath begins to pump out in small, hot gasps and I have to take deep breaths to still my racing pulse. I tap at my temple with my fingers and out of nowhere, a plausible idea implants itself in my brain. *Upstairs*. I need to get upstairs as quickly as I can.

With robotic movements, I make my way up there and into the bathroom where I turn the shower on full blast. The water thunders onto the tray, blocking out the insistent rapping from below. Hopefully they will see the steam coming out from the extractor fan, hear the hiss of the boiler and leave me in peace. I sit on the edge of the toilet seat and think through it with as much rationality as I can muster. They have no reason to think I know anything about what went on. I'm just another resident living a quiet life in a sleepy village. Why would they want to talk to me about it anyway? A middle-aged woman with a disabled husband to care for, and new to the village to boot. Hardly a suspect. I feel a sudden rush of blood to my head and place it in my upturned hands on my lap to stem the overwhelming sense of nausea. I've done nothing wrong. Nothing at all. It was Martyn, you see. And I can't let anything happen to him. As much as I hate him at this moment in time, he is still my husband. He needs protecting from it all and he can't possibly be held responsible for his actions with all the horrors and demons he has whirling around in his brain. So much turmoil. So much misery. He's disabled, mentally ill; call it what you will, but he isn't able to control himself sometimes and quite frankly, it just isn't his fault. And anyway, when things like this happen, I have to help him because his current predicament is partly my doing. He wouldn't be in this state if it hadn't been for the fall on the cliffs. We'd been arguing and he lost his footing and slipped.

I'd like to say that I can't recall what the argument was about but that would be a lie. I remember it very well. As if it was yesterday, actually. It had been an ongoing argument. The whole thing escalated and before I knew it, Martyn was laid on the rocks, his body twisted at a painful, awkward angle, a low guttural moan emanating from his throat. Such a horrid day. A throbbing sensation settles itself behind my eyes as I do my best to blot out the memory. It taunts me, so vivid and unforgettable with its clarity and before I know it, the throbbing has developed into a migraine that I know will stay with me for the remainder of the day.

Staggering over to the cabinet, I locate a couple of painkillers and swallow them down, then lean in and turn the shower off. With any luck, the person at the door will have given up and moved on, decided I'm not worth pursuing. I have been given a reprieve. Or at least my husband has. I hear the familiar thump of Martyn's bare feet as they hit the floor in the bedroom next door and am unable to stop the tears as they begin to roll. He is up and out of bed. Time to face him once again and get on with the day.

12

'When did it happen?'

Callum and Mason are sitting on the sofa, eyes agog at their mother who is twiddling with a strand of hair while she crosses and uncrosses her legs in rapid, continuous, jerky movements. Her nerves are still jangling. Hardly surprising, really. It's not every day things like this happen. Most people go through their entire lives and never be involved in anything like this.

'Some time yesterday, apparently,' Anna whispers, all too aware that the whole scenario will fuel her sons' excitement and curiosity. Teenage boys think events like this are a game: an occurrence played out to entertain them.

'So she just, like *disappeared*?' Mason stretches the word out, highlighting its significance in the stillness of the room.

'So the man said.' Anna stares out of the window at the countryside beyond as if her gaze will suddenly conjure up the missing person, like pulling a rabbit from a hat.

'So, where do they think she's gone to, then?' Callum murmurs and follows his mother's gaze to the rolling hills outside, curved and smooth, layer after layer, like an animal unfurling itself from a deep sleep.

'If they knew that, d'ya think they'd be interviewing all the people in the village, you big thicko?' Mason is staring at his brother, a slight sneer to his contorted upper lip.

Callum rolls over and plants a slap on Mason's forehead, who then dodges under his brother's arm and hurls himself off the couch, landing on the floor in a sharp angled heap. Within seconds, they are rolling about, limbs locked together like a pair of fighting crabs.

'Oh for God's sake, cut it out you two!'

Anna jumps up and stalks off into the kitchen. She can't be bothered to intervene. She would usually drag them apart and have them hanging, one from each fist, but today, she has no energy to manage her two warring sons. It's high time they snapped out of their childlike ways and grew up. The conversation outside has left her drained, wishing it was later in the day so she could justify having a drink to calm her nerves. Sensing her agitation, the boys stop and stare at each other, a slight smirk starting to spread over their faces. This is new to them. The expected slap to the back of their heads hasn't happened. They look at each other and shrug, wondering what's gotten into her.

'Should we go out and help the search team?' Callum suggests as he scrambles up and tucks his shirt back into his skinny fit jeans, their closeness to his skin accentuating his wiry frame.

'That's probably the last thing you should do,' barks Anna over the bubbling and whirring of the coffee machine. She needs something to calm her down, something that doesn't involve alcohol because the way she is feeling, once she starts drinking, she won't be able to stop. Incidents like this make her feel on edge, out of sorts. They make her acutely aware of how quickly life can change from a near blissful existence to an unbearable nightmare in the blink of an eye. That poor lady. Her poor family.

'Who was she, then?'

Callum rummages through the cupboards looking for snacks. Anna glares at him and instinctively hands over the cake tin which he plunges his fist into, grabbing at a scone and gobbling it down, spitting crumbs as he speaks. 'Sorry, I mean who *is* she then? 'Cos we don't know if she's dead yet, do we? Although she probably is, even though that's not what you want to hear. Sorry.'

He wipes his mouth and sits down, his long legs splayed out in front of him. Anna pours a coffee and drinks it straight down before pouring herself another.

'You can get throat cancer drinking hot drinks like that. I read about it online.'

'Oh well, it must be true then. Who needs school when you have Google?' Anna blows into the cup and sips at it, watching Callum intently as she does it.

'So go on then. What's the story?' His face morphs into an expression that is close to maturity. This happens sometimes, as if he is trapped in some kind of indefinable region between being a stroppy, often thoughtless teenager, and something marginally resembling adulthood. Anna enjoys these times, snatches at them covetously before they dissipate into the ether, swallowed up by a mass of seething hormones as they rampage through his system, running riot and wreaking havoc with his emotional capabilities and social graces. Mason slopes into the kitchen to join them, grabs a bag of crisps and slumps into a chair next to her, the sound of his crunching even louder than the coffee machine.

'Apparently, she left home yesterday morning, telling her family she was taking a walk down by the river. Her vehicle is still parked up next to the green and somebody saw her sitting on the bench next to her car but after that, there is no sighting of her. She seems to have disappeared into thin air.'

'Into the river more like,' Mason adds as he slugs back a tumbler of lemonade. 'What?' he cries as Anna's eyes widen and she shakes her head at him, her lips pursed into a thin, disapproving line.

'Gotta admit it, Mum. For once, he's probably right. That's what the police and mountain rescue'll be thinking. They won't tell her family that, but that's definitely what they'll be thinking. They'll have divers here soon looking for a body.' Callum gets up and helps himself to another scone, leaving a trail of caramel-coloured crumbs over the grey tiles as he breaks it open and bites into it.

Anna feels a blackness descend. She doesn't know this lady, and despite her children's misgivings, for all they know, she could still be alive and well. People go missing all the time. It doesn't mean they're dead. Sometimes, they just don't want to be found. Life can get to be too much for them and they simply disappear. But of course Callum and Mason are probably right; here it's slightly different. Here they have the river. Fast flowing and high after a particularly wet winter, it poses a real threat to anyone unfortunate enough to get caught up in it. That's what it is that's making her feel so unsettled and depressed. Anna thinks of how it would feel to be dragged away by the current, the freezing water lapping over your head as you desperately try to clamber to safety, not knowing which way is up in the impenetrable darkness. Any cries for help would be drowned out by the rush of the frothing current as it bubbles up round your neck and washes over your head, slowly filling your lungs until you can no longer speak or yell out and then eventually, not be able to breathe at all. Just a pro-longed, terrifying shroud of nothingness until your heart gives out. And all of that possibly happened just yards from where they are now sitting. A woman out there, struggling, screaming for help, freezing and totally helpless while they were all in here, eating cake and drinking coffee, complaining about how little there is on the TV these days, whining about the internet being too slow. While she was out there, dying.

She stands up and wishes Mike was here. His presence in the house is perversely comforting, annoying at times but a strange source of comfort, nonetheless. Anna stares out of the window, struggling to see beyond the worst-case scenario. She shakes her head. She has to stop it. For heaven's sake, this missing woman might still be out there. She tells herself that she has really got to stop thinking the worst all the time. It's one of her less admirable traits: being a constant worrier. Take this Phoebe lady, for example, who she hardly even knows. She actually loses sleep over the fact that the woman who lives in the big house over the road, who is virtually a stranger, may not be coping too well with her lot in life. Anna lets out a long breath and closes her eyes as she takes another sip of coffee. It is true, though. Looking after a disabled person must be hell on earth. Anna would much rather have her small house and rusty, old car than have to have that to deal with every day. And as silly as it sounds, the only way she will ever be able to stop thinking about her is if she calls round again, which she is going to do, not to interfere or pry, just to be a presence, someone for Phoebe to chat to. But not right now. Right now, she needs this strong coffee to clear her head and calm her nerves. God, she hopes this woman turns up, but no matter how hard she tries, a small, still voice deep within her brain is telling her that something is horribly amiss.

13

The tablets have worked. The headache has lifted. And I do know that although I feel better physically, mentally, I am struggling to cope. If I were to depict an image of how I feel right now, it would be a huge, thick cloak draped over a black canvas. I feel utterly despondent and cannot see any way out of this horrible situation. Martyn is downstairs and I am upstairs, and at the moment, that is exactly how I like it. Everything is still too fresh in my mind, too raw for me to be able to face him, to make pleasantries with him so I am keeping my distance, keeping myself occupied.

The deep pile of the landing carpet is soft underfoot as I pad along to the top of the stairs. I peer over the banister and look down. Martyn's study door is closed. I can hear the faint crackle of his radio from behind it. I hope he stays put. Dear lord, I really hope he stops there for the entire day. I watched him take a plate of toast and a huge pot of tea in there earlier, along with a stack of newspapers, so with any luck, I may just get my wish. I can but hope. Not having to face him will make the rest of the day so much easier to bear.

I head downstairs, the vice around my skull slowly beginning to release itself notch by notch. And that's when I hear it. More knocking. It slices through the still air and freezes my blood. I knew they would come back. Of course they will. A woman has gone missing and they won't give up until they find her. Icicles prickle my scalp and tears mist my vision. Just when I thought I could keep my head up and make it through the day. The stairs blur and move as I take them slowly, one at a time, my eyes downcast, desperate to keep a purchase on the handrail. A voice roars in my ears: *stay calm and keep breathing*. A thousand words flutter around in my brain as I desperately try to form a coherent sentence that I can spill out to this person at the door, to help Martyn out, to cover Martyn's tracks. *Martyn, Martyn, Martyn.* Everything is always about bloody Martyn.

With one hand, I unlock the door and slowly open it. The oak jamb sticks slightly before finally giving to with a dull squeak, allowing it to swing open wide. My knees buckle and I almost want to laugh out loud when I see her standing there before me, smiling inanely, her hair bouncing around her face giving her the look of a small child. *Suzie.*

Relieved beyond belief, I smile at her and step aside to let her in. She reciprocates the smile and marches through to the kitchen where she sits down at my table as if we're good friends and have known each other for years. I fill the kettle and busy myself with finding teabags. It helps to plug the awkward silence that has settled in the room. It doesn't last for long, though. I knew it wouldn't. When it comes to making conversation, I am more than a touch reserved, cautious and careful, unlike Anna, who appears to want to fill every moment of quiet with her relentless chatter.

'Dear God, Phoebe, isn't it just awful? What must you think of our village? Nothing like this has *ever* happened before. It's usually such a lovely place to live. Don't let this incident put you off. I'm sure she will turn up safe and sound.' She shakes her head and drags a small, pale hand through her featherlight hair. It bounces around her tiny face, golden threads bobbing and dancing.

I feel my face burn and move away from her. Turning my back, I busy myself with washing and drying cups and spoons while I wait for the kettle to boil. It's infinitely preferable to having to lie and put on a show of innocence while she goes on and on about how terrible it is and how she hopes the poor woman will be found sooner rather than later. I just need a few more minutes to compose myself before I can face her and speak without it coming out like a stream of incoherent gobbledegook. Because this is one conversation that I really don't want to be having with a woman I barely know. I have no idea where it will lead and I am not a fan of surprises.

'I mean, I don't mind telling you I am absolutely horrified. I spoke to one of them out there and told him I hadn't seen or heard anything. I felt really guilty that I couldn't be of more help really but you can't just make things up, can you? Have they spoken to you yet?' She gabbles the words out, barely stopping for breath. 'Because I think they're trying to ask everybody in the vicinity if they saw her or spoke to her.'

I am rigid, the tea towel scrunched up into a tight ball in my fist as her words ring out in the air between us. I turn abruptly, ready to grasp the nettle. I have to speak. There's no alternative, even if every bone in my body is screaming for it to be otherwise.

'Sorry, I don't quite follow you. Has who spoken to me?' I listen to my own voice. It sounds eerily distant, with a definite echo that whirls around my head. 'Has something happened?' I smile and hand Anna a cup of tea. 'Nothing too serious I hope.'

Her expression changes and she brings a hand up to cover her gaping mouth. 'Oh God, how clumsy of me! I presumed you knew. Bloody hell, it's so awful.'

I shake my head and sit down opposite, my face the picture of innocence. 'Know what? My sleeping pattern's been really erratic since moving in. I walked Tillie early then had a mid-morning nap so I've obviously missed it all. What's going on out there?'

I can tell by her face that I've pulled it off. Her expression never waivers. She sips at her tea, eyes as wide as saucers. The picture of girlish simplicity. So innocent.

'A woman has gone missing. Can you believe it? Round here of all places!'

I shake my head and agree that it is terrible news. Shocking. She swallows more tea and stares at me, then opens her mouth as if a thought has just occurred to her.

'What about your husband? He doesn't leave the house, does he? Did he not hear or see anything?'

I smile sadly and shake my head despondently, hoping it looks genuine.

'He's not been at all well the last few days and has spent most of it sleeping, I'm afraid. He's been in quite a lot of pain and on heavy medication which has completely zonked him out.'

She nods knowingly and pushes a strand of her golden hair back behind her ear with a practised curl of her finger.

'Of course, of course. It's probably just as well really that he isn't aware of what's going on out there,' she mumbles, suddenly flushed. 'This kind of thing can be really upsetting for people like... well, what I mean is, if your husband is feeling a bit, well... you know, and of course it's really worrying and difficult for you and...'

I let her carry on and watch a mesh of scarlet creep over her chest and up her throat. She stops speaking and meekly sips at her tea, the obvious unspoken inference about my frosty disposition and Martyn's physical and mental incapacity hanging heavily between us. It doesn't bother or concern me in the slightest. I'm actually rather used to it. So many friends have dropped off my radar in the past few years, I've had to get used to being alone. I'm pretty well adjusted to a quiet and staid life. Except for Martyn, of course. He's a real drain on me. A full-time job. And anything but staid.

'Do they know anything about her?' I ask, not that I want or need to hear the answer.

'Only that she told her family she was going walking and would be taking the route through the village. Awful, isn't it? I mean, the river's really high at the moment and that only increases the strength of the current...'

Her voice tails off, neither of us sure of what to say next. I actually have lots of things I could say to answer her questions and solve the mystery of the missing walker. I could tell her that the woman was called Nancy, that she was a mother to two grown-up children, that she enjoyed gardening, walking and cycling and was meant to be spending the day rambling with her friend who cancelled last minute, due to illness, leaving Nancy to undertake the walk on her own. I know all of this because this is what she told me before my husband crept up behind her, put his large hands around her throat and throttled her to death. He had been on edge, restless and jittery since the incident with the two teenage boys weeks before and had spent each and every day watching for any signs of strangers in the garden. I had attempted to explain that we would see plenty and he had best get used to it but nothing seemed to sway him. He was neurotic, convinced people were trying to spy on him. People like Nancy.

'Cake?' I ask, my voice breaking. I stand up and bring back a small plate of Victoria sponge, a slight tremor visible in my hand. Anna doesn't see it. She is staring out of the window, a faraway look in her eyes. Suzie used to do that sometimes: disappear into her own little world, oblivious to everyone and everything including Dad's continual struggle with the drink and the hard time Mother had dealing with him. Suzie was impervious to all the goings on around her. Even when he came home one night, so blind drunk he soiled himself and Mother had to clean him up despite being slightly built and only half his size. I remember that evening all too well. I helped Mother get him to bed, hauling him upstairs, dodging his fists as he lashed out, trying to push us away from him, and all the while, Suzie had sat on the bed, styling her hair and painting her nails.

'Oh, lovely. Thank you,' Anna croons as she takes a slice of cake and bites into it, crumbs spurting over the table and onto her lap. I nibble at mine, unable to shake the image that has lodged itself firmly in my brain: Martyn's big, strong hands, clasped around Nancy's small throat, her bulging eyes as she gasped for breath, his thumbs trembling with sheer force as they pressed down on her windpipe, crushing the very life out of her.

He hadn't had a particularly good day. He'd been in a lot of pain with his leg and then a terrible headache had set in. He had stalked around the house, his gait growing more and more unbalanced by the minute, refusing to sit down, too agitated to stay still. I'd tried everything to settle him but nothing had worked, which was when I decided I needed a break from him and went for a brief wander outside, to have a breather on my own. That's when I got chatting to her, this Nancy. She seemed very nice. A well-spoken type of lady. Confident and erudite. I shouldn't have done it really – left him alone in the house, not knowing the state he was in. And especially not knowing what he is capable of.

I can't quite recall how or why it all happened. We were up from the path, closer to the house. One minute, we were discussing the roses and talking about how much she reminded me of one of my old friends, and the next minute... Well, after that is a bit of a blur really. It all happened so quickly. I don't remember Martyn stepping outside and I don't remember the actual attack. I do, however, recall her expression, the look on her face as he pulled her over the step and into the house. And now that's all I can see: her eyes bulging in horror as she gasped for breath, her grey skin and lifeless body slumped on the floor like a crumpled bag of rags.

It was dark when he finally dragged her stiffened corpse through the thickets of our garden and down to the surging swell of the river, unseen by anybody, concealed by the darkness and shadows of the night. I cried for hours, unable to do anything, knowing it had happened again. Because this isn't the first time, you see.

I think of Debra, still missing. My friend, Debra. The rumour mill initially claimed she has run off with a mystery man, started a new life somewhere away from her gambler of a husband, but as time has passed and her bank account has remained un-touched, people are beginning to realise her disap-pearance has a more sinister edge to it. I've always known she didn't run away. Always. It was Martyn, you see, who was the mystery man. There had been an affair, albeit a brief one, but it had happened. I found the receipts and emails. Such an awful cliché. Such duplicitous behaviour. And Martyn had more or less caved in as soon as I confronted him. But

Debra refused to back off, hounding him with phone calls, threatening to make it public if he didn't leave me, trying to ruin his career. And then suddenly one day, it all stopped. No midnight calls, no angry emails. No Debra. Martyn and I never spoke about it again but I knew it was him. I could see it in his face. He had guilt etched into every pore. But people don't just vanish, do they? One day, her body will turn up and the police will start a proper investigation, looking into her life, delving into her secrets. And then everything will come tumbling down. There is nothing to connect us to Nancy but there is everything to connect us to Debra.

'It doesn't feel right this, does it?'

Anna's voice cuts through my thoughts, her words a shrill pitch in the emptiness of the room. No clutter around to soften the edges, no other people to provide a backdrop of sound to her words. There is nothing. Just the slight squawk of my neighbour's tinny voice as it is propelled across the vastness of my new kitchen, rebounding off the magnolia walls and marble surfaces.

'I mean, here we are, sitting here in your lovely new home, eating cake while the Mountain Rescue team are outside looking for somebody who may or may not be in danger. And the river...' She shivers dramatically and pushes another slab of cake into her mouth. 'I can't bear to think about it, can you? Just imagine how cold and frightened she must be wherever she is right now.'

I watch her eat and focus on the jam that has lodged itself in between the crevices of her teeth. She continues, unperturbed by my watchful gaze. My head begins to thump and I have to turn away as my usual twitch takes hold in one of my eyelids.

'How is your family?' I realise it's a silly thing to ask as I don't even know them but I have to say something to stop my mind from going into over-drive and spilling out my secrets to her. I have no idea why I would ever consider doing that. Because despite her proclamations about comprehending the human psyche, there is no way she could ever under-stand my current predicament. No way at all. How can I expect her to when I don't understand it my-self? Protecting a man who is mentally unbalanced and dangerous. And I've been kidding myself that Martyn's problems only began after his accident; they started way before that. His tolerance levels had been on the wane long before he slipped on that cliff. He had become tetchy. More than tetchy. Un-predictable and prone to outbursts. All the accident did was exacerbate his declining mental health and leave us both at the mercy of his deteriorating temper.

Anna seems to slump a little. She puts her plate down on the table and dabs at her mouth with the corner of a tissue. 'They're all okay, I suppose. Mike's working lots of overtime so he's hardly ever around and Callum and Mason are hanging around the house and generally getting under my feet.' Her voice begins to break as she speaks. 'Sometimes, I get quite lonely, with not working. The days can be awfully long.' Her eyes have a faraway look in them and for one awful minute, I fear she might start crying.

I reach over and gently trail my fingers over hers, not an easy thing for me to do. I've never been particularly tactile. It's been so long since anybody has showed me any warmth or affection, I think I'm in danger of forgetting how to reciprocate properly. Martyn and I barely touch now. Once upon a time, many moons ago when we were young and desperately in love, we couldn't keep our hands off each other, but as the years passed, what with Martyn's demanding job in the surgery and me looking after Tom and all the other myriad difficulties that families face each day, we grew further and further apart. I still loved him but we became more like siblings than husband and wife. And now I am his carer. And he is my... well, I'm not quite sure what he is to me any more. But we're bound together, no matter what. *Till death do us part.*

'But you have your studies,' I say quietly, longing for the conversation to move on before she drowns in self-pity. We all have our own problems and like me, Anna will have to learn to deal with hers. That's just how it is.

'Yes, you're right. I shouldn't moan, really.' She nods and sniffs then looks down at my hands, which are resting on my lap. 'Looks like you've been busy in the garden, Phoebe?'

My face burns as she stares down at my fingers, which are cut and grazed. A thin line of mud is encrusted under my nails, dark-brown crescents of telltale dirt from yesterday after helping Martyn to dispose of the evidence, desperately trying to claw at the ridges and furrows left in the soil as he made his way down to the river. Kicking and grabbing at soil to cover his tracks. An unwilling accomplice but an accomplice nonetheless.

'Nothing too energetic,' I mumble, 'just some weeding and planting a few roses.'

'Oh, how beautiful. Roses are my favourites. What type?' Anna picks up the remnants of her cake and stuffs it into her mouth, cream gathering in small globules at the corners of her lips. Suddenly, she isn't miserable any more. I wish I had her positivity. Her moods seem to change with the wind.

I open my mouth to answer but find myself lost for words. I could come out with an endless list of names of roses such as Albertine, Persian Mystery or Compassion but instead, I stand up and walk over to the window, unwilling or at least unable to answer her question directly.

'This garden has been really well planned by the previous owners. From what I can see out there, it will be in bloom nearly all year round.'

'Oh, it is!' Anna gushes as she licks traces of raspberry jam off her fingertips, 'and the snowberries in the autumn are amazing. They liven up the hedgerows with flashes of pure white on those awful, drab days. I get so sick of winter, don't you? It seems to go on for forever. I'm so relieved spring is here. Roll on summer, eh?'

I love how she is so easily distracted. Like a small child, really. Keeping her questions and probing at bay won't be as difficult as I first thought. She seems to delight in being led off on tangents and makes it easy for me to avoid her endless questions and probing.

'Anyway, I haven't even asked how you're settling

in here. You know, it can be a strange feeling moving into a new place.' She stares at me with emerald eyes. Suzie's eyes. 'Feel free to call over to ours anytime if you fancy some company. We've got my brother coming to stay for a couple of days in the next few weeks. Hopefully, he'll keep the two boys entertained. He's a real outdoors type, loves getting dirty and not scared off by a bit of grime, not that you'd think it when you consider his job.'

'Which is?' I'm not entirely sure why I ask. I have no real interest in where Anna's brother goes every day to make money. That's the problem with small talk; it serves no real purpose other than acting as a time filler.

When she speaks, Anna words cut me in two. A cold rush balloons inside my chest and my head is invaded by swarms of angry hornets that batter against my skull.

'He's a GP. He's only recently moved down to Lincoln but for years, he worked locally at a surgery in Richmond.'

I feel physically sick and have to swallow hard to stop the bile rising.

'Richmond, North Yorkshire?' I ask tentatively. Of course it's North Yorkshire. What a stupid question. I clear my throat and push my hair behind my ears.

There are only a handful of doctor's surgeries in Richmond. What are the chances?

'Yes. Forge Hill Surgery I think it's called. We all miss him but at least he visits regularly,' she says, unaware I am finding it hard to breathe. 'Well, as often as him job allows him to, of course.'

Blood roars in my ears. The buzzing in my head increases a hundredfold.

'Forge Hill Surgery?' I ask, suddenly dizzy. I keep my head held high for fear of falling to the floor.

'That's it, yes. Do you know it?'

Somehow, with the greatest degree of control, I am able to shake my head and manage to mumble that I don't. 'I was just curious,' I tell her quietly. It's almost impossible to finish my tea without vomiting.

'You should call over when he arrives and meet him. He's a keen gardener as well.'

I nod and stand up. 'That's lovely,' I say, my voice sounding as if I am underwater. I walk to the sink and throw the remainder of my tea down it, fear clawing at my throat. I will have to lie low for a short while, ignore her knocking, do what I can to keep out of her way as well as avoiding questions from the searchers about Nancy. For once, Martyn's illness has its benefits. I can tell her he has taken a turn for the worse and needs me at home constantly. My fingers feel like blocks of wood as I tap them on the kitchen top. I'll find a way to manage it all. I always do.

'Anyway, thank you for the cake and tea. It's been lovely. I miss having female company around here,' she says before she stops on her way out and gently touches my arm, 'and don't hesitate to ask for anything. Any help, I mean.' She stares at me, and we both know who she is referring to. We don't even need to speak his name now. He is with us even when he is absent from view.

'Thank you. That's really kind. I'll bear it in mind.' I walk her to the door, thinking how soft her hair is and how wet and limp it was the last time I saw her. I remember dragging my freezing fingers through it as her pale body was laid on the riverbank, flaccid and unresponsive.

She turns abruptly and I feel my face flush as if she can read my thoughts.

'Please say you'll call over. I can't bear to think of you here on your own.' She bites at her lip as a tremble takes hold. 'I mean, I know you're not on your own. You have your husband but I mean, with caring for him and everything. It must be really, really hard for you.'

An unexpected lump rises in my throat and I find

myself fighting back the tears, unused to receiving pity or hearing kind words.

'Thank you. I'll definitely be over at some point. It's just difficult to say when, what with Martyn and his needs, you know?' My words come out in a rapid, stilted flow and I find myself praying she doesn't notice.

On a whim, I touch her hand again and feel a frisson of warmth surge through my body. Maybe we are bonding. I can't remember the last time I felt I had a real friend.

She smiles and gives me a small wave. I listen to the crunch of her feet over the gravel and close the door. I lean back on it after she leaves and feel my heart pounding in my chest. Alien thoughts filter through my brain. I think I actually would like to become friends with her but worry about how Martyn will react to that. The light in the hallway suddenly feels oppressive. I bring my arm up to shield my eyes and try to regulate my breathing. It's her face that is the problem. It won't budge from my mind. The paleness of her skin, the blue tinge around her lips, her hair fanned out in the river as she took her last breath. And my voice, drowned out by the almighty roar of the raging current behind us as I screamed out for help.

I pinch the bridge of my nose and breathe deeply. This has got to stop. I need to move on with my life, get a grip, stop torturing myself with things that have passed, things I can't alter. What's done is done and cannot be undone.

I throw my shoulders back and march into Martyn's study. He is sat back in his chair, stretched out while listening to the radio, exposing how long and skinny his legs are and for some reason, his stance infuriates me.

'I'm not cooking or doing any bloody thing for you today so don't even bother asking. Your painkillers are in the bathroom cabinet. You can sodding well get them yourself if you need them. But don't ask me to do anything because I don't want to know.'

And with that, I stride out of the room and slam the door hard behind me.

14

TWO WEEKS LATER

Callum is busy shoving his adult-sized feet into a pair of old trainers that Anna suddenly wishes she had thrown away many moons ago. She gently pushes him up off the sofa with a smile.

'Go on, you lot. I'll do us all something to eat while you all go off and explore or do whatever it is men do when they go walking in the woods.'

'Fishing?' Callum asks.

Toby shakes his head and claps the young lad squarely on the back, 'Not today, laddo. Need to get my stuff unpacked yet. Maybe the day after tomorrow, yeah?'

Anna shakes her head in exasperation, 'Come on lads, give your uncle a break. He's only been in the house five minutes and already, you're pestering the life out of him.'

The boys nod their heads and murmur in agreement as they shuffle out into the warm spring air. Anna watches them as they cross the road and disappear over the road under the shadow of the trees. The sun is dipping behind the branches, casting the earth below in a sinister, dark-amber glow. She thinks of the missing lady and how she possibly took the same route before she disappeared, how the shade of the trees must have developed into an inky blackness as the sun set, leaving her cold and unsure of how to find her way back. Perhaps she stumbled and is still out there on the path further along the river, injured, thirsty, terrified. Although after the amount of time that has lapsed since she disappeared, Anna knows it's unlikely. It's been nearly two weeks since it happened and the longer she stays missing, the slimmer the chances are she will be found alive. Anna knows this. She has thought about it a lot in the past fortnight. An awful lot. She thought about her last night as she lay in bed listening to the owls screeching and hooting, their squawks cutting through the silence of the night air. She thought of her again this morning as she watched her family and friends stop passers-by to ask them if they had seen anything and she will probably think of her again tomorrow.

Sighing heavily, Anna drags her weary body up off the sofa and trudges into her kitchen, her sanctuary. She will prepare something nice for their meal tonight. At least it will help while away the hours and help take her mind off the goings on outside. It's an eerie sensation, having distress so close at hand and being powerless to stop it. In fact, not even being aware it took place at all. She shakes her head and tells herself to stop being so bloody soft. She flings open the cupboard door and winces as it hits the wall with a clatter.

'Right Anna. Let the therapy begin.'

* * *

Mike is home from work by the time Toby and the boys get back in. Within the hour, the house has turned from a vacuum of silence to a cacophony of noise, with teenagers guffawing and play-fighting and people eating, laughing and talking loudly. Anna watches her family as they sit around the table with the clink and scrape of cutlery against porcelain resonating around the room. She smiles. It's reassuring, comforting. She can't fathom why, it just is.

'Don't know about you, Toby,' Mike says, seeing an opportunity and grasping it firmly with both hands, 'but I'm about ready for a drop of the old single malt.'

Anna watches as Mike's eyes take on a twinkle she sees rarely. What with work and decorating and the constant busyness of a household that contains two boisterous teenagers, her and Mike seem to rarely have time to do anything enjoyable. She narrows her eyes and thinks about the last time they did anything together, just the two of them. Apart from a shopping day spent looking for bloody floor tiles, she can't remember when they last ate a meal in a nice restaurant and simply relaxed together. Mike stands up and heads off in the direction of the drinks cabinet and comes back holding a bottle of amber liquid aloft.

'Looks good to me,' Toby whistles as he throws his napkin to one side, pushes his chair back and heads into the living room. He slumps down onto the sofa and kicks off his shoes. 'You pour and I'll drink them, chief.'

They both down the first one with alarming speed. Anna watches in awe, torn between feeling rather envious of their ability to consume whiskey without having to battle a raging hangover the next day and wanting to tell them to slow down, to remind

Mike he is at work early in the morning and needs to keep a clear head. Mike refills their tumblers and before she has a chance to protest, all four males are settled on the couch and the sports channel has been put on, the sound of a roaring crowd bouncing off all four walls.

The chant of the throng of football supporters fades into the background as Anna closes the door and begins to clear the table. She balances an array of plates on her arms, a skill she is still able to manage after spending her student days working as a waitress in a busy restaurant in Newcastle city centre, and loads the dishwasher, pushing the door closed with a deft flick of her foot. A low hum emanates from it, in rhythm with the slow drone of the washing machine that has been on a hot cycle for most of the afternoon as it tries to remove mud and sweat from Callum's jogging bottoms and somehow performs a mini miracle with Mason's football kit. Anna wanders around the kitchen, wiping up imaginary stains and unfolding and refolding tea towels before it suddenly dawns on her that she has nothing to do. She eyes up the half full bottle of wine sitting on the kitchen top, taunting her with its sparkling crimson sheen and alluring label depicting a sunset in a fictional Italian village where tiny fishing boats bob idly in an exotic-looking bay. She picks up the bottle and examines it closely. So tempting. So very, very tempting. She has no intentions of sitting in there with them. Football isn't her thing, sitting amongst a load of sweaty, pheromone-secreting males, all wound up into a frenzy by the match. But at the same time, she doesn't fancy drinking alone.

An idea darts into her head. She considers it and dismisses it just as quickly. Completely daft. She wouldn't want to do it. Or would she? There was a connection the last time they spoke. Tenuous and fleeting maybe but it was definitely there. Anna stands and drums her fingernails on the kitchen top, her eyes focused on the garden beyond. Then before she has time to change her mind, she steps out of her slippers, pushes her feet into her old walking boots that sit by the back step and heads out of the door.

15

I suppose I did it on impulse really, partly because I was fed up, tired of spending day after day, night after night on my own, but mainly because I am so sick of Martyn. Right now, I feel as if I have no life worth speaking of, so when she turned up at my door, I thought, why the hell not? It's been a few weeks since we last spoke and since then, Martyn has kept me on my toes, making demands, his temper constantly on the brink of explosive. It's been a difficult few weeks. Plus there was the lure of the house. *Oh, the house!* The chances of Anna living there and inviting me round must be so slim and yet for once, good fortune has smiled down on me. I'm not about to frown on such an opportunity.

So here I am, sitting at Anna's kitchen table, socialising, back here in the house, *my* house, chatting, pretending all is right with the world and all the while, the body of a woman floats downstream, the marks of my husband's strong fingers embedded into the thin, soft flesh around her throat. It's all so surreal, I actually want to laugh.

I stare at the wall next to where I sit, at the collection of family photographs. Children of all ages stare out at me with toothless grins and messy hair, footballs lodged tightly under their arms. Unlike my kitchen, this one looks lived in: chaotic, with a cacophony of noise filtering in from the living room, pictures hanging on every available wall space and copper pans dangling from beams and rafters overhead. I like it. It's warm, inviting, lived in. I have a more minimalist approach to decor with my cream floor tiles and walls and surfaces devoid of anything remotely resembling normal family life. No pictures, no sentimental knick-knacks. Everything I own is stacked away in cabinets, out of sight. Plain and simple. I sometimes wish I could live like this but it's not in me and there's no point trying to emulate someone else's style, trying to be something I am not. Besides which, my life currently has more than enough difficulties and tensions to deal with and cluttering up my surroundings with ornaments and portraits will just muddy my thinking. And Martyn's. He needs serenity and a calm environment. Sometimes, the calmness and serenity works and sometimes, it doesn't. I blink and feel a tension begin to build behind my eyes.

'How's your coffee? Not too strong, I hope? I have a tendency to drink mine strong. Mike says you can practically stand a spoon up in it.' Anna is standing by the sink, a glass of wine locked into her cupped hands.

'It's fine,' I say looking around me. I suddenly feel envious of Anna's comfortable home with its cosy ambience and family-orientated bits and pieces. Photos, ornaments, lamps of all shapes and sizes, pots and pans. They're everywhere. It's not the clutter I like; it's the sense of fun, the tenderness they have here. It's palpable from the minute you walk in, like a warm embrace. I try to think of where all my photographs of Tom are, and whether or not any of them are even in a frame or ever have been. I suddenly feel quite ashamed of my housekeeping skills. I live in a shell. There's a fine line between being clutter-free and being sterile and I, it would appear after looking around Anna's kitchen, have long since crossed that line.

I'm relieved to see not much has changed. New

units and decor obviously but the general layout of the room is as I remember it. No huge, sweeping extensions, no conservatory or orangery clinging inharmoniously to the back of a 200-year-old house. If I close my eyes, I can see my mother standing at the sink, her arms immersed in the frothing bubbles; I can hear Suzie upstairs, the drone of the old hairdryer whirring furiously as she desperately tries to straighten out those stubborn kinks. The sound of my father's footsteps cuts into my thoughts. I open my eyes before I hear the roar of his anger as he returns from his usual Sunday afternoon liquid lunch, enraged at everything and everyone and the hand that life dealt him.

'Are you certain you wouldn't prefer a wine? Or I have gin or Bacardi if wine isn't your thing? It's not to everyone's liking, is it? I have a friend who simply can't touch the stuff. Gives her blinding headaches. They reckon it's the chemicals in it, you know.'

'No, really, coffee is good for me,' I reply, thinking I would like nothing more than a glass of cold white wine. My head suddenly feels as if there is a furnace in there.

Anna nods and smiles and then flicks a strand of hair out of her eyes, taking my breath away. There it is again. The likeness, those mannerisms. They're uncanny. I feel my heart begin to flutter up my throat and bark out a tight little cough to suppress it.

'Actually,' I say, surprised at myself, 'I've had a rapid change of mind. A cold glass of white wine sounds just perfect. Chardonnay, if you have it?'

Her face lights up as she places her own glass down on the table with a slight wobble. She reaches up to the cupboard for another one.

'I'm so pleased you decided to come over tonight, Phoebe. It's a pity Martyn wasn't well enough to make it but at least you're here,' she says cheerily. I watch her fill my glass to the brim with chilled wine. 'It's good to have someone to chat to, actually.' Her voice dips and she lowers her eyes. 'The boys decided they were going to watch the football and... well, I'm not really into sport so I thought I would see if you...' She takes along slurp of wine and looks over at me, her face childlike and accepting. 'And now here you are!' she shrills just a little too loudly.

I drape my fingers around the base of the glass, unsure what to say next. I'm guessing Anna, despite her bubbly exterior, is actually as lonely as I am. The thought catches me unawares, makes my face burn with self-pity. I sit quietly, mulling it over in my mind. Sometimes saying nothing is the best panacea. I watch as she drains her glass and refills it. I sip at my wine and observe her closely: the way her hair moves, how she smiles with such ease and then before I know it, my glass is empty too. How did that happen? I rarely drink and really should slow down. It's bound to have a powerful effect on me and the hangover will be brutal.

'There you go,' she says with a slight tremor to her hand as she tips the bottle. It clinks against the wine flute and I listen to the satisfying glug as my glass becomes full again. So inviting with its crystal-clear, slightly golden hue. The perfect tonic for a dark, drizzly evening.

'I can't stop thinking about her.' Anna takes another gulp and I watch as her chin begins to tremble ever so slightly.

'I'm sorry?' I say, feigning ignorance, hoping desperately she'll change her mind. I just knew it would come back to this and right now, this is one conversation I really do not want to be having.

'That lady, Nancy,' she whispers.

'Ah right. Yes, Nancy,' I reply and take a deep drink of the wine, feeling the chill of the slightly tart liquid as it travels down my throat. I wish she would shut up, I really do. Why can't she stop harping on about this subject? I came here to relax, not have a discussion about a person none of us even knew.

'What if she didn't go missing of her own accord? What if something terrible has happened to her?' Anna turns to face me, her expression suddenly dark. 'I mean, what if she's dead?'

Her voice is no more than a whisper but it resonates in my head like a clanging bell. I take another long drink of the wine. This time it burns as I swallow it but despite that, I take another gulp, my tongue suddenly feeling too big for my mouth, and then another. I finish the glass before holding it out for a top up. I'm going to need to blur the edges a little if this is where the conversation is heading.

'We just don't know yet though, do we?' I say, trying to think of a million different subjects I can steer our conversation around to without appearing like a cold-hearted bitch. 'We have to stay positive. I'm sure her family won't want to hear anyone talking like that.'

Anna nods sheepishly. I continue on, 'And it doesn't alter the fact that this place is a beautiful village. Just because this awful thing has happened doesn't mean Cogglestone is any worse a place to live, does it?'

'Oh, of course not!' she crows, her face suddenly lighting up. I had forgotten how easy it is to change her focus. It gives me a warm glow knowing I can always be in charge and take the lead without her even realising it. 'Did you know we won the Northumbria in Bloom competition three years in a row?' she coos softly.

'Really? Well, that's marvellous, isn't it? Quite an achievement for such a small place.' She refills my glass and I sip at my wine, a welcome haze beginning to descend.

Anna nods her head emphatically and we sit for a short while in the quiet of her kitchen. Not an uncomfortable silence, more of a natural break in the conversation where we both take time to become acquainted with the idea of each other. I take another drink and then another, followed by a large gulp. I look down to see our glasses are empty once again. Anna refills them and I pick mine up, my fingers feeling wobbly and slightly numb. Shameful. Only a few glasses of wine and already, I am beginning to lose my dexterity. I really must slow down. This time, I take a long slug and then another, a warm fuzziness resting behind my eyes with each consecutive swallow.

The silence is punctured by two wild-eyed teenagers who burst through the kitchen door, their limbs locked in a frenzy as they reach for the large fridge that stands in the corner of the room. Anna sighs deeply and raises her eyes at me, yet I suspect she secretly enjoys this sort of behaviour and being part of a house that is always noisy and hectic. The boys are followed by two men, one of medium height and slightly built and the other more portly, with a receding hairline.

'Oh God, sorry. I haven't done any introductions yet. Too much wine. Very rude of me.' Anna jumps up, moves over to the men, a slight redness starting to creep up her neck and over her face. She points to the chubbier man and looks back to me, her voice beginning to slur slightly.

'Phoebe, this is Mike, my husband. Mike, this is Phoebe, our new neighbour.' Anna points to me like a museum exhibit before stepping aside and moving closer to the taller of the two men. 'And this is Toby, my brother. Toby, this is Phoebe.'

Mike leans over and shakes my hand vigorously. Even though I have drunk nearly a bottle of wine, I can smell the alcohol on Mike's breath as he pushes his body towards me to grasp my hand. Toby stands back and remains still, watching me from the corner of the kitchen, my presence acknowledged by a quick, formal nod. I watch, fascinated, as Mike turns and gives Anna a hug before grabbing a large bag of peanuts and heading back into the living room. The boys wrestle with a family size pack of crisps until Anna intervenes with a loud voice I didn't think she was capable of, and a slight tap to the back of each of their heads. They respond with a guffaw and grab an armful of snacks each. Such pandemonium and noise and yet so relaxing. I look back to see Toby still watching me. His expression never waivers and it suddenly makes me feel hot and slightly uncomfortable. I find myself wondering what the fascination is. He is quite a bit younger than me and I'm not an outstandingly attractive woman. My vision mists up as I begin to squirm under his watchful gaze. And then I remember. It hits me with a hot rush, causing me to shift in my seat.

I quickly finish my drink, ready to flee, to leave this situation and get home as quickly and unobtrusively as I can, but before I have chance to stand up and make my farewells, he speaks. 'Have we met somewhere before? I'm sure I recognise your face from somewhere?'

His voice is soft and sincere. He is smiling at me now but I can't listen to him any more. I need to get out of here right now. I can't allow this to go any further. I should have remembered he was coming. Stupid of me. And careless. Very, very careless. Not like me at all.

'Oh, I don't think so. I'm new to the village.' I try to keep the tremor out of my voice, to keep my pitch steady and confident.

He narrows his eyes, shrugs his shoulders and sighs. 'Ah well, probably the whiskey blurring my thinking. I usually have a good memory for faces but after three glasses of this stuff, I must be getting confused.' He holds up his empty tumbler, tips it from side to side and smiles.

I stand up and smooth the creases out of my trousers, ready to leave.

'Well, you know what they say, don't you?' Anna chirps up rather too loudly as she stares at us both. I shake my head at her, subliminally willing her to shut up. 'If you recognise somebody but you can't recall where you know their face from, it means they're the Devil.' She spits the words out, giggles slightly and leans against the kitchen counter for support, her eyes half closed.

Suddenly sober and desperate to get home, I struggle to hear anything else she says as blood rushes thickly through my ears and around my head. I try to stare at her but my vision is blurry and I feel quite sick. What a stupid thing to say.

'Really pleased to meet you, Toby,' I say, my voice steadier than I hoped it would be, 'but I need to get home now,' I surprise myself at how calm and collected I sound when in reality, I am anything but. I step out from behind the table and make my way over to Anna. I give her a hug and thank her for a lovely evening, then turn around to see Toby still watching me. He has recognised me. I just know it. A pulse judders in my neck as I swallow and tell myself I am jumping to conclusions. I give him a brief smile and slip past him into the chill of the evening, a welcome breeze cooling my burning face as I head back home to Martyn.

He is dozing in the chair when I get back in, and once again I'm furious with him. This is all his fault; the constant need to watch what I say, having to live like a hermit, feeling permanently miserable and fretful about the people he has hurt – it's all down to him, the man I chose to spend the rest of my life with, the man I now spend my days looking after. Everything is his fault.

I close my eyes and try to visualise a life without him, a life where I can visit friends, see my son, have people round for dinner, but no matter how hard I try, all I can see is Martyn's face as he falls on the cliff side, his hands grappling for purchase, the dreadful, guttural moan emanating from the back of his throat and the blood as it seeped from the back of his head in great crimson waves.

He is awake when I open my eyes and is watching me intently. He tries to stand up and wobbles, his gait laboured and clumsy.

'Phoebe. Glad you're back, sweetheart. I was just going to make us both a cup of tea. Did you have a nice evening?'

I let out a small sigh and continue staring at him, tears stinging my eyes. I am trapped. Whether I like it or not, this is my life from here on in. How could I ever leave him? He is totally dependent on me. What would become of him if I simply cast him aside in search of a better life? What would become of me? Martyn and I have been together since our late teens. I can barely remember a life without him.

'I'll get it,' I say, suddenly resigned to it all. Acceptance. That's what I have to focus on. This is my life now and there is no escape, no get-out clause. I created this situation and now I am stuck with it. Whether I like it or not.

'Cheese on toast for supper?' I shout through as I turn on the grill and prepare the food.

They said it was my fault, tried to blame it all on me. It wasn't, of course. What kind of person did they all take me for: some kind of deranged youngster who would deliberately drown their own sister? Suzie had slipped, you see, after the others left us by the river-bank. She had tried to make her way back over to me and lost her footing on one of the stepping stones, a lime-green killer swathed in lichen and moss. I had already turned my back on her, still angry and hurt, but when I heard the almighty splash and her cries for help, I jumped in and waded across to get her out. And that's when it happened. The water was rushing past me, making me feel disorientated and slightly dizzy. It was too high after the rains. All my warnings about the dangers and current strengths had been blatantly ignored and now it was coming back to bite us. I managed to grab her hand and pull her up but found myself falling too. Struggling to stay upright, I planted my feet far apart but in the process, lost my balance completely and landed on top of her, clumps of her hair in my mouth, her fingers still entwined in mine. Every time I tried to move, she somehow became wedged further under me until I ended up standing on top of her slim frame, her bones, hard and resistant like porcelain under my feet. With a shriek, I jumped off her sodden body and tried to drag her up but she was so heavy, so very, very heavy. Suzie was only slightly built but her body took on different proportions when wet. She was slippery and her limbs seemed to take on a life of their own, waving around at peculiar angles every time I tried to move her.

It didn't take long for me to become tired, so exhausted I could barely hoist myself out of the river, let alone the water-drenched body of my older sister. I had just about enough energy to haul myself to the edge of the riverbank, which was where I was when they found me. I had lain there immobile and gasping for breath when a group of fishermen stumbled across me. Suzie was still in the water. Her hair had become wrapped around the debris and stones, trapping her. I could see her from where I lay. Her body was face down, strands of free hair fanned out behind her. They dragged her out and put her on the riverbank, her skin mottled, her lips tinged with blue. One of the fishermen had become agitated, asking me why I hadn't helped her, why I was laid there doing nothing. Why hadn't I shouted? They were only a few yards away; they could have helped us. They could have saved her. I tried to explain but he wouldn't listen. None of them listened. Only my mother, who had always loved me unconditionally, never seemed to doubt my story. She would listen to me, asking over and over again what had happened, how had she become trapped? 'I'm sure you did what you could,' she would whisper tightly, her eyes taking on an empty look as she drummed her fingers on the table and coughed softly. Nothing changed for my father. He was his usual aggressive self. Too absorbed by his own problems and wrapped up in his rapidly declining health issues to notice and too deep in the drink to care.

The funeral directors placed Suzie in our dining room in an open casket for visitors to pay their respects. It filled me with horror, the thought of my dead sister squashed into that narrow oak box, her lifeless eyes staring up at the ceiling. I had no idea if her eyes were actually open or closed because I refused to look. The whole thing felt macabre and contrived. Suzie, the centre of attention even in death. A stream of people traipsed in and out, arms laden with flowers and wreaths, their faces lined with sorrow and anguish, some genuine, many in it just for the sensationalistic gutter-gossip that accompanies the death of a child.

The service was a blur of prayers, hand wringing and tears. I felt numb, unsure of how I should conduct myself. All eyes were on us, assessing our reactions, making sure we did the right amount of crying that is deemed necessary for such a traumatic occasion. Adults I had never met before stood around weeping and talking about the unfairness of it all, hugging my mother and telling her that they would do anything for her. 'Anything at all,' they said as they filtered away one by one, until we were left alone with our black funeral attire and even blacker thoughts.

The weeks after the funeral were hollow, the house silent and vacuous. We rattled around, going through the motions, each of us too locked in our own torturous maelstrom of misery and anguish to communicate with one another. My father's physical condition worsened, putting my mother under unbearable pressure. He could have done more for himself. Even as a child, I could see how he used his illnesses to his advantage, playing the martyr when anything mildly physical was asked of him. He had chronic bronchitis and seemed to revel in his condition. He also turned his anger on me. After Suzie's death, anything and everything was my fault.

The day we went to see Dr Tavel, I thought we were going to see a relative. I have no idea why I thought that. Whether or not I had been told so, I will never know. I have no recollection of any conversations that would have led me to believe that, but I do recall the surprise and mild disappointment when we pulled up outside his surgery, which was surrounded by large conifers. It was eerily dark and quickly became patently obvious we wouldn't be spending the afternoon chatting to cousins and aunts while reminiscing and eating cake.

Looking back, I am not even certain if I knew that it was me he was assessing. It was all very relaxed and informal. We sat on a sofa, my mother and I, while Dr Tavel sat on a large leather armchair facing us, his large, brogue-covered feet shuffling around every time he asked me a question. I remember thinking how strange it was that he didn't have a stethoscope. Every doctor I had ever met always had a stethoscope hanging round his neck. He was clean-shaven and wore expensive-looking clothes. His questions were worded so I could understand them but he often watched my mother when I spoke. I don't fully recall the nature of the questions but do remember how I often struggled to give an answer, or at least the answer I felt he was looking for. Sometimes, after I had spoken, he would sit in silence, tapping his pen against the side of the chair, his eyes flitting between me and my mother. I was too young to understand what was going on. I was more impressed by the comfort of the huge sofa and the vibrant colours of the oil paintings that hung on the walls of his office. I wasn't unduly perturbed by it all – more mystified, really. All I knew was that my sister had died in the most tragic of circumstances and our family, already teetering on the brink of collapse, no longer functioned and was heading for catastrophe. One thing I was certain of, however, despite being only nine years old, was that apart from my mother, who did all she could to make the best out of a bad situation, they all unequivocally blamed me.

16

Her face is everywhere as I take Tillie out for her morning walk. Somebody has been out and about in the village, a family member perhaps, or even the police, and plastered posters on trees and lampposts declaring a small reward for any information that leads to Nancy being found alive and well. I stop and study the photograph while Tillie sniffs at a patch of grass and avidly circles a molehill, her nose buried deeply in the soil, vacuuming up smells with her cold, wet, twitching nose. In the picture, Nancy is leaning against a big, old fireplace, an array of photographs behind her. Her smile radiates warmth and happiness. I surmise it was taken last Christmas, judging by the flickering candles all around her. She will have spent the festive season with her family, surrounded by her children and grandchildren. All happy, all smiling. All together.

I walk further through the village towards the small group of people at the end of the lane. They are gathered around some kind of wagon. As I get closer, I can see it's a low loader. Nancy's car is being hooked onto it by a burly-looking chap in navy overalls and a fleecy jacket, while a policeman stands chatting to a middle-aged couple who are wearing walking clothes. I move closer, keen to mingle and be seen to be doing the right thing, be socially appropriate. The couple bid their goodbyes to the young, pale-faced policeman and head off towards the river as I approach.

I slow down and nod. 'Morning. Still no sign of her?' I shake my head and sigh deeply, hoping my faux concern will be enough to convince him of my innocence. I check myself. I *am* innocent. What I am guilty of is aiding and abetting a mentally ill man who did what he did because of his diminished responsibility. No more than that.

'Not as yet. We're following up all lines of enquiry and some of her family have done their bit as well.'

He points over to the trunk of a nearby tree where Nancy's face beams out at us.

'Yes, I noticed. I hope she turns up soon. Must be dreadful for them. Such a worry.' I lean down and stroke Tillie, who has started to whine and nuzzle her face in against my leg.

'Yes, they're very concerned. And rightly so. This is completely out of character for this lady.' He looks me up and down, sending a small vibe of fear through my veins. 'Do you live locally?'

'Over there,' I reply, pointing to the long, sloping roof of my house with its black slate tiles and large picture windows that overlook the river, completely out of place against the emerging foliage and branches of the nearby conifer trees.

'I don't believe we've spoken yet, Mrs...?'

'Whitegate,' I answer a little too quickly. 'Phoebe Whitegate.' I must stay calm. *Hold it together, Phoebe. Hold it together, old girl.* I watch as he lifts a pen out of his pocket, along with a small, white notepad, and steel myself for a barrage of questions. I decide to pre-empt him. Take control, best way to do it. Who questions, leads. Isn't that what they always say?

'I hope this lady turns up soon.' I look down at Tillie, who is running around in circles excitedly. 'She needs a lot of exercise,' I mutter and roll my eyes dramatically.

Much to my relief, he smiles back and leans down to stroke her. Tillie responds by rolling on her back and wiggling her tiny legs in the air comically. He laughs as he rests down on his haunches and ruffles the fur on her underbelly.

'I have a Labrador. He's as soft as the day is long and as greedy as hell,' he says through clenched teeth. 'Costs us a fortune, he does. Spends all day troughing.'

'Ah, I can imagine. But we wouldn't have them any other way, would we? Man's best friend and all that.'

He stands up and brushes his black trousers down with his large hands.

'I've had Tillie here since she was a pup. I couldn't bear to be parted from her,' I say as I reach into my pocket and bring out a doggie treat. She watches me closely, her eyes fixated on the gravy bone between my fingers. I hold it out to her and she lunges at it, gulping it down greedily without missing a beat.

'We got Laddie from a rescue centre but it's as if he's always lived with us.' He coughs and smoothes his jacket down. 'Anyway, as I was saying, Nancy's family can't state enough how out of character this is for her. I was wondering if you've seen anyone matching her description?'

I shake my head and jut my bottom lip out to express how mystified I am by the whole episode.

'She set off walking by the river by all accounts.' He stares over at the muddy track that leads through the trees, running parallel with the river, then looks over to my house. A pulse taps away at my temple as I watch him narrow his eyes while he ponders the route of the water, trying to work out what happens to the path once it nears the large barn conversion.

'Is there a bridge over there to the other side of the river? Through those trees?' He points to a copse of cedars adjacent to the rear of the house.

I shake my head and smile, hoping I look sincere enough, helpful enough, not too inquisitive or chatty. I need to get the balance right. It's hard work, this lying business, 'No, the path continues straight on.'

He considers this for a minute before speaking. 'So that means it must run past the back of your house?'

I nod. 'Yes. It cuts through my garden. The path was built as a right of way and the house was built around it from what I've been told.'

He stares at me.

'I only moved in a short while ago. I'm new to the village.' Realisation dawns and he smiles again, revealing a set of slightly crooked teeth that aren't completely unattractive despite overlapping with each other.

'Ah, I see. This must be a bit of a shock to you then?'

I widen my eyes and suck my teeth. 'Absolutely. I only wish I'd actually seen her and could help but I've spent the last few weeks unpacking and dragging furniture around.'

'When you're not out walking this one, eh?' His eyes crease up at the corners as he smiles. He looks down to his notepad and begins to write. 'Do you live there alone?'

I don't know if I am imagining it but I could swear his tone has changed, developed an icy edge to it. I feel a sudden rush of blood to my head at the unexpected question. I should have known it was coming and been ready to deal with it but somehow, he has caught me off guard and I feel quite lightheaded and queasy. I can feel my nostrils begin to flare as I inhale deeply to steady myself.

'Yes. I live alone. Too big a house for one person

really but I'm hoping for grandchildren at some point.' I smile and raise my eyes in mock exasperation. 'My son is in his late twenties and settled down with a lovely girl. I'm keeping my fingers crossed.' There, I've said it. No choice, really. I can't have them hanging round the house, quizzing Martyn. Everything would fall apart and then our lives would be over.

The tone of his laugh is much higher than his voice. 'You sound like my wife. Our boys are only in their teens but already she says she can't wait for them to have kids of their own.' He slips his notepad back into his top pocket and I want to clap my hands with relief. 'Women! Give them a houseful of children and they're happy. If only us men were as easy going as the fairer sex, I reckon the world would be a far nicer place.'

I smile and nod and allow him one last stroke of Tillie before saying my goodbyes.

By the time I get home, both the policeman and the tow truck carrying Nancy's small Fiat have all gone. As if she has never been here. Apart from the posters. And left exposed to the elements, they won't last long either. The world will forget about Nancy. And then perhaps, I can relax and not feel as if a damning piece of evidence is about to reveal itself.

I neither know nor care where Martyn has got to when I get in. I unclip Tillie and head to the kitchen then back into the living room. I entertain the idea that he is laid out on the bed upstairs, dead. The thought of it fills me with shivers and I quickly shut it out of my mind, unable to work out if I would be pleased or horrified. No more Martyn. I swallow hard. At the end of the day, he is still my husband and he needs me. I need him. Truth be told, I think I've spent my whole life needing him. He was the one who rescued me from the brink of emotional collapse after spending years bearing the brunt of Suzie's death, taking the blame for it all, spending my childhood in the shadow of my sister's memory. Martyn was the one who taught me how to be strong again, how to face the world with a smile. As a fledgling doctor, he saw something in me; he was able to cut through the veneer I had managed to surround myself with and see straight through it all. Somehow, he was the only person who was able to identify the real me. I'm pretty sure that at the outset, he viewed me as some kind of assignment, a problem he had taken upon himself to solve. That was Martyn all over. Always looking for a new challenge, something to tax him. I didn't mind. I was glad of his help and the fact somebody had shown an interest in the real Phoebe. I was his project. And he was my saviour.

I head upstairs and stop along the way. The sight of my own reflection in the mirror catches me unawares. How is it the lady over the road looks more like my own sister than I do? Quite unfair, really. Suzie looked like my mother whereas I resemble my father's side of the family, with a more sallow complexion and broader features. I stare at the deep grooves either side of my mouth that give me the appearance of someone who is permanently sad and disapproving, and sigh wistfully. Suzie was a natural beauty, her skin like bone china. I turn this way and that, hoping to see a side of me that I like and eventually give up. I am what I am and no amount of yearning is going to change that.

I potter about upstairs, folding clothes, straightening bed linen, doing anything to pass the time. I think of the tow truck outside and am suddenly overwhelmed by a sense of lightness. Her car is gone and soon she too, will be no more than a dim and distant memory. Every year on the anniversary of her disappearance, flowers will be appear by the riverside, the odd poster may reappear, only to be ruined again by the incessant winds and mists. Life will return to normal. As if she never existed.

The sound of an engine draws me to the window. Outside, Anna and her family are off out somewhere together. I imagine they're one of those families who, at the first sign of warm weather, all pile in the car and dash off to the seaside or somewhere in the countryside where hordes of families gather, brash and loud, their faces stuffed full of McDonalds or ice cream. The kind of settings Martyn and I used to avoid. Then I hear Tom's voice in my head telling me not be such a snob, telling me I am hypercritical and disapproving. I bite my lip, suddenly guilty. I'm definitely becoming too insular, locked in my own little world. I make a mental note to be nicer to her next time we meet. Anna has been unerringly kind to me, even when I've been frosty and downright rude to her. That's the problem; I've never been particularly good at this socialising malarkey, even when I was a child. Too frigid and reserved. And as Tom was often fond of telling me, far too judgemental.

One by one, they slide into the back of the car, Mike jumping into the driver's side until there is only Toby left. That evening a few days back still haunts me. The look on his face, his inquisitive expression. It's only a matter of time. I breathe hard and remind myself that he no longer lives locally and in a few days' time, he will be back in Lincoln, immersed in his work, too busy to spend time thinking about some random neighbour who lives near his sister. He stands next to the passenger door and takes a look around him. Then before I have chance to do anything, he looks up and for a fraction of a second, our eyes lock. With a gasp, I try to duck down out of sight, but it's too late and too obvious to escape his attention. He's already seen me. His face doesn't show any expression. In fact, his stare is cold with perhaps a hint of hostility. I check myself. This is silly. I'm overreacting and imagining things. I think back to the other evening, his unrelenting, studious expression as he observed my every move. He can't know me. Can he? I certainly don't recognise him. I'm pretty sure such a handsome face would have lodged itself in my consciousness. I quell the small, still voice that nags at me and sets my pulse into overdrive. The voice that insists he must have worked at the surgery when Martyn did. That is too great a coincidence, surely? I definitely don't recognise him. I was on first name terms with all the doctors who worked there and my memory may not be as good as it once was but know for a fact, he wasn't one of them.

I slink behind the curtains, my face burning with humiliation at being caught out spying like a small child. I close my eyes and think hard. I visualise Martyn's old surgery: a Victorian building with an ugly 1970s annexe that housed the reception area. It once belonged to the local squire and had several outhouses and an extensive garden that is now a huge swathe of concrete. The car park isn't half as pretty as the lawns and rose gardens were, but a damn sight easier to maintain and way more practical.

The faces of all the GPs at Forge Hill are clear and fresh in my mind, each sat in their respective consultation rooms. There was Robin Wright, who had worked there for over twenty years, David Thorpe, a recently qualified young buck who was full of radical ideas on how to change the running of the surgery, Sarah Rushton – or was it Rushy? I can't quite recall. I do remember she had had just returned from maternity leave and teetered on the brink of exhaustion most days, and then there was the new practitioner who...

My head thumps with realisation and a cold rush of fear races through me. Oh God. How can I have been so blind? He had only been there a matter of days when I...

Swallowing down a painful lump, I blink back the tears that threaten to spill out. That day – I've tried my utmost to blank out all thoughts of that day: the day I went to see Martyn at work. But now it burns fiercely in my brain, bright and hot, lighting up and activating parts of my memory I would rather stayed dormant. I slap my palms into my eye sockets and groan out loud. I don't want to remember. I refuse to remember. And if it wasn't for this Toby chap, I wouldn't need to remember. But now here it is, another unwanted recollection, floating around my brain like candy floss, sticking to everything it touches and refusing to budge, making me want to scream out loud with the unfairness of it all.

It wasn't my fault. I was simply trying to save my marriage. I had to do something. I had found the evidence linking Debra to Martyn only days ago and was emotionally fragile. She was my friend and I wasn't thinking straight the day I marched into Forge Hill Surgery and burst into Martyn's room, bristling with fury. He must have been there, Toby, new to the practice and witness to the lunatic ravings of a doctor's jealous wife. Fortunately, he hasn't quite placed me as that barmy lady who had to be forcibly seated and sedated by her husband. Yet. And if I'm lucky, he never will. If I'm not, and he does remember? I scratch at the sides of my bare arms. If he does remember then I guess I'll have to deal with that the best way I can. I'll cross that bridge when I come to it.

I continue to tear at my arms, thinking how much of a relief it would be if I had a sharp implement to hand which I could drag up and down my skin. Like waiting and waiting before finally being able to scratch an itch. The release I would feel as blood escaped through the wounds, purging me of all my pent-up troubles, would be unspeakably beautiful. I shiver expectantly. Such pleasure, so liberating. Yet it would change nothing.

Bile rises up my gullet, burning my throat and blood gushes through my ears. I bring my knees up and rest my head in my lap, then inhale deeply as I try to stem my breathing, which is now rapid and bordering on wheezing. I have to stop this and continue with my normal day to day life. There's absolutely nothing I can do in the meantime. For all I know, Toby may not visit again. Or he may come round every weekend. Or he might ring them every single day...

Stop it, stop it, stop it!

Jumping up, I stomp across the bedroom into the en suite, dizzy with fear and dread. I'm blowing this up out of all proportion and need to get a bloody grip. I've dealt with worse than this in the past. I can do it. I can deal with this and come out of it unscathed. I just need to keep it together. Puffing out my cheeks I decide to take a couple of tablets to calm my nerves. Just some of Martyn's tablets, for his depression, to help me keep a level head. I've seen how they work for him, turning him from a raving lunatic to a pussycat in a matter of minutes. I open the cabinet and grab two of them, throwing them into my mouth, and then stick my head under the tap to gulp back enough water to wash them down. Goosebumps prickle my skin. The ambience in the room has altered. A small but definitely detectable waft of heat filters through the air. He is here. I can feel him. I turn round to see Martyn standing behind me. Tillie scampers round his feet and her innocence stabs at me. If only humans could live like dogs: no questions, no worries, simply accept what occurs as it occurs and do it all with good grace. Every day is a new day, shiny and sparkling and exciting, when you're a dog.

'Where have you been, Phoebe?' His tone isn't exactly accusatory but neither is it friendly. There is an edge to it that scares me, sets my nerves alight. I grit my teeth so tightly, it hurts. My jaw clicks painfully as I set my face into a determined position. Here we go again.

'Walking Tillie, then back here. Where have you been?'

My question catches him off guard and he narrows his eyes and looks around the room. This happens sometimes, as if his thinking is slightly out of sync, playing catch up with current events. He stands stock still, his hands hanging limply at his sides. The silence is deafening. I watch as his fingers begin to shift slightly. He wiggles them about ominously, the momentum spreading up his arms and over his broad chest. A cracking sound breaks the silence as Martyn rotates his large shoulders and moves his head from side to side, as if freeing up his neck muscles. He glares at me, his eyes full of loathing. And then I realise. His medication. The packet was full. Not only has he not had today's dosage; he hasn't had yesterday's either. And it is beginning to show. This is all my fault. I should be monitoring him more closely, making sure he takes his meds regularly. And I used to, but just lately I seem to find it difficult keeping track of time. My head feels muddled, full of worries about Nancy and Toby. And Martyn. He is a constant source of deep concern. I need to be more careful, be extra vigilant when it comes to his medication. It's not something I can tamper with. I do that at my peril.

Martyn moves closer to me, so close I can smell the reek of his breath, see the plaque on his unbrushed teeth. 'Who were you looking at out there?' he snarls.

I shrug my shoulders and try to brush past him but he shoves me back into the wall. 'I asked you who were you looking at?'

This is a split-second decision I have to make. To tell him or not to tell him? Whatever I do, I have a horrible feeling that no good is going to come of it. I decide to come clean. Lying will only increase my chances of confrontation and besides which, he will find out anyway. Martyn *always* finds out.

'It's a relative of Anna's. I think he used to work at your surgery.' I am convinced the sound of my heart thrashing around my chest fills the whole room.

Martyn continues to stare at me. Unblinking. I don't know how he does that or whether or not it's a deliberate tactic he employs to unnerve me. He has a proclivity for instilling fear in me. His eyes bore into me, cold and still. The colour of gunmetal.

'What relative?'

I nod and keep my expression neutral. Martyn is an absolute master when it comes to reading people. Comes with the territory of being a doctor for so many years and since being pensioned off, he hasn't lost his knack for cutting to the chase and disregarding the unimportant stuff. Even if it's really important to other people.

'Anna's brother, Toby. I don't know his surname but apparently he reckons he knows my face from somewhere.'

'That's what he said?'

A tiny pulse hammers at my temple as he watches me. A pain shoots through my jaw. I wiggle it and breathe deeply. 'That's what he said.'

Martyn's booming laugh reverberates around the room. Something tells me I shouldn't have let this conversation get this far. I've got a sickly feeling down in my gut that this isn't going to end well. It rarely does.

'And he saw you that day, didn't he?'

My breathing is ragged, uneven. I seize the opportunity to ask him, 'Do you remember him? This Toby who says he recognises me from somewhere?'

His lip curls up into a sneer and I feel like running away and hiding somewhere until it all goes away. He knows him. Of course he does. What the hell did I expect?

I take a few small, tentative steps out of the en suite, slipping past Martyn, and look around at the huge expanse of bedroom. Plain, nondescript. A king-sized bed, fitted wardrobes and a cheval mirror. Not many hiding places here.

'He did see you, didn't he? That's what you're getting at, isn't it? You're worried he recognises you from that day. Do you remember *that day*, Phoebe? Do you?'

He steps closer to me. I am pressed up against the bedroom wall. Nowhere to run to. Nowhere to go to at all. Trapped in my own home. By my husband. A monster by any other name.

'That day when you turned up at the surgery like a screaming banshee, hollering about me having an affair.'

I'd gone to finish an argument we had had the day previously when I finally realised my husband was sleeping with one of my best friends. After discovering the emails at home, I had confronted Martyn. He had been sat in an armchair in his study reading a newspaper, his demeanour positively jocular when I stormed in, shaky with anger and disbelief.

'Where were you last week? When you were supposed to be at a conference with George?'

He had looked up at me, his pupils slightly dilated, a raw fizz of excitement evident in his expression.

'As you have just said,' he had sighed, 'I was away with George and a few other people. At the conference, remember?'

His gaze had bored into me, unrelenting, daring me to dispute his story. I had dug my teeth into the sides of my mouth, nipping painfully at a flap of skin until it hurt so much, I had to let it go. A metallic taste flooded my mouth, gliding its way over my gums and down my throat, oily and pungent.

'Okay Martyn,' I had said, trying to keep a lid on my anger, 'we can go on playing your little game or you can tell me where you really were. And I mean *really*.'

I had watched as his lips curled up slightly, mocking, so sure of himself. So fucking arrogant.

'Where do you think I was, Phoebe?'

I had stayed silent, too fearful to answer. Suddenly not wanting to know the truth. Time froze in our home that day. Air expanded in my chest. I thought I was going to choke as I watched Martyn's face break into a deceitful grin.

'Yes, that's right, Phoebe. Whatever you're thinking I did, I did it. Obviously. If it makes you shut up and leave me alone then I admit it.'

He had shaken his head and turned his attention back to scanning the newspaper and that was the day my world as I knew it came to a convulsing, grinding halt. I had intended to take a suitcase full of his clothes into the surgery but even that felt too final. Because despite his admission, despite those emails, despite the desperation and the hurt I felt, I wanted our marriage to survive. I really did. And we tried. God knows we tried. He told me he had broken it off with Debra but she simply refused to accept it. She hounded him, threatened to expose their affair, to ruin him. It was a nightmare. And then suddenly, one day it all stopped. The relief on my part was immense. I hoped that would be the end of it, but Martyn's moods continued. He was nervous, edgy. So I decided I would book us a holiday. Just a few days at a guest house in Whitby. Hoped we could get away together, sort it all out, get our lives back on track. How wrong I was.

I turn away from Martyn and not for the first time this week, wish him dead and gone. A pain travels up my jaw and I realise I have had my teeth clenched together tight, so tight I have started to develop a gnawing headache. I close my eyes and steel myself for a raging argument but when I turn around, Martyn is wandering off. The moment gone. This is what he does: comes and goes, leaving a trail of devastation in his wake, a whirling vortex of destruction.

I stagger over to the bed, the medication beginning to take effect. My eyelids are stone pillars, gravity and exhaustion forcing them downwards. The final thing I see before sleep catches me in its clutches is the face of Dr Tavel as he stares down at me, his velvety voice, reassuring and solid. 'Remember Phoebe, lying will only make things worse. Tell the truth and everything will be all right.'

17

TWO WEEKS LATER

Anna idly flicks through the TV channels before turning it off and throwing the remote onto the couch. Such a waste of a life, sitting watching TV all day, every day. She doesn't know how her two boys do it. They seem to spend half their lives glued to the set. It's a miracle she actually managed to prise them away from the screen a few weekends back and get them out of the house. That was partly due to Toby's presence but at least they did something together as a family. A brief visit to Bridget's grave, followed by a walk on the beach with fish and chips on a bench while staring out to sea. A perfect day, really. And such a hard day to follow. And it was invigorating getting out of the house, facing the clean sea air. Since

Toby's visit, she has nagged Mike into spending more time together as a family and at one point, he looked like he might actually be inclined to agree. Tonight's venture to the pub to take part in the quiz wasn't quite what she had in mind.

She gets up, walks to the window and stares at the manicured lawns outside. The weeks have passed by in a blur and already, spring is upon them. The clematis has started its ascent up the side of the fence and the tell-tale swell of the tulips heads indicate that the worst of the winter is behind them. The sun has even made the occasional appearance through the rain clouds and the sky and the trees carry the whispering, low chatter of early birdsong. And still Nancy remains missing. The original crowds of people that searched for her have thinned out to the point where only one person a week visits the village. An older man in his late sixties with thinning hair and a wobbly gait. Probably her husband. Just a lonely, distraught-looking figure who wanders up and down the green, staring off over the river. She can't even begin to imagine what kind of things go through that poor man's head. The posters that clung to the trees through the vicious, howling gales and driving rain have disintegrated to almost nothing, her features now no more than a forgotten, indistinct blur. Every now and then, her face appears on the local news and her family have set up a Facebook page to help find her. But by and large, Nancy has all but been forgotten. But not by Anna. She still thinks of her every day. This village is her home. And she somehow feels responsible for this woman's disappearance. How can people carry on, act as if nothing has happened when Nancy is still out there, waiting to be found? It's an indignity nobody should ever have to bear and an insult to Nancy. Everybody deserves to exist.

Anna looks at her watch. The boys will be in soon, closely followed by Mike. She has nothing prepared for their evening meal and needs to get sorted. And then after dinner, they have the quiz. Truth be told, the last thing she feels like doing is sitting in a pub doing a bloody stupid quiz, especially as she has no female company to chat to. She can always cry off. She imagines Mike's eye rolling and his comments about how it was her idea for them to spend more time together. But a pub quiz in The Crofters hardly amounts to quality family time, does it? They could go on their own, just Mike and the boys. Probably better dynamics anyway. She would just cramp their style.

By the time she starts to prepare their meal, she has persuaded herself that the men would be better off without her. She'll only get the answers wrong anyway. Mike is the brain box and Mason is a whizz kid when it comes to music and media questions. She will be no more than a passive attendee. And Callum is always good with sports questions. They don't need her.

It's while she is setting the table that the idea of how she should really spend her evening implants itself in her brain. And no matter how hard she tells herself she should be out with her family, the idea refuses to go away. It remains there, solid and immovable. That day by the sea, out facing the elements did her no end of good. This year, she hasn't been out by the river. Not once. Nancy's disappearance had put her right off but now she feels a longing to get out there, to embrace nature. It's now officially spring and she has barely set foot over the doorstep.

They are all jostling for food at the table when she breaks it to them.

'I'm thinking of giving it a miss tonight. I'm pretty sure you chaps will have a fine old time without me,' she winks at Mike, who is busy spooning out a hefty dollop of mashed potato which he unceremoniously dumps onto his plate, and hopes he doesn't throw a hissy fit at the idea.

'You sure? Won't you get bored in here on your

own? You hate watching the telly.' His concern doesn't last for long. Callum reaches over for the meat but Mike is faster, helping himself to two large slices before passing it over to the boys, who both complain about the size of his helpings.

'I'm sure. I was thinking of going for a walk by the river, actually. It's April and I've barely ventured outside.'

'A walk at night?' Mason eyes his mother with surprise. 'Wouldn't it be easier just to go during the day when we're all out and it's light?' He watches her from behind his long, sweeping fringe.

'The nights are lighter now. Besides, I fancied seeing the sunset tonight. It's supposed to be a real cracker if the rain stays off.' Anna smiles at them and helps herself to a slab of overcooked beef.

'Well,' says Mike, 'just take it easy and make sure you wrap up warm. It can get pretty raw out there when the wind gets up. And stay back from the river. It's fairly fast at the minute.'

Anna smiles and eyes his belly. Like he knows anything about weather patterns and river currents. She can't remember the last time he walked anywhere, let alone the river path that runs right past the front of his house.

'Don't worry. I'm all grown up now. I can manage.'

* * *

Anna savours the silence after the hubbub of teatime and arguments over who would get the first shower are over. Slipping her feet into a pair of battered old trainers, she grabs her gilet – no need to get dressed up like a real rambler. She's only going out to view the sunset, for heaven's sake. Some of the walkers that pass by here carry their lives in the rucksacks that sit on their backs, forcing them to practically bend double under the weight. All she wants to do is have a stroll, perhaps take some pictures. It's an idea that has rumbled around in her head for a while now: taking up photography. Her OU studies are almost over and she will find herself at a loose end pretty soon. Either that or she goes back to work. And although she has enjoyed being at home for the past few years, the idea has niggled at her that she needs more from life. She had kind of hoped that she and Phoebe might hit it off, spend a bit of time together, but it looks like that isn't to be. Phoebe has made it quite clear she would rather be on her own. After that night in her kitchen, when Anna thought she had at last broken through her neighbour's positively glacial disposition, Phoebe has lived like a recluse. Anna called over a few days later but without the gelling factor of coffee or cakes or all the things Anna likes to do, she found herself at a loss as to how she could connect with her. So she hasn't. She has left things as they were that evening: mildly jovial and pleasant. In fact, if Anna remembers rightly, Phoebe left in quite a hurry. She did wonder if she had said or done something to upset her. They had both had a fair bit to drink so it's all a bit blurry. She shrugs and pushes a packet of tissues deep into her pocket. Ah well. You can't win them all, can you?

Slamming the door shut and locking it, Anna scurries down the path and over the village green, gulping in the cold air, savouring its freshness and the clean sensation she feels as it travels down into her lungs. She breaks into a light run until she reaches the undergrowth and is enclosed by conifers, poplars and fir trees. Hemmed in on all sides. Her very own enclave of anonymity. How lovely. It never ceases to amaze her how much being surrounded by nature can lift her spirits. And the deeper she goes into the woods, the more liberated and lighter she feels. She smiles. Mike was right; it is chilly. Not freezing. Just bracing. That's fine. She can handle bracing.

Marching on over the sloping green, she stumbles down a stony bank and finds herself on the river path. She looks up. Clouds are gathering overhead but with any luck, she might get some decent pictures of the expected sunset before they release their contents. A small surge of excitement wells up in her chest as she sets off at a rapid pace – too fast to keep up for an indefinite period but for now, it suits her. She is feeling energetic, full of beans. Her skin prickles and there is electricity flowing through her veins. She finds herself wondering why she doesn't do this more often.

Up ahead, she can see the giant hogweed already at waist height. Come mid-summer, unless somebody lops it down, it will be the size of a grown man, if not higher, with sap that can blister and burn the skin of anybody unfortunate enough to come into contact with it. Sometimes, it blocks the river path and villagers, covered with elbow length gloves and as many layers of clothing as possible, take it upon themselves to cut it down. And then the following year, it's back. Bigger and stronger than ever before.

Anna breathes in deeply. Too many smells to differentiate. Her favourite is the Himalayan Balsam that lines the riverbank. Even taller than the hogweed, its overpowering fragrance fills the air and Anna stands stock still, just letting it fill her nostrils until her olfactory system becomes so inured to it, she can no longer detect its powerful scent. On a whim, she turns and follows the path in the opposite direction. She rarely takes the route that runs behind Phoebe's house as it involves climbing over a number of stiles and getting snarled up in bramble bushes that have been left to grow wild by the local council. But today, she feels ready to confront anything.

She makes a point of not looking up at the back of Phoebe's house. Not that it matters. She's gotten quite used to being ignored of late. She's completely over it.

The path is longer than she remembers, uneven and muddy. Her breath comes out in a series of small, ragged gasps as she climbs over a stile and fights through the overgrown foliage that has encroached the path to the point where it is almost inaccessible. She refuses to let a few weeds stop her and dips her head, ploughing through the brambles, her hair becoming entangled, thorns snagging at her hands and face.

It takes almost an hour of walking and climbing and fighting her way through the undergrowth before she can properly lift her head again and see daylight. She emerges into an open field, into a curious stillness that sends a creeping sensation over her burning skin. She looks up to the sky and notices the clouds are gathering force, blocking the sun. Sinister and draped over the horizon, they will make as good a photograph as any sunset. Anna dips her hand into her pocket and drags her phone out. The flashing battery sign catches her eye. Damn. She holds it up to the bubbling, grey clouds and presses. The screen turns black and a small vibration tells her she has missed her chance. She pushes it back into her pocket with force. Bloody stupid thing. She only charged it last night as well.

Her feet are rooted to the spot as she scans the area for something that will tell her she's still on the path. This is fairly big expanse of land with no indicators as to where she should go next. Slowly, she turns her head and stops when she spots a small, wooden arrow that tells her to keep going forwards. Of course, she should have guessed, really. The path follows the course of the river. This will be worth it, photograph or no photograph. She smiles and feels a tiny flurry of excitement at being out here on her own, being able to discover the world beyond her own front doorstep and be independent – no teenagers, no telephones, no TV blaring in the background, just the occasional caw of the crows circling overhead and the dull drone of insects as they hover over the water, dancing and swaying in its rising mists.

Behind her, a sudden boom takes her breath away

and sends a buzzing sensation through her skull. Anna raises her eyes and watches as a streak of jagged white lightning blazes its way across the darkening skies. The grey, looming clouds have fulfilled their promise. Another crack reverberates overhead. She counts the time lapse between the flashes and each clap of thunder. Ten seconds. The clouds are heading westwards which means the storm will soon be right above her. She huddles down into her collar for warmth as the temperature takes a sudden and unexpected dip. A brief sun shower is all it is. She will be fine. She feels sure of it. She's a grown up, for goodness sake; if she can't handle being caught out in a storm practically on her own doorstep then there's something seriously wrong with her. She does, however, need some shelter out of the oncoming downpour. A copse of trees at the far end of the field suddenly looks inviting. She can wait there until it all clears. Which it will. That much she is sure of. The wind is picking up. It will all blow over fairly soon.

She sets off at a lick but the heavens open before she gets there and by the time she manages to find an area she can hide under, she is sodden. Droplets of rain slip between the branches as the downpour gains in momentum and begins to fall in great sheets. Anna shivers and tries to crouch further under the canopy of trees but ends up standing in an area of thick mulch. Almost immediately, the damp begins to seep through her canvas trainers. She looks down at her feet and swears under her breath. Bloody stupid British weather. Always guaranteed to let you down. Water drips on her lashes, misting up her vision, more circles the rim of her collar before running down her back, causing her shirt to stick to her skin like an ice pack.

Within a few minutes, the dark clouds have bunched up into a huge, black, sinister mass and the remaining daylight has all but disappeared. Cursing loudly, Anna makes the decision to carry on walking otherwise she could end up stuck under these trees all night. After all, you can't get wetter than wet, can you? The cows in the field turn to watch her as she dashes back out into the storm, across the grass into a nearby churchyard. With any luck, there might be a doorway she can stand in. The church might even be open and she can go inside and wait.

The heavy, ornate lych-gate lets out an almighty groan as she pushes it open, dips under the over-hanging bramble bush and into the graveyard. The church and its grounds are slightly elevated and as she peers over the fence in the far corner. She recog-nises her home village in the distance and the trajectory of the river. She sucks in her breath. It is miles back. Much farther back than she expected it to be. She shivers, suddenly aware of how wet her clothes are and how cold she is. And now she has been starkly reminded that she is a long way from home. Once she loses all the light, she could easily get lost and stumble into the water. She stares up again. The sky westwards is almost black and this weather is just getting started. So much for a brief shower.

Battling the small, still voice that is telling her set back off home, Anna grasps the large handle of the church door. She stops and issues herself an ultimatum. If it's open, she will go inside, wait a bit, see what happens with the weather. If it's locked? Well, if it's locked, she will turn right round and head back home. With slippery, freezing hands, she rotates the huge, metal handle that is almost twice the size of her fist. Nothing happens. She leans against it and pushes hard with her shoulder. Nothing. Definitely locked. Damn. It's a lovely old church, dainty and pretty and she really did want to stay.

Another thunderclap sounds overhead and a huge drop of rain catches the side of her face with a smack and traces its way down her neck. Reaching her hand round her back, Anna flicks her hood up, only to realise that it too, is soaked through and contains a puddle of water which slaps the back of her hair and pours over her neck and down her between her shoulder blades in huge rivulets. A quiver pulses at her stomach. It looks like the decision has been made for her. Glancing over to the village in the distance, Anna shudders. How is that possible? It seems even further away than a few minutes ago. At least two or three miles. Maybe even further. Her eyes close as she concentrates on her breathing. All of a sudden, she feels rather scared. She kicks at the ground angrily, sending a spray of water up over herself. This is stupid. She is a grown woman, for God's sake. All she has to do is brave the elements and follow the path back the way she came. How hard can it be?

The water has risen a huge amount even in the short time she has been out. Anna tries to stem the quiver of mild panic that is tapping at her insides as she heads back over the field and into the woods. The light is almost gone, save for a slash of burning sky that straddles the horizon. Her sunset. Her reason for being here. She laughs. There has to be some irony in that.

Huge puddles litter the path as she sets back off home. Stumbling through the bracken and foliage, Anna waves her arms about to bring down any low-lying branches that could tear at her skin or get snarled in her hair. Her brisk walk breaks into a trot and before she knows it, she is running through the darkness, suddenly desperate to get home. She lowers her eyes to the ground. One wrong step and she could lose her grip on the path and be down on her backside or worse still, break a bone. The thought of being stuck out here in the dark and the rain almost makes her physically sick. She thinks of the missing lady and has to stop to overcome a bout of dizziness. *Out here. In the pitch black. Alone. Thirsty, cold and dying.*

A small sob escapes from her throat as she picks up her pace again and breaks into a run. She is now so very, very cold. The temperature has plummeted in the last few minutes even and is continuing to drop. Bad idea. This was such a bad idea. Her saturated trainers slip and slide along the wet path, her legs scissoring wildly as the rain hammers down onto the ground, turning it into a mud bath. Not daring to stop to catch her breath, she continues on, clambering over stiles, her freezing hands slipping on the slimy, wet wood, staggering through the dark. She forces herself on, head down, determined to get home.

Stepping to one side to avoid a pile of logs and a

huge pool of water, Anna feels herself sinking, her entire body leaning over to one side as she slides down an embankment. She leans forward, grabbing at anything she can find to stop her fall. A searing pain stabs at her fingers and runs up her arms as she inadvertently seizes a hawthorn branch, the spikes violently tearing at her skin. As if burnt, Anna shrieks and lets go, hanging onto the branch of a larger nearby tree to stop her inevitable slide down to the river. Her breath shudders out of her chest with a deep rumble and she does her best to clamber back up before realising one of her feet is firmly lodged, trapped under something solid. She tries to look backwards but it's so dark and the shrubbery is so dense, she can't see what is stopping her from moving. Turning to one side, Anna manages to twist her foot and extricate it but the trainer remains firmly jammed. She brings her leg up and massages the ball of her foot. What now? If she had thought to charge her phone up before leaving, she would at least have some light and be able to retrieve her shoe, perhaps even call for help, but as it is, she risks falling further into the thickets and darkness by leaning too far down to get it. *Shit!* Her head is fuzzy with fear and for a second, she thinks she may even pass out.

Hauling herself up on to the path, Anna tentatively puts her foot down on the mud. It's bearable. Wet and deeply unpleasant but bearable. All she needs to do is watch out for stones and gravel and she will be fine. She needs to just keep going. She needs to get home. Her untidy house, her husband, her children – all the things that normally irritate the life out of her are now all she can think about.

Putting all her weight on her shoe-covered foot, Anna hobbles on, careful to avoid any raised areas that may have stones embedded in them. Her gait is unsteady and she slips, the floor coming up to meet her as she lands on her hands in the thick sludge. As rapidly as she can, she hoists herself back up, frightened that if she stays down there for too long, she will never get back up. She can't stop. It is now really dark and she absolutely must get home no matter what. She sets off and once again, finds herself down on her knees in the middle of a filthy, cold puddle. Tears get the better of her and begin to roll, her small gasps and sobs filling the night air. Tears and snot mesh into each other and drip off her chin as she grabs hold of a clump of wet grass and hoists herself upright.

She stumbles on for what seems like hours, slipping, falling, getting snagged by thorns, squinting in the darkness, sobbing. Her shoeless foot is so cold and wet, she can no longer feel it, all sensation gone from the ankle down. By the time she spots a dim light in the distance, she is practically slipping and sliding along on her hands and knees, her hair a mass of knots and tangles from the shrubbery and her face covered in God knows what. She lets out a small, dull grunt of relief at the tiny, glowing window. A beam of hope, its radiance so magnificent and so welcome, she has to stuff a dirt covered hand over her mouth to stifle the scream before it escapes unchecked.

Slowly and painfully, she shuffles towards it, not entirely certain where the light is actually coming from. She no longer cares. It's a window and a window means a house. And a house means safety and warmth. She is determined to crawl towards it, no matter what. That light is her saviour, her beacon. At this moment in time, she would haul herself over hot stones to reach whatever it is that lay beyond that pane of glass.

There is a rustle a few feet ahead. Anna stops, her heart fluttering around her chest like a small, caged bird. She waits until the sound comes again. Tries to work out what it is. A pigeon perhaps or maybe some type of small predator like a kestrel or a hawk? No, it's too late and too dark. A badger or a stoat even? *A per-*

son? Her throat closes up at the thought. Nancy's face flashes in her head. Oh Jesus, what the hell is it? She desperately wishes there was more daylight. What on earth possessed her to even do this?

Her breathing vibrates through her ribs in short, jerky bursts as she hauls her leaden legs along, doing her utmost to remain silent. Her eyes ache as she shuts them momentarily to gather her thoughts. She has never been so frightened. One wrong move and this thing hiding in the bushes could spot her and they may even have a weapon and...

She stops herself. This is stupid. She can't think like that. This is a safe place. A tiny village in the north of England, not Los Angeles, for God's sake.

The noise is louder, closer, moving towards her. She wants to scream but something inside her stops it from erupting out of her throat like hot lava. A flicker to the side causes her to turn. She is met with a pair of staring, amber eyes. This time the shriek finds its way out and Anna watches as a small fox trots out of the bushes and swaggers on up the path, completely unruffled by her presence. Almost gasping with fear and relief, her head aflame with a hard, intense buzzing sensation, Anna staggers the last few paces to the quadrangle of light, suddenly realising she is behind Phoebe's house. Her laugh borders on

the hysterical. She has made it. She is home. At long
last, she is home.

'Who is that? What are you doing out there?'

Anna's knees buckle and an icy tremor runs down
her spine before realising she recognises the voice.

'Phoebe? Is that you?' Her words come out as a
whisper and her throat contracts, closing up like a
tightened fist. She fears she may burst into tears again
at any minute.

A thin, conical beam of ochre light travels over
her head and circles on the trees in the distance before coming back and illuminating the right-hand
side of her saturated and filthy body. Anna looks over
to its source and can just about make out Phoebe,
standing on the patio. The tears escape and she begins to sob hysterically. With no way of stopping it, a
deep howl forces its way out of her gut and into the
dense, eerie blackness of the surrounding woods.

'Anna? Oh my word, Anna you poor thing! What
on earth has happened to you?'

Within a matter of seconds, Phoebe is by her side,
propping her up, holding her steady as they both
slide about in the quagmire beneath their feet. The
path is almost swamp-like as Phoebe holds Anna's
arm and half shuffles, half drags her up the garden
and onto the patio which, with the flick of a switch,

lights up like a football stadium. They are suddenly drenched in its luminosity. Too tired and distraught to speak, Anna allows herself to be led inside into the warmth of the house. The door clicks closed behind her and she slumps to the floor in a deluge of hot, unchecked tears.

18

Freda leans on the door with her shoulder and rotates the key with as much force as she can muster after a fifteen-hour shift. She curses Alan and all his promises to get the bloody thing fixed. It's been such an exhausting day as well. The key finally grinds into place with a snap, almost taking all the skin off her finger in the process. She rubs her hand vigorously and, muttering an inaudible stream of expletives, shoves the old brass key in the side pocket of her handbag. She can't remember the last time anything in this shop worked as it should. What with depleted shelves, a wheezing and groaning chest freezer that sounds as if it is about to spontaneously combust, and a till that by rights should be in a museum, many would be forgiven for thinking the old place should be bulldozed. She has thought it herself on more than one occasion. Wished it, actually. Most days, if the truth be known. But apparently, there's not enough in the pension pot to allow them to hang up their hats just yet, or so he keeps saying. She wonders how much will ever be enough as she huddles down against the rain and makes her way over the road to their neat 1950s bungalow, a squat little edifice sat amongst the trees, close enough so Alan can keep an eye on the till and his precious little shop even when the place is locked up for the night.

She hurries along, thinking how lovely it would be to have a holiday somewhere away from A&F Stores and all its problems. Away from the draughty old window behind the front counter that hurls all kinds of inclement weather their way during the autumn and bitter winter months, away from the complaints of, *Why don't you start stocking up a bit more? There's nowt in here for me tea*, just anywhere away from it all.

Freda stops and stares over beyond the trees to the cluster of holiday cabins beyond and thinks even one of those for the weekend would be a welcome break. A lump forms in her throat as she thinks how sad her life is when she considers somewhere just a couple of hundred feet from her own front door an actual holiday. Rummaging in her pocket for a tissue, she thinks about her sister and wonders what time it currently is in her part of Queensland. She never can get to grips with all this time difference carry on. Whatever the hour, Dorothy will probably be having a damn sight more fun than she ever has. If only she'd heeded her sister's warnings about staying in the area she grew up in.

'It's a big wide world out there, Fre. Life doesn't begin and end in Durham, you know.'

And now all these years later, Freda can see how right she was. Too late now though, isn't it? And it's not as if Simon has shown any interest in taking over the business. Not now he's got his degree and everything. No doubt he'll be another one to go off globe-trotting, leaving her behind with Alan, who actually truly believes that the north of England is the epicentre of the universe. They waited so long to have Simon as well, and pretty soon he'll leave. Just like all the others. The thought of it brings a lump to her throat.

She shakes her head miserably and heads home, trying to think how many people have stayed in the village they all grew up in besides her. A horrible, murky sensation settles in the pit of her stomach as she realises there's only her and Alan left. Everyone else has moved out, gone up in the world, while she is left running a measly corner shop that hasn't kept up with the times, relies on local farmers to provide them with fresh produce because the bigger suppliers won't give them the discount, and doesn't even take plastic. A sea of faces run through her head as she tries to recall them all: the Harrisons who now live in Peterborough with their grown-up daughter, John and Mary Halston who moved to Norfolk after he got a massive promotion in sales, Sally Metward who ended up married to a rich American and now lives in California. And then there was...

The idea hits her with a thud. She dismisses it, telling herself not to be so ridiculous. It couldn't possibly be, could it? That face has stuck in her mind for weeks now, driving her mad and no matter how hard she has tried to forget it, the features kept coming back, evoking distant memories that danced on the periphery of her thoughts. Now it has come to her with a thump, crashing into her brain making her remember things she would sooner forget.

She dumps her bag on the bottom step and hangs her jacket over the newel post, suddenly noticing with a certain amount of shame how dirty her coat actually is. Not like her sister's cashmere and silk ones that exude wealth and a life of leisure.

'That you, Freda?' Alan's voice bellows through from the kitchen. She sighs and kicks off her shoes. Who else is it going to be, for goodness sake? 'Your tea's ready when you are. Did you manage to lock the safe up?'

She slips her feet into her loafers and heads into the kitchen, where a waft of billowing steam and the unmistakable aroma of steak pie and boiled veg meets her. If her husband has any redeeming features, it's that he is the cook in their house and he does it far better and with a greater vigour than she ever could.

'Safe's all sorted. Where's Simon?' She reaches up into the cupboard, grabs two mugs and stuffs a teabag into one of them before filling the kettle.

'Upstairs on his laptop doing something or other with some new software, apparently. It's all beyond me that kind of new-fangled computer stuff.' He starts to spoon out a heap of carrots onto the plates.

Freda opens the fridge and pulls out the milk carton. 'Do you remember that family from years back who had the bother with their daughter?'

'You'll have to be a bit more specific than that

love, I'm afraid. The old grey matter in't what it used
to be.'

'They had a couple of young lasses. He was a bit
of a drinker, used to knock the mother about. Lived in
one of the terraced houses opposite the river.' Freda
watches Alan as he continues to ladle out the food.
His memory isn't that bad and he has a knack for remembering faces. He would know if it was her for
sure.

He stops for a second and scrunches his eyes up
then glances at her. 'Oh aye, I remember that lot.
Awful carry on it was. By, that was a good while back
now. Why do you ask?'

She stares down at her nails and shrugs. 'Not sure
really. Thought I saw her last week in the shop.'

'The mother?' Alan stops and stares at her. 'It
can't have been the mother, you daft apeth.'

'No, not the mother, obviously,' Freda murmurs,
an uncomfortable jolting sensation beginning to
niggle at her, 'the young lass. Could have sworn it
was her. Much older, obviously, but she had a look
of the old man about her. Said she'd just moved
into the big barn conversion further down the
village.'

'The Parker's place that backs onto the walkway?'

'That's the one.' Freda sits at the table and fiddles

with her knife, turning it over and over, willing the knot in her stomach to loosen a fraction.

'Well, I can't see why she would move back 'ere. Not after all that trouble. Would have thought this place held nowt but bad memories for her.' Steam billows in his face as he opens the oven door and lifts out a hefty ceramic dish with pie crust spilling over its sides.

'Maybe,' Freda whispers. She watches as his knife cuts into the pastry with sharp crack, releasing another burst of steam.

'Mother was a lovely woman. Mind, she had her own fair share of problems after all that business, didn't she? Which is hardly surprising when you consider what happened. And anyway, the young lassie left this place when she was no more than a bairn.' He steps back to allow the heat to escape before grabbing a spoon and delving into the dark, rich gravy. 'I doubt it was her, love. You'll have to tell me if you see her again. We see so many people every day, it's easy to get faces mixed up.'

'Perhaps,' she murmurs, hoping he is right. Because if it was her, it makes Freda wonder why she's back. She never could quite get to grips with that one – very different from the other kids round here: sullen, prone to temper tantrums that just about bordered on the hysterical. And the arguments and fights she had with that sister of hers, well it was bloody embarrassing to witness. That poor mother and the things she had to put up with, and then of course what happened to her was absolutely dreadful. Nobody in the village had ever had to encounter anything of the sort before and she's pretty sure they haven't since. A terrible state of affairs it was. Terrible. She picks up her cutlery and hopes it wasn't who she thinks it is. Because loathe though she is to say it about somebody who was just a child at the time, she was a magnet for trouble, that one. It followed her around and if she's back living here for good – well, Freda doesn't like to think about what could happen. This village has been a peaceful, as well as monotonous, place for the past thirty-odd years and despite her moaning about how drab her life is, that's exactly how she'd like it to remain.

19

I had been in the dining room polishing the silver when I heard it. Such a ridiculously antiquated habit really but one I can't seem to let slide. I quite literally dropped everything to see what was going on out the back of my house. Not in a million years did I expect it to be her. Anna. And she was in such a terrible state too. Covered head to foot in mud, soaking through and so distressed, sobbing and choking. By the time I was able to help her inside, she was just about inconsolable.

I stare down at the heap before me and lean down to help her up. Her body is shaking and I am concerned she may be suffering from hypothermia. Not that I would know. Martyn is the one with medical knowledge round here. I touch her arm. She is freezing. How on earth did she get in such a state? Guilt pricks me. I have made a point of avoiding her lately. And all because of her brother and the fear he might recognise me. Ridiculous really but I didn't feel I had a choice. Anna whimpers and my first thought is to run over the road and fetch her husband but something stops me. What if she went walking after a family argument? God knows, I can identify with that sentiment: that desperation to be alone, the absolute need to be your own person without the hindrance of family members questioning your every move. So instead, I fetch a large towel and an even bigger blanket which I wrap around her, and then with as much ease as I can, I lift her up and lead her over to the small sofa at the far end of the dining room. It doesn't matter how dirty she is. Cushions can wash. Anna's teeth chatter violently as I gently guide her over to the couch and sit her down.

'I'm so sorry about this.' Her eyes are red-rimmed and glassy as she stares up at me. 'It seemed like such a good idea at the time, going for a walk on my own, but then the weather turned and it got dark so quickly. I wanted to get a picture of the sunset, you see.' Her hair is as soft as I remember, even the bits that are plastered to her face by the rain still manage to free themselves and bounce around as she talks.

'Oh, don't be silly. I'm just relieved I heard you. I thought at first that it was a fox. They can be so noisy out there sometimes, howling and screaming. Quite an awful and unnatural sound when you're in here on your own at night.'

My words don't seem to register with her as she continues to stare off into the distance. Her voice is croaky, barely more than a hint of a sigh.

'And although I tried to not think about it, Nancy, that missing lady was in my head all the way back. Some of that river bank is quite steep you know, and really, really unsteady. And it is so dark. No light at all – just pitch black everywhere.'

She stares down at her foot, which is shoeless and as dark as the mood I feel descending on me at the mention of Nancy. Why does Anna always do this? She witters on incessantly about things that don't concern her, making me feel miserable and on edge. It spoils everything and she just doesn't seem to get it. When I've just about managed to eradicate all memories of that bloody awful day from my mind, Anna goes and rakes it all up again.

'I'll go and make us some cocoa. It will help to

warm you up,' I say through gritted teeth as I shuffle off to the kitchen, my anger clawing to be let out.

She is sitting in the same position, the same help-less expression on her face when I return.

'There you go. At least you're back now and in the warm.' I hand her the cup and she grabs at it grate-fully, a definite tremor visible in her hands, 'Once you've drunk this, I'll go and fetch your husband and he can help you back home.'

I wait to see if she has an adverse reaction to my suggestion but she appears to be locked in her own world, oblivious to me or anything I say.

'I've been thinking,' says Anna as she blows on the cup, 'do you think we should go out there with your torch and have another look for her?'

Is she mad? Or am I being tested here? I hope my steely glare is enough to deter her and make her re-alise she is talking nonsense. Maybe she's more dehy-drated and exhausted than I first thought. Or perhaps she really is the naïve type: the mousy housewife I took her to be when we first met. I clear my throat and make sure my voice is loud enough to convey what I actually think of her stupid idea.

'I think we should clean you up and get you home Anna, and let the police carry out their own investi-gations.'

As if she has suddenly been catapulted back into reality, Anna sits up with a start, a light of recognition behind her eyes.

'Yes, you're right. I'm sorry. Silly idea. It's just that I can't stop thinking about her. She's on my mind all the time. All the time...' Her eyes are clouded with sadness, her mouth downcast.

'You're beginning to warm up. Finish your drink and I'll help you back home.' My voice is sharper than I intend it to be. Good God, why can't she stop going on about this? She looks up to me, a look of gratitude in her face. 'I was chatting to Toby about you last week.'

I stand stock still, waiting for whatever is coming next. A barrage of accusations? Laughter at my predicament? My legs are jelly as Anna continues on, suddenly renewed with a swell of energy now she is warm and safe inside my house.

'He still can't place you and it's driving him half insane. He said he almost googled you to find out. Imagine that!'

Yes, imagine that. My head swims as I try to find my voice. I feel a headache coming on and take a long swig of cocoa, its gritty residue coating my teeth. The barren, cream walls of the room begin to close in on me as I swallow the last dregs of my drink.

'But of course he didn't know your last name. He asked me and I told him I didn't know either.'

The silence is prolonged, crackling with unanswered questions. What is this, some kind of trap?

'How are you feeling?' I ask dully. My patience is wearing thin now.

Tears well up in her eyes once more as she speaks. 'A bit better, I suppose. It was just so awful out there.' I want to sigh out loud at her dramatic behaviour and tell her to get a grip. This woman seems to revel in feelings of marginal misery and exasperation. What does she know about being unhappy anyway? She should try being me.

'Funny, isn't it? You moving here and then Toby thinking he has met you before. Such a small world, don't you think?'

Her voice has a sourness to it and I wonder what it is she is really trying to get at. If she has something to say, she had better just come out and say it. I'm not in the mood for silly mind games. I shrug my shoulders to indicate that these things happen but she just will not shut up. Some people don't seem to know when to give their mouths a rest. Especially her.

'Toby is in the area again. He's going to a conference in the city centre. He'll probably come back to ours afterwards. He might even stay over for the night. You should pop over and put him out of his misery.' She chuckles lightly. 'Your face is driving him mad, apparently.' She stares up at me with her filthy, tear-stained face and smiles.

I almost choke on my own spittle. I would rather chew my own arm off than see him again but find myself smiling politely. All I want to do is be back near my sister and lead a quiet existence, not be re-minded of all the angst and worry that went before. I moved here to leave it all behind me, to have a fresh start, just me and my husband, to be left alone to piece the fragments of our marriage back together. And here she is, this woman, this person in front of me who is virtually a stranger, and she seems abso-lutely bloody determined to put a stop to it all. I feel a rage begin to build and I have to take a few deep breaths to stop it bursting out, a grotesque explosion of pent-up anger. How dare she? Who the hell does this Anna woman think she is?

I stare down at her. She is totally unaware of what is going through my mind, which is just as well really. It's time to get her home before I say something I will probably regret. It's been a long and busy day and I am now extraordinarily tired.

'Or I can arrange another get together? The last one was fun, wasn't it?'

Before I even have chance to reply, I hear a noise behind me that turns my limbs to stone. I am rooted to the spot as I listen to Martyn scuffle his way towards us. Anna smiles at me, oblivious to his approach. He is right behind her and I realise that I'm more attuned to his presence than she is. He actually moves very quietly and rather than hearing him, I suddenly realise I am able to sense his entry into a room. Time stops as, out of the corner of my eye, I see him pick up the heavy, silver candelabra I had been vigorously buffing up before rushing out to help Anna, and watch in horror as he raises it high up in the air and brings it down onto the top of my neighbour's skull with a deep, sickening thud.

Blood pulses through my head and fear grips me as her body sways for a second before slumping forward and landing at my feet in a deep scarlet puddle. I turn to look at Martyn. He is standing next to me, the candelabra still in his hand, Anna's blood smeared over it, his knuckles white as he clasps it with force. Dear God, it's happening again. I want to scream at him. I want to fill the room with the sound of my own wails, to howl at him that his actions repulse me, but instead I stand mute, terror pummelling at my temples. I cover my mouth with my cupped hands and turn to look at Martyn but when I do, he has already walked away, leaving me to deal with his mess. The candelabra is at my feet, red and oily with blood, the smear of fingerprints evident over the polished surface.

I quickly grab Tillie, who has scampered through from the kitchen when she heard the thump of Anna's body as it hit the tiled floor. She yelps and I smooth down her fur and murmur in her ear to reassure her. Then I dash through to the utility room, pop Tillie in her cage with a bowl of water and click the door closed behind me.

I follow the sound of Martyn's footsteps as he moves into the study. When I find him, he's in the same position he was the day I confronted him about having the affair: sat back in his chair with a smug look on his face. I step forward and shake my head at him, my brow furrowed into a deep, angry line.

'Why Martyn? For God's sake, why?'

'I don't need a reason, Phoebe. You know that. Now go away and leave me be.' And he laughs and turns away as if we have just discussed the weather or talked about what we should have for lunch.

I want to throw myself at him, pummel his chest, kick out at him, but it's pointless. He is beyond any kind of reasoning so instead, I trudge back in to see Anna, to work out what I should do next. Pain hammers behind my eyes as I stare down at her lifeless body, her pale, pulpy face pressed down into the tiles. The world tilts precariously on its axis as I watch her shoulders shift and squirm ever so slightly and hear a tiny moan emanate from somewhere underneath her crumpled, bloody body. My hands fly up to cover my mouth and tears mist up my vision. Despite having her head cracked open by a heavy piece of silver by a psychopath, she is alive. Dear God. That poor woman. She is still alive.

20

'It stopped days ago.' Callum looks up from his phone which he is completely engrossed by.

'So it's what – 11.30?' Mike says as he stands next to the antique mechanical clock that sits on their mantelpiece, squat and remarkably unattractive with its tarnished gold effect rim and dirty face. He tips it sideways and listens for the dull knock of the pendulum as it swings into action before standing it back down and winding it up until it can turn no more.

'Probably something like that,' Callum murmurs, his face contorted into a grimace as he is disturbed from reading a series of particularly amusing or gross memes that he is guffawing over. He continues scrolling and re-reads a message he received from

Sammo from last week that he didn't take any notice of when he first got it. Not after Sammo had acted like such a dickhead. Callum had been too pissed off to take any notice of anything Sammo had to say.

Your neighbour's a fucking nutter!

Callum clicks the delete button and watches it disappear. Probably chased out by the old guy for breaking into their shed or doing something similarly stupid. He and AJ were both out for bother that day. Whatever it was, it served them right. Arseholes.

'For God's sake, Callum! You've got a bloody clock on that stupid phone of yours, haven't you? The least you can do is check the time for me.'

The young lad looks up from his phone, an unmistakable expression of mild annoyance on his face as he looks over to his brother as if to say, *What? What the hell have I done now?*

'It's 11.39, Dad, if you must know. And there's no need to shout.' Mason is sitting on the couch with his feet tucked under him and the remote in his hand. When it comes to TV viewing, nobody else gets a look in, especially when his favourite car programme is on. *Speed*. There's something about it that fascinates him. He can't wait until he's old enough to start having driving lessons. When that happens, he'll pass his test and show his dad how that car of his should really be driven. It should be given a good blow out every so often, a good de-coke, not driven like somebody's nana is behind the wheel. That's how his dad is with it. It's a waste of a good car. Anyway, he doesn't know what's the matter with the old man tonight. Grouchy as hell, he is. And there's no need. He should chill the fuck out. It's not Callum's fault their mam hasn't come home yet, is it? Or that they didn't win the quiz. Taking it out on other people is bang out of order.

Mike stares at his two sons and hollers over at the pair of them, 'Get your shoes on, the pair of you. We're going out to look for your mother.'

'What? Go out looking for her where?' A flush takes hold of Callum's face. He's waited all week for this particular episode. They're rebuilding an old VW and fitting it with a Jaguar engine. He's been looking forward to it for ages.

'Not that you've noticed but your mother went for a walk when we went out and she hasn't come back. It's nearly midnight, pitch black out there and if you're not concerned, then maybe you should be.'

'Ring her,' Callum says dismissively and turns back to the screen.

'Tried that. Cuts straight to the answer machine. Now do as I asked and get your shoes on.'

The boys glance at one another, shrug resignedly and slope off into the hallway to retrieve their trainers.

'She'll probably be over the road at that woman's house.' Mason pushes his arms into the sleeves of his well-worn denim jacket and peers out at the darkness.

'What woman?' Mike growls. He is tired, has had too much to drink and is mystified and bloody worried. This isn't like Anna. She's a creature of habit and is always in before it gets dark. Always. When she said she was going for a walk, he thought she meant for an hour or so. Not this.

'That new neighbour over the road,' Callum replies. 'You know, the one who was here a few weeks ago. The weird one.'

Mike scowls and shakes his head dismissively, 'Oh right, yeah her. I doubt it.'

Callum points to the phone in the corner of the room where a pale-green light winks at them. 'There's a message on the answer machine. Problem solved right there.' He smiles at the fact he has sorted this mini drama before it's barely begun. A small achievement but a noteworthy one all the same.

Mike marches over and presses the button down, his eyes dark with expectation. The machine whirrs before a crackling, distant voice fills the silence of the room. 'Hi, it's me, guys. The conference has been brought forward so I'm in Durham for the night. Should be finished by 3.30 tomorrow so I can be at yours for about 4 to 4.30. I wouldn't mind a bed for the night if that's all right? Don't fancy the drive back in rush hour traffic. See you all tomorrow.'

A thin beep follows Toby's voice and Mike shakes his head and whistles with relief. 'God knows why she didn't leave a note to say she's gone to see him but at least we know where she is now.'

He picks up the receiver and punches Toby's mobile number into the handset ignoring the small, still voice in his head that's telling him she wouldn't usually visit anybody this late, especially in the city. He stares over at the boys and thinks out loud while his call connects. 'She must have taken the train. That's where she'll be now. On the last train back from Durham city centre.'

A groggy voice answers after three or four rings. 'Yeah? Hello?'

'Toby, it's Mike. She's obviously left you and is on her way back here?' He taps his fingers on the side of the phone expectantly, his breath becoming laboured as he waits for his brother-in-law's reply.

'Huh? Who left me?' A rustling sound fills Mike's ear and he pictures Toby propping himself up in bed, rubbing at his eyes.

'Anna. She *has* been to see you tonight I take it?'

'No. I've not heard from her. Should I have? Did she say she was coming through?' His voice is raspy, slightly breathless after being dragged from sleep.

Mike detects a sudden note of concern in Toby's voice and regrets ringing him, putting him through this when he's got an important day ahead of him tomorrow. His eyes suddenly feel heavy. If she's not with Toby then where is she?

'Sorry Tobes. My mistake. Get yourself back to sleep and we'll see you tomorrow when you're done.'

'No! Hang on.' He is suddenly awake and not about to hang up. 'What's going on there, Mike? What's all this about Anna?'

Mike reluctantly begins to explain, torn between feeling guilty for involving him and being scared witless by his wife's disappearance. Out of the corner of his eye, he sees the two boys beginning to get restless, the absence of their mother now something tangible. Not a simple misunderstanding or something that can be easily explained away but a situation that is gathering momentum with a sickening and gut-churning rapidity.

'Right, I'm getting dressed and will be with you in half an hour,' Toby says, exuding an air of calmness he definitely doesn't feel. His stomach is in knots. He knows his sister and can tell when something is up. And something is definitely up. She wasn't herself the other week – subdued and drinking more than she usually does. Not like her at all.

'No Toby. It'll all be okay. You've got a big day tomorrow. We can manage just fine here. She'll be back before you even get here and...'

But the line is dead before Mike can finish his sentence. With a trembling hand, he slams the receiver down and slumps onto the sofa, staring at the window directly ahead. *Come on, Anna. Show your bloody face!*

* * *

The roads are thankfully practically empty, bar the truckers who just seem to keep going all night, and Toby pulls up outside Mike and Anna's house in just over half an hour, announcing his arrival with a slight screech of the brakes and the metallic rattle of his handbrake as he pulls at it with a little more force than is necessary.

Mike notices Toby's hair first – still ruffled from sleep, sticking out at peculiar angles, he resembles the small boy he has seen in photographs when he and Bridget and Anna were small. Three tots sat next to each other wearing wide grins and colour co-ordi-nated outfits.

'Still no sign, I take it?' Toby rushes in the room, his eyes scanning each of them in turn as he searches for an answer.

Mike finds it difficult to summon up enough strength to answer so doesn't. There's no need any-way; the dead stares of the three of them convey enough despondency to tell Toby everything he needs to know. He looks at each of them in turn. 'Nothing?'

'No, nothing. We've tried her phone again. Still no answer.'

'Have you been out looking for her yet?' His words seem to cut through the stillness of the room. Callum and Mason are sitting on the sofa staring at the screen but neither of them appears to be really watching it. 'Right, we need to get out there,' Toby says. 'You got any torches?'

Mason jumps up, dips his head into the cupboard

under the stairs and comes out holding three small torches aloft. 'Will these do?'

'Perfect,' Toby says as he takes two and gives one to Mike and keeps one for himself. Something seems to suddenly slot into place and without hesitation, Mike hurls himself up and begins barking out orders.

'Right, you two lads, Toby and I are going to have a look down by the river. Why don't you both head up to the shop? Stick to the path and don't split up. And keep your eyes peeled. She might be on the other side of the road.'

Mason widens his eyes. 'The shop? Dad, it's nearly one in the morning. And anyhow, it shows how often you walk anywhere. There isn't a path on the other side of the road. It's all fields, remember?'

Mike sighs and checks his torch is working. 'She might have gone to use the cash machine. I'm trying to think of every possible place she might be. Just do it, okay? Stick together and meet us back here in an hour.' He walks to the door and shouts over his shoulder, 'And take your phones so we can ring you if need be.'

The grass squelches underfoot as Mike and Toby clamber through gorse bushes down to the path.

'Which way?' Toby is looking down towards the sound of the river as it gushes past them, steady and fast. Mike stares into the vast darkness and swallows back his fear. He won't allow himself to think anything other than the fact that Anna went for a walk and is sheltering from the rain under a tree somewhere. They've just passed a ragged, fading poster for a missing woman, likely to have fallen in the water and been dragged away by the current. What are the chances of another incident like that happening in the same place? He isn't at all religious and doesn't believe in a greater deity but finds himself praying that Anna will come striding out of the woods at any minute with a huge grin on her face, full of apologies for scaring the shit out of them all. He begins to question why they ever moved here in the first place. Stupid fucking river. Such a hideous death trap.

The rain falls in great sheets, drenching them in minutes.

'Should we shout her name? I was just thinking that if she's a way off and disorientated, we might actually scare her. Two grown men screaming at the tops of our voices. What do you think?' Toby is staring at his brother-in-law, the beam of light illuminating his face, highlighting his pale skin, putting every blotch and mark under the spotlight. Mike shakes his head and his chin quivers slightly. He swallows and wipes the water from his face.

'Let's just stick together and keep sweeping the area with the torches. She may have slipped and be stuck somewhere.' He doesn't relish the thought of his wife alone and frightened out here at night but has to keep his options open. He prays she has visited a friend, decided to stay over, tried to ring but couldn't get through for any number of reasons. A stream of outlandish and bizarre scenarios fill his head because quite frankly, the alternative is too grisly to contemplate. They head further into the darkness, the wind from the river beginning to gather force. Even through the protection of the trees and dense shrubbery, it pushes them sideways, howling around their necks, biting at their faces.

'If it wasn't so bloody wet, we might have been able to look out for footsteps and follow her route.' Toby trudges along the mud, shining the torch at the ground every few seconds to keep to the path while Mike waves his about amongst the trees, then very slowly and deliberately, along the riverbank. Even with both beams of light, it's almost impossible to see anything. The hedgerows and shrubbery provide darkness and shade even during the brightest of days, such is their density. Attempting to locate anything in them at night time is hopeless.

Mike feels a dull pounding in his temples. If

Anna is out here then what the hell is she thinking staying out so long? Is this something to get back at him because he doesn't help out around the house enough? Or because he spends too many hours at work? He hopes not because enough is enough. If it's payback she's after then this little jaunt of hers wins hands down.

'I'm going to give one of the boys a ring. See if they're okay out there.' Toby pulls out his phone and punches in a number. He puts it to his ear and listens. Straight to voicemail. Shit.

'I'll bet there's no signal where they are. It's a right bugger round here. We have to go to the back of the house to get texts,' Mike says, aware his voice is rising in pitch, making him sound as desperate as he feels. Where the fuck is she? Their voices echo in the quiet of the night. Somewhere in the distance, an owl hoots then all is quiet again. Only the surge of the water as it flows past them somewhere down below. A raging current. Freezing and deep and strong enough to defeat even the strongest of swimmers.

'Anna!' Mike's voice resonates around them but is suddenly drowned out by the clap of thunder that booms overhead. He waits and then shouts again and again and again but the rain is torrential and the sound of his voice is overwhelmed by the noise nature makes when the clouds become too heavy, rip open and release their contents in a great deluge.

'For fuck's sake!' Toby slips as the path turns into a swamp. His leg becomes tangled up in the branches of a low-lying bramble bush. It snags at his ankle as he pulls his foot free and he ends up on his backside in a huge puddle. 'Where the hell is she?' He drags himself up and hollers into the impenetrable darkness, 'Anna!' Still, the downpour continues to crash down around them, forcing them to crouch under the branches of the larger trees.

'Wait!' Toby calls out to Mike who stops abruptly, his body frozen with anticipation. 'It's Callum calling me!' Toby holds up his phone to show Mike the screen. He shrugs. It's too wet and dark to see it even with torches. Toby presses it and holds it to his ear, his eyes scrunched up against the raindrops.

'Callum? You see anything?' He nods vigorously but Mike can tell by his tone, they haven't found her. 'Right, okay. Well at least we know she isn't there. You get yourselves back home and get dry. Thanks for trying.'

Toby slips the mobile back into his pocket and looks up.

Mike turns to look at Toby, who shines the light directly on to his face. Panic and fear are written across his contorted features. 'What now Toby? What the hell do we do now?'

'Keep going. We haven't covered much ground. She could be just around the next bend. We'll go on a bit further and if she's not there, we go back and start knocking on doors.'

Mike seems buoyed up by this idea and storms on ahead, water bouncing off his head as he ploughs through the sludge and mud. The stink of wet soil and sludge fills their nostrils as they trudge on through the darkness. On and on and on for a good twenty minutes, finding nothing.

Mike is becoming frantic. Toby can see by his gait, his great big strides, how his shoulders are dipped, that he is losing hope. He wonders how long they should keep going for before heading home. What if they turn back and Anna is just up around the bend, injured and freezing? At what point do they call for help from the professionals?

Toby thunders on, trying to visualise Anna sitting in a neighbour's house, swigging back wine and chatting happily. If it weren't so serious and scary, he would laugh at the image. As it is, he finds himself fighting back tears.

It takes them another twenty minutes to realise their search is proving to be fruitless. By the time they turn and head back, they have been out for over an hour looking for her.

'We need to knock on doors,' Toby splutters as he walks into an overhanging branch and comes away with a mouthful of wet leaves.

Mike runs his hands through his hair. 'Where the hell is she, Toby? What the fuck is going on round here?'

'Let's not jump to any conclusions. We need to get back, dry out and then speak to some locals. For all we know, she could actually be at home, waiting for us.'

Deep down, they both know this isn't the case. The boys would have rung by now. She would have rung.

'Come on, we need to head back and start talking to the neighbours.' Mike follows Toby's voice as they swing round and plough through the inordinate amount of water and dirt that, up until half an hour ago, was the path that followed the curve of the river. They walk slowly, ankle deep in it, careful not to slip. Toby's trousers are already soaking and filthy. Mike picks up a stray branch and every few paces, drags it through the bushes, hoping it lands on something solid, something more substantial than twigs and piles of rotting foliage. Nothing. He keeps it up until they are almost back at the house, patting the ground for anything, any sign is wife has passed this way.

'Right, you go and let the boys know we're back and I'll start asking people if they've seen her.'

Mike nods as Toby makes his way to the end of the road and starts hammering on doors. He goes inside, wondering all the while what the hell he is going to say to their two sons. *Your mother has disappeared? Your mother has left us?* Mike freezes. Fuck. What if she has pulled the wool over their eyes and actually left him? He dashes upstairs and yanks open her wardrobe door. Still full. Sitting by her bed is her handbag. He rips it open and feels relief wash over him as her purse topples out on to the floor, along with her car keys. The relief is short lived. Apart from her phone which, knowing Anna, will be dead, she has nothing with her. This wasn't planned. She is in trouble. Somewhere, she has fallen foul either by something or someone and isn't able to come home. Fear stabs at his insides. He feels his eyes fill up with tears and swallows hard to suppress them. What he needs to do right now is be the strongest he can be, for the boys, for himself and Toby, for Anna. He has to stay sharp, stay focused so he can find his wife and bring her back home.

Taking the stairs two at a time, he lands at the bottom with a thump.

'Callum! Mason!' Mikes voice comes out as an un-intended roar and both lads hurtle through to the hallway, a look of disappointment on their faces when they see him standing there on his own. 'I'm off out with Toby to see if any of the neighbours have seen your mum.'

Callum's face becomes panic stricken. This is serious. Two hours ago, it was just a case of mum being bloody dippy and not realising the time but he can see with the passing of each hour and the awful weather outside, that there's more to this than sheer forgetfulness. He feels a lump rise in his throat and his cheeks feel as if they are on fire. Where is she?

'I'll come with you. They're not gonna be happy being knocked up at this hour.' Mason tries to side-step his way past his dad but Mike blocks his way.

'No. Stay here with your brother and keep the door locked. I'll take my key. There's only a dozen or so houses so we shouldn't be too long. And as for knocking them up – tough shit. Your mother is missing.'

'And what if she isn't with any of them? What do we do then, Dad?'

'Like I just said, stay here with your brother and keep the door locked. We won't be long.'

The door slams before Mason has a chance to protest, to shout that she's his mother and he should be able to help look for her too. He hears the key being turned in the lock and slopes back off into the living room with Callum following behind. The black screen of the television stares at them from the corner of the room.

'Where do you think she is, Mase?' Callum is staring at his younger brother, willing him to have an answer.

'Fuck knows,' is all Mason can manage as he slumps down onto the sofa and wipes away an unexpected stray tear.

21

It didn't take me long. In less than five minutes, I was able to mop up around Anna's twitching, groaning body, leaving virtually no trace of any blood. None visible to the naked eye, anyway. If an army of forensic investigators were to wade on in here, then I'm sure it would be a different matter. But they're not going to, are they? Absolutely nobody knows she is here. I check the floor to make sure it is spotless and am only left with the candelabra, which I shove in a bin liner and stuff in the cupboard under the sink. I will pull it back out later and clean it up. Right now, it's the least of my worries. The biggest job by far is moving her body and working out what I am going to do next. My breath comes out in ragged chunks as I drag her across the kitchen floor and into the hallway. I have wrapped her head wound in a large towel and for now, it seems to have stemmed the flow of blood. My bedroom is the first at the top of the stairs. I will take her in there. I can use the en suite to clean her up and at least make her slightly more comfortable while I work out what my next move is going to be.

Behind me, I can hear Martyn cackling with laughter and hollering sarcastic comments designed to upset me. This is what he does. His only source of entertainment. He has so little going for him now, you see, that events like this restore the balance of power between us, making him feel imbued with an element of supremacy giving him the control he craves. Today, he refused his medication. Even slipping it into his tea proved fruitless. He wouldn't drink it unless he watched me make it from scratch. So I should have expected something like this. I should have been prepared. I imagine he will be laid back in his leather chair right now, arms placed behind his head, a sickly smile plastered across his smug face. I blot the image from my mind. Right now, I need to get Anna upstairs and sorted before anybody comes knocking. Which they will. People don't just disappear into thin air. They are out there somewhere, and friends and family and the police do their utmost to try to find them. I want to be ready when that happens. I need to be ready.

Dragging her up will be too difficult. Heaving her body over each and every step will be torture for both of us so I lean down and lift one of her lifeless arms around my neck and place my right arm around her waist. She is surprisingly light and before I know it, I have managed to haul her up over each step and am at the top of the stairs and pulling her into my bedroom. Martyn has slept in the guest room for the past few nights which suits me fine. Perfect, really. I prop her up against the side of the bed, her legs stretched out straight across the rug. Her head flops to one side and a line of saliva is working its way down the side of her face. I rub it away with my sleeve and lightly trace my finger over her creamy skin then wrap a strand of bloodied hair that has fallen out of the towel, around my finger. So much like Suzie, it's breath-taking. So very much like Suzie.

Her eyes flicker, sending my heart into a flutter and I snap into action. I look around the room for anything to help me. Grabbing at the tie-backs hanging up at the window, I quickly pull Anna's arms behind her back and fasten her wrists together. Not too tight. I don't want to stop her circulation, but need them rigid enough to stop her getting free. Then I do the same with her feet, making sure I use a soothing voice as I bind her up. I tell her how sorry I am about all of this and assure her it won't be forever. I have no idea if she is conscious or not but I need to salve my conscience. This is partly my fault. But it is also partly hers. I tried to warn her away from us when we first moved here, to tell her that Martyn wasn't a well man, but she just wouldn't listen, insisting she could help him when all the while I knew she was wasting her time. He is stronger than that. Martyn is the strongest man I have ever known.

Finally, after locating it from the cupboard under the sink, I use the leftovers of the tape I used to stick the removal boxes together and press it firmly over Anna's mouth. She moves slightly so I pull a longer strip off and push it in place over the existing one. Then I stand back and admire my work. Even Houdini would have the Devil's own job to escape from that lot. I look around. There are some objects placed on the bed: a few items of laundry, some pieces of jewellery and my keepsake box. Carefully, I pick them all up and put them on the floor, then haul Anna up onto the quilt. She will be less likely to roll about knowing she could fall off and injure herself. As a precaution, I close the blinds and then pull the curtains closed. I usually only have them tied back for show but need to be extra careful tonight. I don't want any prying eyes catching me out. I head into the bathroom and come back with a wet flannel which I dab on Anna's bloodstained face. She is remarkably pretty with her childlike features and full mouth. Suzie was always the pretty one, the fun one, the confident one, whereas I could hardly bear to look at myself in the mirror. I'm not outstandingly ugly but neither could you consider me good looking either. As Suzie was so fond of telling me, I am average. Even my mother struggled to use the word *pretty* where I was concerned. *Quiet, intelligent*, but never pretty. It's taken years for me to be sure of myself, but I find I am more confident now, not as awkward as I used to be. Strategic use of make-up has allowed my face to morph into something more presentable and mirrors no longer hold the fear for me that they once did. Even the wrinkles and deep lines that have started to develop on my skin and around my eyes and mouth don't scare me. I'm not proud of them but neither am I ashamed of them. I am what I am, no longer living my life in my sister's shadow. I am me.

By the time the knock comes, I feel confident, equipped to deal with whatever they throw at me. Anna is sleeping soundly on my bed upstairs, my house has been cleaned of any evidence and Martyn is holed up in his study at the side of the house, a streak of dim light from under the closed door the only indication he is here at all. I have wrapped myself up in my dressing gown and pulled my hair back in a tight hairband. My face is scrubbed free of lipstick and mascara, and I am prepared to meet whoever is behind the door, whether it be Anna's husband or even the police. This time, unlike a few weeks back when they came looking for Nancy, I am ready. The house is practically cloaked in darkness as I make my way towards the hallway.

A small gasp of breath leaves my throat as I swing the door open to see Toby, Anna's brother standing there. *Him*. His face doesn't alter as I greet him and try to look shocked when he tells me Anna is missing.

'Missing?' I ask, narrowing my eyes in confusion. 'But it's the early hours of the morning! How long has she been missing for?'

He shrugs and looks at his watch. 'Apparently she went for a walk while Mike and the boys were at the pub and she hasn't come home.'

I suck my teeth and shake my head as his eyes bore into me. His stern gaze is unrelenting and I wonder if he is still trying to work out where he recognises me from. I feel a prickle begin to take hold in my armpits and at the back of my neck. I will need to keep this brief without appearing uncaring or brusque. I don't want to unravel in front of this man. I absolutely must keep it together.

'But it's pitch black out there,' I gasp and widen my eyes dramatically. 'Where did she say she was going to?'

I'm not sure if I imagine it but Toby seems to slump a little, his shoulders drooping as he speaks. 'Just off for a walk to see the sunset. We were wondering if you've seen her at all?'

'Gosh, no. I was busy doing housework in here most of the evening and then I had an early night.' I peek my head out of the door a little and look up to the sky. 'Where would she go to in this weather? It's awful out there.'

Toby shrugs and I can't swear to it, but am certain his voice changes slightly, develops a warble to it that wasn't there before. 'That's what we can't work out. It's not like her at all. She's usually a real home bird. We've been out and walked down that way by the river where she usually likes to go but the weather was so horrendous and it was too difficult to see anything so we had to turn back.'

I cover my confusion well. At some point, Anna must have turned around and walked in the opposite direction behind my house. This is good. It will throw them off the scent and give me more time to plan my next step. Because I have to have one. I can't leave her up there in my bedroom indefinitely.

'I really wish I could help you...'

'Toby,' he replies quickly and gives me a small smile.

'Toby,' I add and return the smile. I am so adept at lying, I surprise myself. 'I have to say I'm really worried now. Does she have her phone with her?'

He nods and begins to retreat down the path. 'Yes, but Mike seems to think the battery is dead.'

I roll my eyes and purse my lips. 'Awful, just awful.'

'Anyway, thanks for your concern. You know where we are if you hear or see anything.'

'Absolutely,' I shout after him. His feet crunch on the gravel and I watch as he leaves my drive and heads to a row of terraced cottages further up the road. 'And if there's anything at all I can do to help, you know where I am.' I wait until he disappears from my sight completely before closing the door and leaning against it to catch my breath. The room spins slightly as I head towards the stairs and take them two at a time, a small amount of vomit rising in my throat. I'm almost certain I've pulled it off so have no idea why I'm so nervous. Delayed shock. That's what it is. And the thought of what I am now going do with her. That's the tricky bit. The dangerous bit. I should be used to picking up the pieces of Martyn's destructive streak but it never gets any easier. And now I am left with an injured, semi-conscious lady who is bound and gagged in my bedroom. If I release her, she will undoubtedly go straight to the police. And who can blame her? But the consequences of that will be too great to bear for me and Martyn. Completely unthinkable. So I can't let that happen. It's out of the question.

I flick on the landing light. A small groan is coming from beyond the closed bedroom door. I turn the handle slowly, not entirely certain I really want to see her if she has regained consciousness. Bracing myself, I open it and through the darkness am surprised to see that she is laid completely still, her hands and feet still tied up and the tape still in place. As softly as I can, I step forward and drop to my knees at the side of the bed to check the gash on her head. As I lean over, her eyes snap open and I find myself looking deep into her jet-back pupils. Startled, I jump back, my throat thick with alarm.

'You're awake,' I whisper hoarsely as I move away. Her gaze is remarkably steady for someone who has just been bashed over the head with a heavy object.

She mumbles something from behind the tape and for a moment, I am tempted to remove it to hear what she has to say, to find out how much she remembers, but then think better of it. Taking off the tape will give her the chance to scream and then we would all be done for. No, I will keep her warm and dry and take care of her, just like I used to do with Suzie. I will be the sensible sister again, the thoughtful one, the good one. I will take charge and this time I will do it properly. Make sure she stays safe. Make sure she stays alive.

The bedclothes begin to get snarled up as she starts to wriggle about, kicking her bound legs like a fishtail, frantic and graceless.

'Shh,' I say, pulling the duvet straight. 'You shouldn't move about too much. Your head might start bleeding again. You don't want that to happen, do you?'

Her eyes widen and it suddenly occurs to me that at some point, she will need to go to the toilet. She set off just after teatime so it won't be long before nature calls and I certainly don't want the mess all over my bed. I look down at her clothing. She really is quite filthy. Muddy trousers and a grimy, wet sweatshirt. The trousers are fairly loose fitting and shouldn't prove too difficult to remove and put back on again.

But all in good time. Anna is a grown woman and can hold on for a bit longer. I need to calm her down first, make her more compliant; less feisty. Martyn's medication is in the bathroom cabinet and there is plenty spare since his refusal to take it. I pad over to the en-suite bathroom, open the door and pop two capsules in my hand, then just to be sure, take another one. I open each capsule in turn and tip the contents into a small container and mix it with a tiny amount of water. The next bit will be the trickiest part. I want to catch her unawares, leaving her unable to fight back. I carry the vessel that contains the mixture to the side of the bed and place it on the bedside cabinet. She is watching my every move. I have to ignore her staring presence. I know what her little game is and refuse to let her gaze unnerve me. Anyway, this is as much for her benefit as it is mine. At least if I let her relieve herself while she is less alert, her dignity will remain intact. Quick as a flash, I pull the tape off and tip the liquid into her mouth. Before she can protest or spit it out, I stick the strip of tape back on and press down hard enough to ensure she swallows all of the mixture.

She gags slightly but then within minutes, her writhing slows down and her eyes begin to droop. If I am going to do this, I need to do it now before she falls into a deep, drug-induced sleep. She tries to focus on me as I lean close enough to speak to her. 'I'm going to let you go to the toilet now, Anna. Please don't struggle. I'm doing this to help you. Squirming about will only result in you wetting yourself and you don't want that, do you?'

Without giving her chance to protest, I drag her up off the bed and over to the bathroom where I yank her trousers and pants down and sit her on the toilet. Like a sleepy child, Anna gives in and relieves herself. By the time I get her back onto the bed, she is almost unconscious and I am exhausted. Although she is fairly light, the exertion of dragging another person around has taken its toll on me and I need to rest. I slump in the chair by the bed and feel a comfortable slumber begin to descend.

* * *

Light is breaking through a tiny crack in the curtains when I wake up. Anna is lying opposite, staring at me, a pleading expression on her face. It's too early for me to deal with her needs right now. Firstly, I need to check on Martyn and sort Tillie out and then I will bring her a drink of some kind. Preferably water as tea will be too hot and it's also a diuretic, and although getting Anna to the toilet wasn't as traumatic as I initially anticipated, I don't want to do it more often than is necessary.

Martyn is in the kitchen when I go downstairs. His hair is ruffled and I imagine, like me, he slept all night in a chair. Is this what our life has come to? Living separate lives, co-existing under the same roof with no real purpose? I wonder how much longer we can go on like this. As soon as I sort out the problem of Anna, I will make more of an effort to help Martyn. God knows he needs it. He's a monster; of course he is, I realise that, but he too is a victim of sorts and needs me as much as she does.

I let Tillie out into the garden where she pees for England and then I feed her. While she is eating, I make some tea and nibble on a slice of toast. Martyn is sat at the kitchen table, looking out of the window. We don't speak. There is no need. What is there to say?

After I have showered and got dressed, I take a glass of water through to the bedroom. Anna is laid on her back staring up at the ceiling. She turns to face me as I walk in and I am disturbed by a lone tear that rolls down her cheek and drips onto the quilt. I don't want to give her any more medication just yet so I squat by the bed and hold her gaze.

'I know you're upset but don't worry. Everything will all right soon enough. I'm going to take the tape off your mouth so you can have a drink. Are you thirsty?'

She nods vigorously and another tear falls from her eye. This is good. She is upset but not angry. I hold the glass up and she watches it carefully, her face full of neediness. I place a hand behind her neck to lift her head and rip the tape off. She winces and before she has a chance to yell, I hold the glass to her lips and watch as she drains it in one go. While she is still swallowing, I push the tape back down firmly and let her head fall back onto the pillow. As a precaution, I take another length of tape and set it over the layers that are already on her mouth. She struggles slightly and cries some more as I push my hands down to make sure it stays in place.

'Don't worry. This isn't going to go on for forever. It's just for a short while. Everything will turn out for the best, you'll see.'

Hot air rushes out from her nostrils which flare as I kneel close to her to speak. She is frightened. I understand that, I really do, but she needn't be. We're friends after all, aren't we? I try to placate her by gently stroking her flawless, creamy skin.

'I knew you would come back to me, Suzie. I just knew it.'

I remove her remaining shoe and dirty socks and without untying her, wash her feet with a warm, soapy flannel, taking care to rub between her toes. She needs to be clean. I *want* her to be clean. I dry her off and slip a pair of my best slippers on her feet. I don't want her to be cold or uncomfortable.

'There. Doesn't that feel better?'

Her eyes are full of fire and without warning, she begins to buck and writhe. So once again, I make a concoction of Martyn's tablets and a touch of water. I need her to be still while I administer it. I simply cannot do it while she is bouncing around on the bed like a feral animal. Bending over her, I grab a handful of her hair and kneel on it. She stops immediately and while she is pinioned to the bed, I rip off the tape and shove the contents down her throat. I'm not happy about doing it but have no other option.

'There, there. It wasn't so bad, was it? You have to stop jumping about or Martyn will hear you and come up. You definitely don't want that to happen, do you?'

I hope she can see that all I'm trying to do is protect her. He is a violent, vengeful man and the longer he goes without his medication, the greater his fury will be.

Within seconds, she becomes sleepy and lifeless, her head lolling to one side. So much better. I'm nearly fifty years old and don't have the energy to be dealing with a person who chooses to thrash about like a wild stallion when all I'm doing is helping her. Once she is fully asleep, I will clean up the cut on her head and maybe even wash her hair. Eventually, she will thank me for it. Until that time, I guess I will just have to put up with her tears and anger.

There is a noise outside which draws my attention to the window. My heart beats a little too quickly as I shuffle over and peek through the side of the blinds. It's as I expected, really. Mike and Toby are standing at the front of Anna's house, talking animatedly to each other. I squint and try to get a good view of them. Stubble covers both of their faces and Mike looks utterly exhausted. If only they knew she was up here, safe and warm. Not down in the freezing river with its raging current, high and fast again after yet more rain. A tall and young-looking man steps out of the house and stops to speak to both of them. A police officer, perhaps? He isn't from Mountain Rescue. Not properly kitted out for it. They glance around and point in various directions before turning to look over at my house. I watch as the young man nods to Anna's husband before setting off over the road. I hear the familiar crunch of the gravel and brace myself for the knock on the door. When it comes, I take a kind of devilish, perverse pride in fooling them all. If they insist on being so clueless then maybe they don't deserve to have her back. I head downstairs, thinking I managed to quieten her just in time. Sometimes lady luck can really play her part and today, for once, she is definitely smiling down on me.

22

Time passes too quickly and each hour that slips by leaves Mike feeling more and more hopeless. He imagines Anna being swept downstream, her head bobbing up and down, her small body slamming into all kinds of detritus – old tree trunks, gnarled branches, loose rocks – all of which could injure her really badly. That is, if the power of the current hasn't already dragged her under, overwhelming her, filling her lungs with freezing cold water. He fights back the tears. How the hell did this happen?

He looks around the living room which, without Anna's magic touch, is already beginning to look markedly dishevelled. Cushions sit crumpled and squashed on the floor. He can't think how they got there until he remembers that one of the boys used them as a pillow while trying to take a nap. They had all refused to go to bed. Somehow, sleeping on the floor of the living room seemed more fitting. Warmth and comfort felt so very wrong when Anna is out the cold and wet and probably terrified. Cups of half-drunk tea litter every surface, everyone too sick and worried to finish them.

The knock on the door sets his heart battering wildly. Anna? There is a surge of movement within the house as Toby and the boys jump up simultaneously, running to open it.

'I thought I would come and help you. I heard Anna was missing and felt I had to do something...' The lad at the door is a lot younger than Toby but older than Callum and Mason – Toby guesses early twenties – and tall and slim with a sincere expression. 'One of the neighbours came in the shop and mentioned that you were looking for her. Everyone is worried sick. Mum wanted to come and help but she's serving in the shop and couldn't get away. Anna's a lovely woman and my mum and dad are really upset and I said I would – well, I just want to help...' His words tail off as he watches the solemn faces of Mason, Callum and Toby scrutinising him, listening to him with intent.

The boys give him a nod of recognition and step aside.

'Simon!' Mike's hand reaches out through the three bodies and gently pulls him inside. They head into the living room and perch on the edge of the sofa.

'Simon's mam and dad own the village shop,' he says to Toby whilst nodding his head as if to assure him of this young lad's identity. 'Anna worked there for a short while after we first moved here.'

'Wish she still did,' Simon breaks in with a slight smile. 'My father needs dragging into the twenty-first century and Anna was the best thing that happened to that place. She nearly persuaded him to set up a website and start taking visa cards which is more than me or my mum have been able to do.' He laughs softly then stops and rests his hands on his knees, looking at the sets of watchful eyes on him. 'Anyway, that's not want you want to hear right now, is it?' He clears his throat quietly. 'So, have you called the police yet?' Simon looks from one to the other.

'An hour ago. We have to wait twenty-four hours apparently and then call them again. She's not considered vulnerable,' Mason replies, his anger palpable.

'Really? That's bollocks,' Simon states flatly. 'I

know a bit about forensics from my degree and I can honestly say that's not true. When did she go missing?'

'Sometime last night. Probably about seven-ish but we don't know exactly. We went out to the pub. She didn't want to come. Fancied a walk instead.' Mike dips his head. He should have insisted she join them. Hindsight is a wonderful thing, isn't it?

'And they're saying you have to wait till seven tonight to ring back? Jesus.' Simon dips his head and looks away, his distress beginning to show.

'We're not going to, though,' Toby cuts in. 'This is totally out of character and they have to take that into account, don't they?'

'Yeah, especially as she's not the only one,' Callum pipes up. His cheeks flush up as he speaks. A small area of acne covers his chin and his hair has a shine that suggests it's in need of a good wash. At only thirteen years of age, he is still a boy but right now, feels haggard and well beyond his years.

'The only one what?' Simon asks, looking over to Mike.

'The only woman who has disappeared round here lately,' Mason adds dejectedly. Dark rings sit under his eyes and his voice comes out as a low squeak.

Simon nods as he recalls the other lady. He was still living away in his digs at the time but remembers his mum telling him about it. He wants to curse some people's stupidity when it comes to being near rivers and stops himself just in time. There was a student that tripped and fell the river while he was at university. Swept downstream by the full force of the freezing, swollen current. She hadn't had a drink like the papers had reported. It was just a tragic accident on a cold and wet winter's night. Such an awful waste of a life.

Mike rolls his eyes and suppresses a sob. He hardly gave the other woman a thought at the time. He, like most other people, presumed she had fallen in the river and got dragged away. It happens, especially during bouts of heavy rain when the rivers are high and the currents are strong. You see it all the time on the news: people going missing, last spotted near the Wear or the Ouse or the Tyne or the Tees or any number of rivers throughout the north east and most likely the rest of the UK. People fall into them all the time. Unpleasant but true. But two of them going missing within such a short space of time. Could there be a connection? He hopes not, because if there is, it doesn't bode well. Thoughts gallop through his head, none of them palatable. The chances of a tiny village like theirs having a madman running loose must be pretty slim. So what *has* happened to them both? He closes his eyes. His mind goes back to thoughts of the river and that bloody current...

'Yeah, Mum told me and I saw it on the news. It's a bit mad, isn't it? Two of them disappearing. You really need to ring the police again and tell them this stuff. They don't always make the connection, you know.' Simon's eyes are wide and he suddenly looks very pale.

Toby nods and pulls his mobile out of his pocket. He didn't make the connection either. Lack of sleep. Shock. They're all running on empty.

Simon leans towards Mike. 'I know this might sound a bit daft but do you have any outbuildings? 'Cos that's what the police'll ask when they arrive. In fact, it's probably the first thing they'll do.' He touches Mike's arm and nods towards the patio doors and the garden beyond.

Mike looks over towards the shed and the old coal bunker and feels a tad stupid. She wouldn't be in there, would she? Why didn't he think to check them? 'We have an old shed. It's full of garden furniture and tools. There's also a coal bunker. It's dropping to bits and completely filthy. There's no way she's going to be in there. Why would she be? If she wanted shelter, she would just come back into the house, wouldn't she?'

Simon shrugs his shoulders and tries to keep the tremble out of his voice. Studying this stuff is one thing but actually being part of it is another thing entirely. He clears his throat and looks at the forlorn figures in the room. He needs to stay calm and help them out. He can see they're in no fit state to cope. Probably been up all night as well. He runs his fingers through his hair and sighs. This whole thing is shit. Stuff like this shouldn't be happening right here in the village he grew up in. 'Might have forgotten her key. Just trying to cover every possible angle.'

Mike stands up and gathers all the relevant keys together. 'Right. Good point. Mind you, the door was locked when we got back last night so...'

'She could have lost it while out walking,' Simon says flatly. 'I take it you've asked everybody around the area, see if anyone heard or saw anything?'

Mike nods. 'Toby and me did the rounds last night. Woke them up but nobody saw or heard anything. It was a waste of bloody time.'

'At least you asked. Every little bit of information helps, doesn't it? And word got back to me and Mum and Dad so at least it's got people talking. Made them aware, you know?'

There is a short silence as they listen out for Toby talking into his phone in the next room. His voice is raised and it's quite obvious he is on the point of losing it.

'You okay, lads?' Mike asks Callum and Mason, who sit quietly hunched in the corner of the room. What must be going through their minds? Simon stands up, strides over and gives Mason a firm pat on his arm.

'It'll all come right, lads. You'll see. She'll be back before you know it.' Simon watches them. Poor kids. They nod appreciatively and for the first time in many years, lean in to one another for support, their heads barely touching.

'Should we go and speak to the neighbours again?' Simon asks Mike. He came to do something and feels pretty useless sat here.

'Can't harm, can it?' Mike whispers. He too feels bloody ineffective. 'Tell you what, you two lads check the back garden and the shed and stuff while we go and speak to the neighbours again.'

Toby strides in the room, his face flushed with anger. 'Said they will send somebody over later in the day. There's an emergency in town, apparently. A gas leak. Like a missing person isn't just as bloody important.'

'Right. Well, why don't we all go out and have another look around? Talk to neighbours again. Worth a try, isn't it?' Simon smiles at them all. 'And by the time the police turn up, she may well be back home, telling you lot off for not looking hard enough, eh?'

Mike laughs, a short, sharp bark. *Better than crying,* he tells himself as they slope off outside.

23

After my father died, I hoped things would improve. He passed away the winter after Suzie's death, on a day when the snow was so deep, the ambulance took over two hours to reach us. Ironically, it wasn't his liver that gave up. His bronchitis had developed into pneumonia and doctors told us that even if he had got to hospital sooner, there was nothing they could have done.

Mother and I spent the next few weeks rattling around in our suddenly too large house, Suzie's old bedroom a constant reminder of our predicament. My visits to Dr Tavel ceased, the only positive to come out of it all. What little money my mother had received when my father was alive appeared to have

stopped and everything suddenly became too difficult to manage. The days were dark and long and in-
exorably miserable. There were many times when
Mother struggled to get out of bed and I would find
myself on my own, wandering around the house
searching for clean underwear and uniform,
scratching around for food before getting myself off
to school. Usually, by the time I came home on an
evening, she had managed to get herself up and
dressed and the house was marginally less messy. She
would push my plate of food over to me with a weak
smile and a stream of feeble, half-hearted apologies
for oversleeping, assuring me it wouldn't happen
again. It did. Of course it did. Day after day after day.
And then as if being ordinary-looking wasn't difficult
enough to deal with, I began to look grimy. My
clothes were unwashed, my hair dirty, my fingernails
bitten and ragged. I was one of those children in the
playground who stood alone, friendless and ignored,
too grubby for even the most unpopular pupils to be-
friend. Nowadays, I would be counselled for my be-
reavement and referred to social services for neglect.
But of course that didn't happen. What did happen
was that I was subjected to bouts of prolonged bul-
lying for simply existing, for the dreadful crime of
having a mother who was undergoing a complete

nervous and mental breakdown after the death of my sister and father in quick succession.

I had hoped that as the winter passed and the memory of two funerals in such a short space of time lapsed into the further recesses of our memory, she would improve but unfortunately, it was not to be. It was a bright, crisp day when my mother left me. Daffodils were pushing up through dark, saturated soil and snowdrops were peeking their heads up towards the thin, feeble rays of sunlight on the day she died. Spring was most definitely in the air. I was left to cope alone after a concoction of painkillers and vodka were found at her bedside. She had taken the extra precaution of slicing open her wrists in case the huge amount of killer drugs she had ingested didn't quite work. And that was how I found her upon returning from school one sunny afternoon in late February. The previous day, she had seemed better. She had chatted and smiled and that evening, we had even sat and watched TV together. She had asked me about my day, told me things were about to improve. I hadn't realised she meant only for her. She had it all sorted in her mind. Her death was a *fait accompli* and I was no more than a helpless onlooker.

The house was silent when I entered, which wasn't unusual. Untroubled by the quiet, I had wandered into the kitchen, expecting to find her standing in front of the sink washing pots or sitting at the table staring at the wall with a blank expression on her face. Unfortunately, that too was the norm. But she wasn't there. It was at that point, a certain amount of trepidation began to tap at my brain. I dropped my schoolbag onto our battered old couch and ran upstairs, expecting to find her napping in her room. I opened the door and saw the familiar form of her body under the sheets. But unusually, the whole of her body was covered, including her head. As quietly as I could, I tiptoed over and gently tapped a lump which I assumed was her back. No response. The curtains were drawn and it was difficult to see clearly so I wandered around to the other side of the room and pulled them aside, telling myself it was the right thing to do. She wouldn't want me to leave her sleeping. Not this late in the day.

As I moved closer to her, I could see a discolouration seeping through the pale-blue sheets. I knew they wouldn't have been changed for some time and was mentally trying to work out how use the washing machine when I noticed the smell. A metallic, sour odour that seemed to be emanating from where my mother was laid. I slowly padded over to her lifeless form and let out a small gasp when I saw the scarlet pattern spread over the blankets. As carefully as I could and with trembling fingers, I peeled back the coverlet. It must have been my wails and cries that alerted the neighbours to my plight, as that was where they found me, hunched over the blood-drenched body of my mother, dumbstruck and quivering and almost on the point of collapse.

Life in the care system wasn't brilliant but neither was it awful. My foster parents were adequate; I was warm, fed and clean. The other children didn't take kindly to me but by that time, I had learned to grow a second skin. Their hurtful comments about my being an orphan and not having any nice clothes worth speaking of simply washed over me. My grandparents and aunts and uncles were either too busy or too poor to take me or as was the case of my Aunt Sadie, my mother's sister, stated outright that they simply didn't want me. When approached by social services for assistance, she apparently told them that I was trouble and best avoided. With hindsight, she most probably blamed me for the death of her sister – the sister she didn't attempt to help when her mental health deteriorated after my father's death.

I knuckled down at school and learnt to ignore those around me. My schoolwork was my haven and by the time I left, I had gained A's in all of my exams.

My first foray into independence was when I received a grant to go to university in Newcastle. And although I loved the work, my own mental shortcomings finally caught up with me. An overwhelming sense of loneliness suddenly hit me and twice, I ended up being admitted to hospital after attempting suicide. That was where Martyn came in. Prior to meeting him, I was rudderless, unable to focus. He gave me a new lease of life, took me under his wing, and took care of me. Falling pregnant with Tom in my second year wasn't what I had planned but I soon realised it was what I needed. I had a new tight family unit. My very own people, people who were mine and mine alone. It may not have been ideal for most but for me, it was just perfect. I had Martyn and my newborn son and nobody would take them away from me. Nobody.

24

He doesn't stay for long. I'm so good at it now, you see: this lying caper. As soon as I open the door, I can tell by the expression on his face that he will believe every single word that comes out of my mouth. Why would he not? I'm a middle-aged, middle-class lady, new to the area and hardly a threat, am I? The person I live with is, but he is tucked away in his study at the other end of the house. I feel confident enough to say that before this young man even opens his mouth, this conversation won't take long.

'Hello there. I was just wondering if you've seen a woman around here? Anna from number eighteen.' He points over to her house, *my house*, and I smile and shake my head.

'Has she still not come back?' I say, sucking in air in mock astonishment.

His lips are a firm, thin line as he speaks. 'I'm afraid she isn't. I... well me and my parents know Anna quite well and I thought I would come and help out till the police turn up.'

The police. My eye flickers slightly. I blink it away. He is self-assured, this young man, I'll give him that. But then so am I.

Tillie comes running through to complete the picture. I need him to see what kind of family we are. Reserved, harmless. I mean, what kind of household would keep a pet and be cruel to others? She stands obediently at my feet, looking up to me and then back to the man. I shake my head and tut. 'It's so odd. Not like her at all. But I'm sure there's a rational explanation behind all of this. Anna is a very sensible lady.'

'I take it you spoke to her family last night?'

I nod and reach down to pet Tillie. She responds by running round my ankles enthusiastically.

'But obviously, I expected her to have returned last night. I presumed she had taken an evening stroll to the shop or for a brief walk by the river to clear her head.'

He shakes his head. 'She definitely didn't go to the shop. We would have seen her. Clear her head?' he says and his face creases up, a furrow forming between his brows as he watches me. 'What do you mean, clear her head?'

I sigh and look behind him then back to his eyes. So innocent, so full of hope. 'Well, between you and I, I think Anna and her husband have been having some problems. At least that's what she implied whenever we spoke. I know she was also fed up with running around after them all.' I bring my hand up to my mouth and shake my head some more. I only wish I could conjure up fake tears. 'I'm sorry, I shouldn't have said that. It's just so upsetting,'

The man on her doorstep closes his mouth, an embarrassed flush beginning to creep up his neck. 'Erm, right, well, anyway if you see or hear anything unusual, you know where she lives. Mike and the kids are worried sick so anything at all...'

I nod sagely and am about to close the door when he speaks again. 'The path runs through your garden, doesn't it?'

I keep my face impassive as I reply, 'Yes. Yes it does. Why do you ask?'

His voice is brighter, his awkwardness at being

privy to Anna's marital problems now forgotten. 'I was just thinking that she might have gone right past your house if she went walking. You didn't see her, then?'

I keep my irritation under wraps, conceal it well. 'Do you not think I would have told you if I had seen her? We get lots of walkers along that path Mr...?'

'Simon,' he interjects. 'And I know all about the walkers who come through here. I've lived here all my life. So have my parents. They know everyone in the village. Everyone.'

I feel my guard begin to slip and hope he can't see the redness that I feel creeping up my face and over my ears which are beginning to burn.

'They run the local shop so we know every inch of this village.' He keeps his eyes on me. His mouth is set in a firm, tight line. I feel my heart begin to flutter up my neck at his words. That lady in the shop who spoke to me on the day we moved in. The way she followed me around, the way she watched me long after I had left. Has she always worked there? Does she remember my parents? Does she remember me? I blink hard and run my fingers through my hair to hide the tremble that has taken hold. So what if she does recall my face? I haven't done anything wrong and never have. All she will remember is a scrap of a child who led a blighted existence and left the village shortly afterwards, never to return. Until now, that is.

'Right. Well as I was saying, Simon, there are loads of ramblers who pass through here. I don't sit at the window, watching them all. And if I had seen Anna, I would obviously have said so, wouldn't I? She is a friend.'

His stare is unmoving, his features impassive. He is confident; I'll give him that. 'Of course, sorry to have bothered you. Well, I'm going to stay and help for as long as I can so you know where we are if you see or hear anything. Anything at all.' The last sentence hangs in the air as he waits for me to say something in return.

I simply nod and accept his apology with good grace, telling him to keep me informed of any updates. He assures me that they will and heads back up the village.

I close my door and lean back against it. The police. They're waiting for the police to turn up. And it's highly likely they will put more effort into finding Anna. Not like the search for Nancy. That particular investigation was a half-hearted attempt. It was as if they presumed the river had taken her before the search had even begun. But a second disappearance? They will move heaven and earth to find her. But that's okay. She is safe here with me and absolutely nobody will find her. I'll make sure of it.

I watch from the living-room window as he continues knocking on doors and is confronted by a series of helpless old ladies who can barely stay upright, shrunken and disabled by age and arthritis. He will have nothing to report back, no leads to go on. There is nothing around here except for the power of a bulging, raging river that swallows the innocent and the unprepared. It's the main killer round here, the obvious killer.

I let Tillie out in the garden to do her business before the police descend. I would much prefer to keep a low profile while they conduct their search. She will last until mid-afternoon before needing to go out again, by which time they may well have given up and left.

I make a pot of tea and smile. Everything is working out perfectly. I look at my watch. I have at least another two or three hours before the medication wears off. And loathe though I am to do it, I will have to administer some more. Just until the police leave the village. That's if they even turn up.

I spend the next hour or so drinking my tea and

cleaning the kitchen. Not that it needs it. It's just a way of passing the time, giving myself time to gather my thoughts, get my plan sorted in my head. I wipe and wash and drag cloths across each surface until they gleam.

I hear the familiar noise of Martyn's walking cane as he tap, tap, taps his way into the kitchen. He takes the mug of tea I have made for him and swills it back. This is good. Now that I have stopped badgering him to have his medication, he is more willing to take things I've prepared for him, unaware that it is laced with his pills.

'Where is she?'

I am startled. I didn't expect him to ask after Anna or even remember the incident. That's so typical of him, you see: to cause a major ruckus and then forget all about it. His mental health is becoming much worse, along with huge holes in his memory. I need to be careful here. I don't want him to go racing around the house looking for her, just when I've got it all under control.

'Don't worry. I've sorted it. There's nothing for you to be concerned about.'

'How is she?'

'She's fine. A bit bruised but on the mend,' I say

thinking how ridiculous this all sounds. An impartial observer would think us mad.

He nods and becomes immersed in his newspaper. He is happy. That's good. A happy Martyn is an amenable Martyn which in turn makes life easier for me.

The sun makes an appearance and floods the kitchen in shades of yellow and warm ochre. I flop down onto an armchair at the edge of the dining room. Telling lies might be getting easier but it's tiring. Ribbons of dappled sunlight rest across my lap, making me feel relaxed. I could sit like this all day. What with me sitting here all calm and collected and Martyn quietly reading the paper, anyone would think we're a normal family.

It's the thump from up above that alerts me, drags me out of my languor. I spill out of the chair, my scalp prickling. I hear it again – another crash and a low moan. *Anna.* Taking the stairs two at a time, I charge into the bedroom and am confronted by the sight of her body on the floor and my papers scattered around her. Somehow, she has managed to roll herself off the bed and has landed on my things. The laundry is strewn over the rug and my wooden box gapes open like an angry mouth, its contents on display for Anna to see. And judging by the look on her face, she *has* seen them. Seen them, read them and devoured each and every word. So now she knows. Now there is no going back. My head throbs as I kneel down beside her writhing body and look her in the eyes. She continues to buck about like a wet fish until I raise my hand and slap her hard across her face.

'Now look what you've made me do,' I gasp as I gather up the newspaper cuttings and fold them back up. 'You see, I'm not a violent person but you really shouldn't have touched my personal belongings.'

She is still at last, her eyes wide with shock and fear, a red welt starting to form on her cheek just below her eye. I suppress any pity or feelings of regret. She shouldn't have done it. Invaded my space and read what wasn't hers. This changes everything. And it is all her fault. All of it. If she had managed keep her mouth shut, stopped harping on about Nancy, she probably wouldn't even be here at all. Silly, silly woman.

I put everything back in place and this time I snap the clasp shut on my container, then I drag Anna back up onto the bed, noticing how dirty her hair is. I was going to wash it last night and didn't get round to it. I might be cross with her but I don't want her to feel unclean. Her usually fair, slightly curly hair is caked with dried blood and sticks to her head in great dirty clumps.

'Stay here. I'm just going to get some things to clean you up with.' I give her a stern look and her face crumples. Putty in my hands. Excellent.

I notice how small and slight she is and suddenly something clicks in my brain. Food. She hasn't had any. Or a drink. I mustn't let her get dehydrated. Somehow, I am going to have to feed her. But first, while she is weak and still slightly sleepy, I will sponge down her hair, restore its usual bounce and shine. I gather up some shampoo, a bowl of warm water and a small sponge and sit down beside her on the edge of the bed. She winces as I dab the sponge on the cut on her head and gently clear away the dried blood.

'Shh. I won't hurt you, Suzie. I'm just washing your hair, trying to make you look pretty again. You'd rather look beautiful than greasy and grubby, wouldn't you?'

She doesn't move or respond as I massage the shampoo onto her scalp and softly rub the bubbles through the knotted fibres of hair. Slowly but surely, each lock gradually springs free until at last, I am able to draw my fingers through it without hitting any tangles or knots. I squeeze the wet sponge over thick strands of her golden hair until all the bubbles have gone and each lock is gleaming. I towel it dry and hear her grunt as I inadvertently touch her scar. I notice it is still bleeding. Not copious amounts but it is definitely there. A constant weep of blood and mucus.

'Sorry about hurting you. It's all finished now. You can rest here while I get you a drink and some food.' My mouth is close to her ear as I gather up the bowl of dirty water, the sponge and shampoo bottle. 'And please don't roll about or I will have to hurt you again.' I raise my hand over her face to show her I mean it. She widens her eyes in fright and shakes her head. Her eyes plead with me to not do it. Finally. She is starting to get the message.

I hurry downstairs and gather up a few snacks and a glass of water. When I get back, she is in exactly the same place. Good. She is starting to understand me. We are going to get along. I prop her up slightly and quickly rip the tape back. Her lips are pursed and she closes her eyes against the sting. I lean down to grab the glass and when I look back, she is staring directly at me. I push the glass to her lips before she can speak. Water runs down her chin and her mouth appears static. It's the tape. Her skin will feel sore and numb. This is advantageous for me. If I work quickly,

I can get her fed and watered and have her gagged again before she has chance to speak or make any incriminating noises.

She finishes the water and I quickly slip a slice of banana between her contorted lips. She presses down on it and I insert another, then another. I refill the glass from the jug by my side and tilt her chin while she drinks some more water. It's while I am reaching over for a segment of orange that I hear her. It's faint and her voice is low and croaky but I definitely hear it. 'Phoebe. Help. Please help. Won't tell anyone. Promise.'

I sigh and put the glass to her lips. She is shaking and I touch her arm to reassure her.

'Oh Suzie. If only I could believe that but you see, it's too late to let you go. You've read my most precious documents and now everything is too far gone to turn back. Nothing will ever be the same again now. You can see that, can't you?'

Before she can protest, I rip off a new length of tape and push it back down on her mouth nice and tight.

'There. We don't want you making any unnecessary sounds, do we? Not with all the activity going on out there at the minute. This is our little secret and we want it to stay that way.'

Her eyes fill up and her cheeks redden and puff out in protestation. Two flawlessly formed tears spill out of each eye and roll down her face in absolute symmetry. Even when she cries, she does it faultlessly. Her beauty knows no bounds. She is perfection personified. I sit on the edge of the bed and run my fingers through her still-damp hair. Silky and clean, it bounces through my fingertips like liquid gold. There is a noise outside and her head turns to the direction of the window, a frantic expression on her face. I lean down and whisper gently in her ear, the heat of my own breath bouncing back onto my face as I speak.

'Shh. There, there. Don't try to fight it, my darling. I knew we would find a way to get back together. I've waited many years for this but I just knew you would come back to me, Suzie. I just knew it.'

* * *

I feel a frisson of excitement and contentment as I head back downstairs and into the living room. Such an amazing feeling. At long last, it's all coming together. And not before time. I've had years of loneliness and heartache. I deserve this piece of utopia. Some people spend their lives bathed in happiness, with everything always going their way, but not me. I have had more than my fair share of misery. This particular moment in time is mine for the keeping. I've earned it. I finally have everyone where I want them. Martyn is in his study, happily reading and Suzie is upstairs, resting after our lunch together. The only piece of the puzzle missing is Tom. A surge of excitement pulses through me. I will ring him. I don't know why I didn't think of it earlier. I grab my mobile from the kitchen drawer and am dismayed to see it needs charging. Damn. Undeterred, I pick up the landline and punch in his number. He picks it up after only a few rings.

'Yeah?' His voice is slurry, groggy. Not like him at all.

'Tom?' I shrill down the phone, a little too loudly.

'Mum? What's up?' He sounds faint.

'Nothing, darling. Just thought I would give you a call to let you know how well things are over here. And see how you are, obviously.' I snort a little as I giggle. Gosh, it feels good to laugh. In fact, it feels bloody marvellous. Long may it continue.

'I'm... we're fine. Is everything okay?' He is livelier now. I have his attention.

'Yes sweetheart, why wouldn't it be? Am I not allowed to ring my only child?'

'Well, yeah, but it's just that it's the early hours

here.' I can hear him murmuring to Mya, no doubt. Her again. It's always about bloody Mya, 'It's 4 a.m. Mum. What's up?'

I chuckle again, determined to stay upbeat. Nobody is going to drag me down, especially my son's girlfriend, the woman who is keeping him from me. Because that is obviously the only reason he has stayed over there. To see her. She is to blame for my little family unit being incomplete.

'I have a visitor here.' I stop and gasp a little. I didn't mean to say it. It just slipped out. Fortunately, he doesn't seem to hear me.

'Mum, can I call you back when we get up? Mya and I have an early start and really need a few more hours' sleep.'

'Of course, darling, of course.' I hear a sound behind me and turn to see Martyn pointing to the phone. Exhilaration grips me. He wants to communicate with his son. At long last. My heart batters around my chest at the thought of it. They haven't spoken since... well, I can't remember... since Martyn's accident, I suppose. I smile and nod at my husband. 'Tom, I have some exciting news for you. Your father's here and he wants to talk to you.'

There is a stony silence at the other end of the line. When he does speak, Tom's voice is a whisper, a thin, reedy squawk that sends a chill across my skin. 'Mum? What are you talking about?' I hear his breathing become laboured and a rustle of fabric as he moves closer to the phone. 'Mum, what on earth are you saying? What the hell is going on?'

25

After speaking to Tom on the phone, I guess I got a bit carried away and had a rush of adrenalin, or something that made me uninhibited. I have no regrets, though. For all I know, it may be the last time I will ever get chance to step foot in there. Martyn and I have pretty much burnt our bridges now, haven't we? And besides, isn't it the 'done' thing to help neighbours with the search? I've seen it on TV. All the locals out combing an area when somebody disappears. Not that I did help with the search; I was more of a shoulder to cry on, a friendly face in time of need. But of course, it didn't go as well as I would have hoped. When does it ever?

I called around, leaving Anna and Martyn alone

in the house together – a risk, I know, but after speaking to my son, I was gripped by exhilaration and before I knew it, I was on their doorstep, asking if they needed any help. They were very polite and welcoming, if a little puzzled by my appearance. The house was a mess. Crockery and clothes strewn everywhere, cushions laid on the floor, shoes littering the hallway. Complete chaos. And no Simon. That was good.

'I was wondering if you needed any help with anything?' I asked, trying to appear as humble and sincere as I possibly could.

'Not unless you fancy making yet more tea?' Mike had said, his voice cracking as he spoke. 'That's just about all we've managed to do,' he whispered before turning away and wiping his eyes with a crumpled-up tissue.

I should have felt some sort of guilt at that point, a modicum of remorse at his predicament. But that's the strange thing. I didn't. If anything, I was suddenly elated. I had power over these people. They were all there because of me and Martyn. Puppets on strings and I was the puppeteer, the master of their futures. And it felt good.

I offered to tidy up, keep the house in some sort of order.

'After all,' I had said, with a forced note of positivity in my tone, 'when Anna gets home, she would
hate to see the house like this, wouldn't she?' They
had all nodded and with a murmur, stepped aside
while I gathered up coats and sweaters and hung
them all in cupboards. The cups I placed in the sink
before washing up and wiping down surfaces.

'Where do these go?' I had asked as I walked back
into the deathly hush of the living room where they
were all standing in a huddle, their faces the picture
of misery and wretchedness. I held Anna's gloves and
scarf aloft and headed towards the stairs. Mike
nodded as I made my way through and slowly
climbed up. They had been in a drawer but after a
quick rummage, it was what I had needed to get up
there. Just one little look in my childhood bedroom.
That was all I had wanted. Too much of a temptation
to resist.

I had mounted the stairs as quietly as possible
and quickly worked out which room was Anna's. I
quietly placed the items on the bed and backed out
before padding along to my old bedroom. It had two
single beds on either side and was quite obviously
the room of Anna's two sons, with modern electrical
gadgets stuffed in every corner and crevice. I looked
out of the window and sighed. Apart from the growth

of shrubbery and trees blocking some of the view, the river was still visible. Ferocious and mildly threatening, it rushed past, rumbling over rocks and stones, frothing up into a ragged circle of white water before moving on downstream.

Behind me, I had heard Suzie's voice, a whisper, telling me it was an accident, that despite what everyone thought, it wasn't my fault. I had replied that it didn't matter any more because she was home now; we both were. Back where we belonged. She agreed and suddenly, feeling as if a weight had been lifted, I had lain down on the bed. Just for a second to let the moment pass. I hadn't intended to do it and was almost certain I had only been there a few minutes but maybe it was longer because when I opened my eyes, one of Anna's sons was standing in the doorway, staring at me. His expression had said it all. It was a mixture of horror and bewilderment.

'Sorry,' I had mumbled, sitting up abruptly and swinging my legs off the bed, 'I had a sudden dizzy spell and needed to lie down to let it pass. It's probably all the upset.'

He nodded, his eyes still wide with shock, my words doing little to alleviate a horribly awkward situation. I stumbled past him, my legs liquid as I made my way downstairs and into the living room where Mike and Toby were stood talking.

'Remember to contact me if you need anything,' I managed to say hoarsely. They nodded and gave me a smile. It was fine. They hadn't noticed my absence. They were too wrapped up in their own dilemma to care about me.

I stepped out the front door and headed home. It was just as I had got in that I heard them: a group of youngsters hollering about finding something. I had assured myself that at least this new find will help that boy forget about what he had just seen. In the grand scheme of things, a lonely old neighbour taking an unexpected nap on his bed won't register as a threat. Finding his mum is all he will be interested in. If only he knew.

26

Mike feels his chest tighten when he hears it. Something has happened, something of significance. A couple of the younger neighbours are helping Simon, taking the river path both ways to see what they can find. They made Mike stay here. Forced him. Said he would need to be here for when the police turn up. Mike prickles at the thought of them. *Where the fuck are they?* His wife is missing. He wants Mountain Rescue, a team of police officers, a search helicopter. The whole frigging shooting match. But now he can hear Simon's voice, clear as a bell, carried on the thermals, drifting towards the house.

'We've found something!'

Mike fights to suppress a wave of nausea that

grips him. They've found something. Jesus Christ. He hangs onto the sofa for balance as the floor slopes off at a painful angle and the walls tilt. An image of Anna's bloated, dead body fills his head. No, for God's sake. They wouldn't be shouting it across the entire village. So what have they found? Hair, perhaps? Or a piece of clothing? He tries to picture Anna's outfit before he left the house. He has no idea. She could have changed clothes to go walking. She probably *did* change clothes. He tries to think. What does she usually wear? Dark jeans or joggers, maybe? A sleeveless jacket? Why the fuck didn't he stay in or insist she go to the pub with them?

Callum comes hurtling through and grabs Mike's arm breathlessly, saying, 'You need to come outside and have a look at a trainer that we've found in the bushes, Dad. See if you recognise it.' His eyes are dark, his voice a harsh screech.

Mike's stomach flips. Where would she be with only one shoe? He doesn't move. Panic clasps at his stomach. Anna has dozens upon dozens of pairs of shoes. Sandals, running shoes, sling backs, stilettos, boots. What if it is actually hers and he doesn't recognise it? What kind of husband doesn't know his wife's clothing? Jesus, this is absolutely fucking unbearable.

'Toby reckons it might belong to that other

woman.' Callum looks at his dad hopefully, willing him to say that his mum didn't own any trainers. Mike looks at his son, is able to read his thoughts. He too, finds himself praying that the other missing lady was wearing trainers and that this one belongs to her. As bad as he feels for the other woman's family, right now he has to look out for himself and his two boys. He hopes to God this trainer isn't Anna's. He nods and disappears into the utility room and emerges a couple of seconds later wearing a pair of dark-green wellies.

They walk together towards the others in silence, the squelch of wet mud under their feet the only sound to be heard. The drizzle runs down Mike's neck. He pulls his collar up and dips his head, acutely aware that his every move is very probably under scrutiny.

They follow the path, pass through a garden and continue on up through a series of overgrown bushes and thickets. It isn't a pleasant walk, far from it, and he wonders why ramblers would want to take it, why Anna took it. It needs a thorough cutting back. Thorns and spikes snag him as he passes through. He tries to imagine how it would look in the dark and suppresses the thought.

'Just down here if you can manage to get through.'

Simon is on his haunches leaning into a dense patch of shrubbery. 'We didn't want to move it till the police get here. Any sign of them yet?'

Mike shakes his head and closes his eyes, wanting to put this moment off for just a little bit longer. He opens them again and looks over the top of the surrounding foliage. The bank leading down to the river is staggeringly steep. The sharp drop down to the thunderous river below them that is on the point of bursting its banks takes his breath away. Anyone who lost their footing around here would stand absolutely no chance whatsoever. A painful lump sticks in his throat and he finds it hard to drag his eyes away from the fast-flowing water far below them.

'It's just here if you want to take a look?' Mike reluctantly steps over to an area beside his feet. He gets down next to Simon and Toby, who push a clump of branches to one side. And there, trapped between two thick, gnarled branches is Anna's training shoe. Mike recognises it immediately. Of course she has some. How could he have forgotten? They're not what he would think of as trainers, the sort of shoes people wear to go jogging or to go to the gym. These are the ones she wears every day for what she calls her 'scruffy jobs' such as sweeping the path or cleaning the windows or even just walking to the local shop.

Anna's shoe. Here, by the river, up a high bank. A pain pulses behind his eyes as he scans the nearby area. The rain has saturated everything in sight. The path is sheer sludge and parts of the bank look so slippery and wet, they look liable to erode and slide away at any minute.

'Jesus,' is all he can say.

Simon looks at him, his eyes dark with dread, Mike nods and walks away. His legs are liquid as he makes his way back home. He needs to be alone. Just for a few minutes. That's all he wants so he can sort all this out in his head.

The garden is empty as he staggers up the path, in the front door and upstairs where he collapses on the bed and howls like an injured animal. Toby and the boys are standing at the doorway when he looks up. He hates being seen like this – weak and ineffective – but can't seem to summon up the strength to do anything any more. He is sapped of all energy after seeing that shoe and the almighty strength of the current. There is no way anybody, even the strongest of swimmers, could survive that.

Nobody says anything. What is there to say? Toby quietly turns and guides Callum and Mason away and downstairs. Mike sits up and wipes at his eyes. How the fuck did this happen? It's his fault, of course.

He should have stayed in with her. He knew as soon as they got in and the house was in darkness that something was wrong. No more visits to the pub. That's it. No more drink for him. Ever.

*　*　*

Toby stands staring out of the kitchen window. Where in God's name has Anna gone? This whole thing is surreal, like something off a TV drama series. Stuff like this shouldn't be happening to them. They're an ordinary family, bordering on the mundane. Razor blades slice at the lining of his stomach every time he moves and his head feels as if a herd of cattle are stampeding through it. Lack of sleep. And lack of food.

He turns the gas on and finishes cooking. They all need to eat. Despite the awful circumstances, people still need to be fed. Tea will still get drunk, bacon butties will get eaten. Life goes on. Just as it did after Bridget died. He remembers feeling infuriated after his sister's funeral that people were mowing their lawns, heading out for picnics, laughing. Mike was there for him then, listening to his woes, forcing him to see the positives even on the greyest of days. Now it's his turn to do the same.

He flips the bacon, the sizzle from the pan the only sound to be heard. Toby watches it mesmerised, his mind in momentary shutdown until Mason hurtles past him and grabs Toby's arm, eyes wild.

'Mountain Rescue are here. And the police. And there's bloody loads of them.'

27

I am downstairs, bustling about, trying to compose myself after the silly moment in the bedroom, reassuring myself that it will soon be forgotten, when I hear the bang. I rush up, wanting to get there before Martyn makes his way up. If he finds her messing about again, prying, there's no telling what he will do. She knows his temper is unpredictable at the best of times. I have told her over and over what kind of a man he is. Just when I thought she had started listening to me, she goes and starts playing up again. I'm just thankful that she waited till I got back otherwise goodness knows what would have happened if she had done this while I was over the road in her house.

When I get to the bedroom, she has somehow managed to stand herself upright even though her hands and ankles are still tightly bound, pulled the blinds apart, and is looking out of the window at the throng of people outside. She has seen that the search party has upped their game. I need to take action.

I drag her back onto the bed, a fistful of her delicate golden hair wrapped tightly around my knuckles. She makes a strange, strangled crying sound beneath the tape as I lay her down and lean over her.

'Don't move again, Suzie. You're making this way harder than it needs to be. You really need to start cooperating, you know.'

I turn her over and tighten the cords around her wrists, then fling her onto her back. Time for more sedatives. Not too many. I don't want to kill her. Not when I've waited for so long to have her back. I mix them up, slice off some more tape and go through the procedure. *Rip, drink, re-apply.*

Standing up, I walk over to the window and peer out at the activity around the front of the house. They've got plenty of bodies helping out now. I can't help but laugh. I wonder what is going through their minds at this moment in time. If only they knew. It's so empowering, having this level of control. I can't remember ever feeling so confident, so strong and euphoric. I had no idea this calamity would leave me feeling this way. Isn't it funny how a spontaneous and potentially catastrophic event can turn to one's advantage so quickly?

When I look back over at her, she is almost gone, her eyelids flickering as she tries to battle against the effect of the drugs. It is useless. She may as well relax and let them do their thing. Fighting it all is futile. And anyway, why would she want to? She is back home now, back to where she belongs. Back with me, her sister.

It doesn't take long at all for her eyes to become sealed shut and for her body to go limp. I could sit here all day staring at her, marvelling at how beautiful she is. And she is. I can't quite believe how fortunate I am to have her back. And in time, she too will feel the same way. I am sure of it.

The noise outside draws my eyes over to the window. Yet more movement out there. And the police. Lots of busy people scurrying about like ants. I doubt they'll come over here to speak to me again. Why would they? I've been over and shown my support, done my bit as a good neighbour and friend. And apart from our proximity, there is nothing to link her to me. I look over at her unconscious body and can't suppress a smile. She's all mine now.

Over the road, a line of uniformed officers trudge into the house, leaving the door open behind them while some men from the Mountain Rescue get kitted up to go walking. They can search all they like. They won't find her.

I leave the room, closing the door with a light click, and head back downstairs. Martyn is in the dining room, exactly where I left him. He looks up as I go in and smiles before returning his attention back to his food. I leave him be and wander into the kitchen. This is my favourite room in the house. It is always flooded with light, no matter what time of day it is. I also have an excellent view of the river. What more could anyone want? Such a perfect day.

And it is too. Suzie remains asleep and Martyn and I spend the rest of it chatting and reminiscing. We even get some photograph albums out and sit together perusing them, laughing at the terrible fashions and dreadful hairstyles. I let out a wistful sigh as we find our old wedding photographs – me in an ivory shift dress, looking relaxed and slightly overweight after having only given birth to Tom six weeks prior, and Martyn, as handsome as ever in his navy, close-fitting suit. And of course, there are the photographs of Tom as a baby. Such a sweet, sweet boy with his rosy cheeks and chubby little fists. I used to love tracing my fingers over the row of dimples on the back of his hands: tiny indents where his knuckles should have been. Such happy times when we were all together. How life changes, I think as I gather the array of pictures up and slide them all back into the folder.

There is no noise from upstairs but then I didn't expect there to be. I've given her enough medication to fell a horse. But soon, I'm going to have to see to her ablutions, make sure she is fed and properly hydrated. I've waited too long for her to lose her. I have to take care of her. She's my responsibility now. All mine.

I gather up some bits of food and take a bottle of water upstairs. She will need toileting first. Poor woman must be desperate for the loo.

She is placid when I get in there, pliant and in need of a drink. Getting her on the toilet is easy enough, her system still full of drugs, dulling her resistance. I lay her back on the bed and gently stroke her hair.

'We're going to get along just fine, Suzie. No point trying to fight me, is there?'

Her eyes flicker as she watches me. Not fear any more. Trust and recognition. That's what it is.

'We're a team, you and I, aren't we?' I nestle my body close to her on the bed and wrap my arm around her waist. 'Nothing to be frightened of now, sweetheart. I'm here to make it up to you. All those years apart will soon be a distant memory, just you wait and see.'

I stay there until the light begins to fade and then very slowly, extricate myself and slump wearily into the chair where I stay until the morning.

28

The throbbing pain in her head makes her want to vomit, every slight movement causing her to heave. She stays completely still. Being sick could be deadly. Nowhere for it to go. She could so easily choke and die. And there is no way she is about to let that happen. Not here, in this place. With her.

Anna twists the lower half of her body, trying to alleviate the dreadful dull ache that is setting in at the base of her spine after being laid for too long in the same position. Light is filtering in through the blinds where she knocked them to one side to see out of the window. And she will do it again as soon as Phoebe leaves the room. As long as she doesn't give her any more of that medication. She has no idea what it is but it terrifies her, the thought of being so heavily sedated, she can't think who she is, let alone what day it actually is.

Anna bites down on her lip as a shooting pain travels up her arm into her shoulder. Concentrating hard, she tries to focus her mind elsewhere until it subsides. She is tied so tight, it feels as if her arms are becoming dislocated. She has never known such pain. All over her body but especially her head. Why her head? That's the thing. She can't remember how she ended up here. Blinking back tears, she thinks back to the last thing she can recall. Walking. She was walking somewhere. It was muddy, it must have been. She can smell it on her clothes. And it was raining. There was darkness. So much darkness. But that's it. Nothing else will come to her. Her mind is completely blank.

A noise disturbs her. Slowly and meticulously so as to minimise the pain, she rolls over and focuses on the dark shape in the corner of the room. *Her.* She is asleep, propped up in a chair. A cold sweat covers every inch of Anna's skin. She watches, her eyes wide with fear as the shape begins to move, wakes up and lets out a small, muffled groan. Anna snaps her eyes shut. Pretend to be asleep. It's the only way, otherwise the medicine gets poured down her throat. Problem is, her bladder is bursting and she is thirsty. So very, very thirsty. She freezes as the shape lets out a strangled yawn and the floor creaks beneath her moving feet. Anna senses her presence next to the bed. She stays still, fearing her hammering heart will be battering so violently, it will show through her sweater. A tell-tale pulse of unadulterated terror.

'Sleep well, little one,' the voice croons, a sickly sweet lilt to her tone. 'I'll be back up soon to give you some breakfast.' There is a pause before she speaks again. 'Actually, I guess you need to go to the toilet, don't you?'

There is a sigh and Anna feels herself being hoisted up off the bed. She keeps her body as floppy as possible to emulate sleep and a drugged state while her pants are yanked down. She is grateful for the familiar, cool sensation of the toilet seat and has no option but to let it go. So undignified and unseemly but better than wetting herself. She is put back on the bed, the cord on her wrists and ankles cutting into her skin. Breath wafts close to her face, sour and hot.

'I know you're awake now so don't try anything.'

A cool finger traces its way down the side of her face and Anna wants to retch. Her blood stops pulsing while she waits for her to move away and leave the room. Only when Phoebe finally shuffles off and goes downstairs does Anna let go, the tears pouring down her cheeks unchecked, an unrelenting river of fear and dread.

29

Martyn is sitting eating toast when I go down. I spend the next few minutes tidying up and loading the dishwasher before preparing some breakfast. A yogurt and some juice. Should be enough for now and nice and easy for her to digest. I'm on my way to the hallway when the shrill pitch of the landline cuts into the silence of the morning. I scowl and reluctantly put the tray down to answer it. Bad timing. Probably somebody wanting to sell me something. They will get short shrift, disturbing my time with Suzie. She is hungry and thirsty and needs some sustenance. I pick it up and answer it with more than a touch of reticence in my voice, and am surprised to hear Tom speaking at the other end.

'Hi Mum. How's it going?'

'Going?' He has caught me unawares and I find myself struggling to make sense of what he is saying.

'Yeah. You know, how are you?' I can hear people talking in the background – voices. Lots of them.

'I'm fine. Are you at work? Sounds very noisy.'

He laughs softly, a gentle rhythmic sound. Poetic. 'Well that's the thing you see,' he says and my pulse races as he speaks, thrashing round my ears making me dizzy, 'I had a last-minute conference come up at work and it was in London. I don't get back to the UK that often so I thought, why not?'

I look down at the floor, trying to keep my balance. 'I'm sorry, Tom. I don't quite follow you?'

I do. I follow him completely. I just don't want to hear it. Not now. Any other time, but not now.

'I'm on the train, Mum. I left Kings Cross fifteen minutes ago. I'll be getting into the station in just over two hours. Don't worry about picking me up. I'll get a cab.'

The floor moves beneath my feet, the wood grain swirling violently as I cling onto the table top to stay upright. Of all the times to visit, why now?

'Mum? Are you still there?'

I nod and clear my throat. 'Yes, of course. That's fabulous, darling. I'll get the kettle on ready.' My own words rattle around my head, empty, hollow, meaningless.

There is a long pause before he speaks again. 'Truth be told, I'm a bit concerned about you, Mum. You don't seem yourself at all.' His tone is careful, deliberate. As if I am some kind of idiot who needs looking after.

I try to laugh dismissively, be unconcerned, but it comes out as a low growl, giving him more reason to doubt me. 'I am absolutely fine, Tom. You just caught me off guard, that's all. I haven't even had my breakfast yet.'

'That's what I mean,' he says lightly. 'It's after nine and you haven't eaten. You're normally up with the larks.'

It seems that whatever I say he is going to have a comeback.

'Just overslept, that's all.' I am trying to stay calm but panic tears at me, creeping up my neck, buzzing around my brain. Time is passing as we speak. I need to get moving, get things sorted.

'Okay. Well, I hope that's the case. Anyway, I'll see you in a few hours.'

We hang up and the enormity of what is about to happen suddenly hits me. Terror cramps my gut. I race upstairs and lean over the toilet, where I am violently sick. Again and again and again. I wait until my stomach stops heaving, then stand up and look in the mirror. A haggard woman stares back at me. No make-up, uncombed hair. I am a complete mess. I've been so busy dodging questions from prying neighbours and caring for Martyn and Suzie that my own needs have been sorely neglected. I quickly rinse my face, then think better of it and step into a steaming-hot shower. The water pummels my skin as I scrub away the grime of the past few days. I step out feeling clean, invigorated, ready to face the world and whatever it decides to throw at me.

By the time I've combed my hair and applied a slick of lipstick, my plan is hatched. I will need to be quick, though. Time is against me. I have two hours before Tom arrives. Suzie has to be fed and watered and hidden from view. And I have to do it now.

30

She flinches as I approach her with a small bottle of water. So typical of her. She always was a smart cookie.

'We're going on a short journey. Call it a holiday. For you, anyway. Don't worry, it's not for long,' I say as I unscrew the lid and sit on the edge of the bed. She tries to flinch but I see it coming and am ready to pre-empt her every movement. I straddle over her, pinning her tiny frame beneath me, my knees pressing hard on her shoulders. This shouldn't take long. I don't rip the tape off completely but pull it to one side and force the neck of the bottle in her mouth. The small amount of water empties into her mouth and I quickly press the tape back in place. Her cheeks puff out in protest. I move off her and apply another strip of tape. Can't afford to make any mistakes. Not when I've come this far.

As soon as I can see she is completely unconscious, I pull my boots on and go outside to reverse the car into the garage. There is plenty of space to manoeuvre so I make sure I position it with the rear end close to the door that leads into the house. Once I am satisfied that everything is ready, I go back inside and take the stairs two at a time, excitement beginning to grip me. Everything is going to be fine. More than fine. It's going to be perfect. Once Tom gets here, I will have all of them with me. My family. All together. As if we've never been apart.

Getting her back down the stairs feels a great deal more arduous than taking her up there. She is floppy and her head keeps lolling around. I hang onto the handrail and end up bumping her down, our legs becoming entangled as I take each stair one at a time. It's a cumbersome process but in the end, I manage it, out of breath and with a slightly sore head after we clash temples on the last step.

I briefly consider putting her in the back seat, laying her out flat, covered by a blanket but decide the risk is too great so do something I would rather not do, and put her in the boot. It feels cruel putting her in there, indecorous and unbecoming, especially after I have cleaned her up and made sure she looks nice. It's small and dark too but at least we don't have that far to travel.

We get there in just over fifty minutes and I'm pleased to notice that the road leading up to the house is empty. All at work, I imagine. I fumble around the bottom of my handbag for the key. I feel a tug of panic at the passing of time. I have to get her in and sorted before the drugs wear off. And before my son turns up and wonders where I am. I feel the familiar shape of it at the bottom, lodged underneath a sea of tissues and old receipts. Relief washes over me. I really must keep it together. It would be stupid to get this far and then spoil it all because I lose my nerve and come undone. Very, very stupid indeed. What on earth would Martyn think of me? What would Suzie think of me, come to that?

It's far easier getting her out of the boot and into the house than it was dragging her down the stairs and getting her in there in the first place and I almost want to weep with the exhilaration of it once I position her in a comfortable place. A long driveway and tall conifers surrounding the property all added to the ease. No worries about who would see us. The question of how I will keep her fed and tend to her ablutions nags at me. I ignore it. One thing at a time.

I cover her with a warm, fleecy throw and lay her down, her back resting against an array of carefully plumped up cushions. I'll explain everything to her when she comes around and once she sees what my plans are, I just know she will understand. I close the blinds, switch on a low power lamp and turn the heating up. I don't want her to be cold when she wakes.

I feel a need to say goodbye to her, to tell her why I've gone. She'll be worried when she wakes up in a strange place on her own. I don't want her to be frightened. Couldn't bear the thought. I lean forward and place my head close to hers, so close I can feel the heat of her body as it pulses out of her skin in hot, rhythmic waves.

'I'll be back to see you soon, my love. I have to leave you here because Tom is coming to see me. He thinks I'm not managing very well. Silly of him really because I'm managing perfectly well. Of course I am. Especially now I have you back Suzie. My Suzie.'

On impulse I place my lips next to her warm cheek and kiss her. Her skin is as smooth as porcelain. So beautiful, so precious she is. And all mine.

31

Toby makes more sandwiches. The boys will eat them even if nobody else is interested. Or maybe they won't. Those poor lads have worry etched over their faces. Deep grooves of anxiety that are plain to see. He fills the kettle and wanders into the living room while it boils. Callum and Mason are out the front, watching what is going on, keeping an eye on the police and the search party, and Mike is napping. Poor Mike. He was dead on his feet and Toby had to practically force him to go to bed for a few hours.

Two nights she's been gone now. Two fucking nights and they are no further on. All they have is their suspicions and a fucking training shoe. The police have taken it for forensics but have said not to hold out any hope with the amount of rain and mud that has shifted along the river in the past few days. And they've given up on talking to the neighbours. It proved to be a waste of time and that's something they don't have a great deal of. They were all either half dead or more interested in discussing the possible closure of the nearby post office. He's glad the media haven't gotten hold of the story just yet. They always seem to give people who go missing an air of finality. He can't ever recall anyone who has ever made a miraculous reappearance after their faces were plastered all over *Sky News* or the front page of *The Daily Mail*. Media interest signifies almost certain death. They wouldn't run with the story otherwise. All the public want are the grisly ins and outs that come with the aftermath of a tragedy. He cranes his head further towards the window and peers outside. Anyway, there's hardly any passers-by through here who could have witnessed anything and the old dears locally may be harmless but they're also about as much use as a chocolate fireguard. The only one round here with any common sense worth speaking to, who isn't decrepit, is that lady over the road, the new one that's only recently moved in, and they've already spoken to her. She's even been over to help and it's quite apparent she knows nothing. He idly bites the side of his mouth. It's still niggling him where he's seen her before.

He wanders back in the kitchen and stares at the kettle. Bloody thing is taking ages. He pulls out his phone and scrolls through his messages. Too many to read and lots of work-related emails. He wonders what to do about work. At some point, he is going to have go back, let everybody know what's happening. He will wait to find out the latest updates from the police later today and decide. It's not going to be an easy decision to make given the circumstances and it will be even more difficult to break the news to Mike and the boys. Maybe he can go back for a few days to catch up on things and then come back here, make sure they're all fed and resting properly. Especially the boys. They're only twelve and thirteen and still need lots of nurturing, despite them thinking they are adults. The police have searched just about every inch of the house and questioned all of them relentlessly, sitting them down in the living room, going over the night she disappeared in minute detail. It's been exhausting and they are all dead on their feet. He wonders what else there is left to do. The thought of divers turning up soon fills him with dread. That's the concluding part. A part he isn't yet ready to think about or contemplate.

Desperate to change his train of thought, he finds himself typing in the name *Phoebe* and *Cogglestone* into the search engine on his phone. Nothing. Of course not. She's only lived here a short while. A couple of months at most. And he doesn't know her surname. God, he wishes he could place her. Things like this drive him nuts. Even under the most stressful of circumstance, his brain won't stop functioning, thoughts churning about, torturing him with hidden memories that refuse to reveal themselves.

He pours the boiling water from the kettle into the teapot, which is already full of soggy, used teabags, and puts the lid on. It's while he's searching for clean cups that it comes to him: a sudden moment of clarity that punctures his thoughts. Why does your memory do that? Hide things from your consciousness and then throw them out at you once you've turned your attention elsewhere? Dropping the cups onto the top with a clatter, he punches something into his phone. It can't be her, can it? Surely not. The facts don't add up. She has a husband, doesn't she? He waits while the website loads up, a small niggle of doubt present in his mind. He's probably barking up the wrong tree. But that day was so memorable, so bloody outrageously embarrassing, it has stuck in his mind. Because of course she made such an impact. Oh boy, did she make an impact! And then there was the dreadful accident shortly afterwards. Poor man. The article loads up and he squints to read it properly. It won't make for pretty reading anyway. He remembers all too well the details of Martyn's injuries. They were horrific. It's her face he wants to look at, to see if it's her. He drags the picture outwards using his thumb and forefinger. It enlarges and takes a couple of seconds to readjust. He narrows his eyes to stare at the blurred image in front of him. And then suddenly it clears and there she is, smiling out at him from the screen on his phone. A picture of her and Martyn taken shortly before the accident. Before she stormed into the surgery like a banshee, hollering all kinds of abuse and threats. A sickly sensation settles in the pit of his stomach. Stupid really, focusing on something as unimportant as this when his sister is still missing. He should be out there helping with the search. Something isn't right though and he won't settle until he gets it sorted in his own mind.

A noise causes him to look up. Callum is standing in front of him looking decidedly worse for wear. His hair is lank and a film of grease covers his forehead and nose. The top he is wearing looks as if it's just been dragged out from the bottom of the pile of dirty washing that is undoubtedly festering in his bedroom at this very minute. Poor kid.

'Can I ask you something, Callum?'

The boy eyes him warily. That's how it is now. They're all on edge, dancing round each other, exhausted, distressed, unable to deal with any more bad news. They're ready to snap at any given moment. He nods and flops into one of the chairs around the table.

'That lady over the road? The one opposite who lives in the big house?'

Callum nods, his skin suddenly prickling. He wonders if this is about the carry on with Sammo and AJ. Pair of daft twats, coming here and acting like they own the place. He hopes she hasn't complained. It's the last thing his dad needs right now, the last thing they all need. Because she looks like a complainer, the type who would get offended by the slightest little thing.

'Did I hear somebody say she has a husband living with her?'

The young lad relaxes. Not a complaint about his mates then. That's good. He has enough to deal with at the minute.

'Yeah, so Mum said. He's disabled, apparently.'

'And she saw him, your mum?'

Callum shrugs his shoulders and stares at his shoes, already losing interest. What has any of this got to do with his mum? 'Dunno. Why?'

'No reason. Did she say what his disabilities are?'

The young lad narrows his eyes in thought. 'An accident, I think. Yeah, that's it. He had an accident while—'

'—out walking. That's how it happened. An accident,' Toby murmurs softly, his spine suddenly stiff with unease.

Callum looks up, a vague look of recollection on his face, 'That's the one. Broke his hip and stuff. Still in a really bad way from what Mum said. Completely unable to do anything for himself. Why?'

Toby shakes his head and leans on the table for support. 'No reason. Just wondering.'

Out of nowhere, a heavy lump works its way up his throat and tears sting at his eyes. Mike isn't the only one who is exhausted. And as for considering going back to Lincoln – who is he kidding? Anna is his only remaining sister and he will do whatever it takes to help find her. That's all there is to it.

* * *

Mike is waking up as Toby enters the room and places the steaming mug of tea next to him on the bedside cabinet. Toby eyes up the bed. God, it looks inviting. He could sleep the clock round at the minute. Mike blinks and drags himself up by his elbows. He wearily runs his fingers through his hair. His shirt sticks to his stout belly and his trousers are badly creased and concertinaed where he has laid with his legs drawn up to his abdomen.

'No news?'

'No news,' Toby replies. He wonders if the police have done a sweep of the river. Is there a set routine for these things or is each case different? Every bone in his body wishes that Anna would skip through the door at any minute, flustered and apologetic at having caused such a furore. He is trying to stay positive for Mike, Callum and Mason but at some point, they are all going to have to face up to the fact that something dreadful, probably even fatal, has happened to her. The sensible medical practitioner in him tells him as much but as her brother he has to keep some hope. He would do anything – *anything* – to see her smiling face again.

Mike twists his heavy frame off the bed and sighs loudly before taking a long swig of the tea. He winces as it burns its way down his throat.

'What now, then?'

Toby bites his lip and shakes his head. 'I don't know, mate. I really, really don't know.'

They head downstairs in silence, each of them too deeply locked in their own thoughts to say anything. Mike looks around. There is an unnatural stillness in the house. Even with all the bodies that have trooped in and out all day and night for the past two days, Mike has never known the place be so quiet. No television blaring in the background, the boys not yelling or laughing, no sound of Radio 2 filtering in from the kitchen as Anna spends the day baking, preparing a sausage casserole or trying to work out why her lemon drizzle cake hasn't risen properly. Anna is the heartbeat of this house, the glue that binds them all together. And now she is gone. The words rattle around his head and catch in his throat. He turns and stares at the door, picturing her standing there, rolling her eyes at something he has said, or shouting up at the boys for them to stop stomping around, telling them that they sound like a herd of elephants up there. The image blurs his vision. He blinks and swallows hard. It's not over yet.

'That was the last we've got,' Mason says, eyeing up his dad's mug.

Mike stares at him. 'Eh?'

'We're out of coffee and teabags. I was gonna make some for everyone outside. They're parched.'

'Right, well I need to get out of here for a break. I'll nip to the shop.' Mike tries to sound positive and in control but it comes out as forced, aggressive even.

'Too late,' Mason mumbles as he stares at the clock. 'It's just about to close.'

'And Simon's gone home I take it?'

They all nod. The thought that they could knock on his door, get Freda or Alan to open up the shop, looms in his mind. He dismisses it. Simon's been a massive help. He doesn't want to bother them any more. They have a shop to run, early mornings to contend with. The last thing they need is people banging on their door when they have to be up at 4 a.m. to sort the morning papers out.

Toby shrugs his shoulders and intervenes. 'That's what neighbours are for, isn't it? Borrowing a cup of sugar and all that? Anyway, it's my fault. I used the last. Should have noticed, really.'

'I'll go.' Mason gets up, is standing behind them, his hands slung deep into his pockets. 'I could do with getting out of this place for a short while.'

Mike nods and watches as his son slopes away. He feels useless. What kind of a father is he putting his kids through something like this? A fucking pathetic one, that's what. If he were an outsider looking in, he would want to punch a dad who was as stupid as he is. Letting his wife wander off down the river on her own while he went out drinking. A fucking worthless tosser is what he is.

They are all still standing around in a daze, watching the police milling about outside, when Mason comes back holding a half-filled jar of coffee and a handful of teabags.

'Who do we have to thank for these?' Mike shuffles across and takes the jar before it slips out of Mason's grip.

'Jocelyn. She said she sends her best wishes and to call on her if we need anything else.'

Mike nods gratefully and watches as his son heads off into the kitchen. His voice echoes as he shouts through to them from behind the cupboard door. 'I called at that Phoebe's house but nobody answered. I was glad, actually. I know Mum feels sorry for her with her disabled husband and everything but she's really weird. Bit of a head case if you ask me.'

Mike frowns and scratches at his scalp. He brings his fingers down and stares at them in mild disgust. His hair is greasy and he is in desperate need of a hot shower. 'Why? What makes you say that?'

A small pulse thrums at the side of Toby's face, an insistent twitch that won't go away. He rubs his hand over his face and surreptitiously wiggles at his jaw to stop it.

'Well, he made me swear to not tell anyone, but AJ messaged me the other night and told me that when him and Sammo went in her garden a few weeks back, she threatened them with a knife. And then earlier when she was upstairs...' Mason shakes his head, exhausted and unable to formulate the correct words. Instead, he retrieves his phone and scrolls through his texts to try to find it before giving in and sticking it back in his pocket.

Mike shakes his head dismissively. 'Is this the same AJ who told everyone his grandma had won the lottery and that his dad was related to the Royal Family?'

Callum thinks of the message he deleted and frowns. He tries to say something but Toby's voice breaks the silence. 'Whitby,' he says ruminatively as he chews at one of his nails, 'they were out on a walk up the cliffs at Whitby.'

Mike stares at him and shrugs his shoulders. 'Who was?'

'Phoebe and her husband. They were up on the cliffs, walking. And he fell.'

'You know about it then?' Mason is looking at Toby quizzically.

'Oh, I know about it all right.' A fist tightens somewhere down in his stomach. He has heard about people doing this kind of thing, read about it in medical journals, but never actually encountered it. He once dealt with a patient who had Complicated Grief Disorder and couldn't function properly, but has never come across anything as extreme as this.

'How come? Is he one of your patients?' Mike has suddenly taken an interest in the conversation, not because he actually knows or cares about Phoebe or her husband but because at the minute, there is little else going on to engage him. He just needs the police to do their bit now and bloody well find Anna.

'Not a patient, no. A colleague.'

'Retired, I guess after his accident?' Mike replies, his sudden curiosity now waning. At the minute, other people's problems don't rank high on his agenda. God knows he has enough of his own going on. A retiree living in a huge house with a hefty pension doesn't need his help or his interest.

'Not retired.' Toby's face has turned a sickly shade of grey, the colour leaching out of it as he tries to tie all the loose ends together in his mind.

'Not retired, yet disabled and house bound. How does that work then?'

'Give me a minute to think this through.' Toby taps at his forehead, his fingers tracing a line above his eyes cutting through the deep groove that sits above the top of his nose. 'I just need a second to think.'

32

It shouldn't be like this, people carrying on as if everything in the village is normal when it is anything but. Freda stares out at the fading light from the corner of the window that isn't plastered with 'for sale' signs. Faded yellowing scraps of paper and plain white postcards put up asymmetrically without any thought to aesthetics or light blockage, cover the pane of glass. She sighs and wishes she could rip them all down. How many lost cats and parakeets can there be round these parts? And if she sees another shabby chic dresser or art deco sideboard for sale, she swears she might just scream. This is such an insular place. Or is it simply that everything is getting on top of her lately? This shop, the long hours, their bloody huge overdraft. Some days it all seems too much for her. And now another disappearance. And not just any person either. Anna. Lovely, quiet, gentle Anna. She swallows the lump back that sticks painfully in her gullet. Bloody government and its cutbacks. That's what it is. If they hadn't slashed the budgets for the Environment Agency then the river would have been dredged but as it is, it gets clogged with branches and sometimes even entire trees that have been uprooted in the floods and all kinds of other crap that swills about and traps anyone who slips into that stretch of the river. And then there's that ruddy useless path – well, they call it a path – more of a mudslide. The whole sodding place is a death trap.

Freda rubs at her eyes wearily and decides she has had enough for the night. She is going to lock up and without telling Alan, she is going to go and help Anna's husband and his family and whatever search party they have got going. Simon tried his best but he's just a young lad and did what he could to help out. But at the end of the day, she is the one who knows Anna. They were friends and she might just remember something that can help find her. Any bit of information will be welcome, won't it?

The setting sun emits a feeble trickle of warmth

as she flicks off the lights and locks the door. Alan will spot the fact that the place is in darkness no doubt but quite frankly, she is beyond caring. If he wants to keep the place lit up in case one measly customer decides they need a packet of toilet rolls then he can come over here and serve them himself. She has more important things to do.

* * *

The walk to the other end of the village provides Freda with some much-needed therapeutic relief. It's rare she gets chance to do the simple things lately. Even walking feels like a treat. She passes the hubbub of noise emanating from the holiday cabins – the same ones Alan had insisted would use the shop regularly, be their main source of income. Turns out the camp has its own small shop on site. And anyway, the place is frequented by yuppies who arrive already armed with their own supplies of feta cheese and hummus and clinking bottles of the sauvignon blanc they consume in huge quantities once their little darlings are safely tucked up nice and safe and warm in their John Lewis quilts. They wouldn't be seen dead venturing off the site to visit the ramshackle old shop that only sells

cheddar cheese and cheap Bulgarian wine at £3.00
a bottle.

She finds herself glad of her wellies as she hits
the path that runs through the fields that separate
one end of the village from the other. She misses
being in the centre of the village. It's good to catch up
on the odd bits of gossip, sneaky snippets that make
their way into the aisles of the shop or are exchanged
at the front counter but feels out on a limb once the
darkness sets in. Just her, Alan and Simon now he's
back at home after finishing university, and the
whoops and cackles of holidaymakers as they down
yet another crate of craft beer and cider.

By the time she manages to drag her feet out of
the squelch of the mud that once passed as the path,
the sky has a baleful look about it. A ridge of clouds
hangs ominously overhead, low and threatening, perfectly matching the sinking, dull sensation that is sitting at the pit of her stomach as she spots the
uniformed officers dipping in and out of the trees,
torches in hand as the light begins to rapidly fade.
Soon they will give up and Anna, just like Nancy, will
be no more than a face smiling out from a newspaper
or a Facebook page, set up to try and find her.

Doing her best to ignore the crowd of official-
looking bodies and the bloody huge Mountain

Rescue van that is parked by the verge of the green, Freda heads over to Anna's house – easy to spot – the one with the police in the front sliver of garden, looking bedraggled and wearing expressions that tell her all she needs to know; Anna is still missing. Dread tugs at her as she stops and tries to kick wet mud off her boots. Her heel hits the kerb, sending splashes of soft mulch over the path. A noise stops her and she looks up as a small car pulls up at the junction and stops before it swerves into the village and onto a driveway ahead, mounting the pavement with speed and screeching to a halt behind the high privet that surrounds a large house. The old barn. Not so old now it's had a ton of money poured into it. Freda feels her skin prickle. *Her.* It's her. The more she thinks about it, the more certain she is that it is definitely her. It might be nearly forty years ago but it's something that has stuck in Freda's mind for many years. Her heart patters about her chest. Alan is right, though; so what if it is her? People often end up back where they started. Some never leave in the first place. She suddenly feels overcome with exhaustion and wishes she could sit down on the pavement without appearing like an old, mad, bag lady. Casting a glance in the direction of the river, Freda shivers.

Come on Anna, show yourself. Don't be dead. Please don't be dead.

* * *

The hoard of people turn to face Freda as she attempts to head into Anna's garden. A tall officer holds his hand out to her and places his entire body in front of the gate.

'Can I help you?'

'I'm a family friend. I run the corner shop – A&F Stores? I've come to see if Mike and the boys are okay.'

The officer glances at her for longer than is necessary before nodding and stepping aside to let her in. She heads into the kitchen where she sees the two boys and Mike. Another man is there who she hasn't seen before but something about him is familiar. The set of his jaw and the shape of his eyes puts her in mind of somebody. It takes her a few seconds to realise he looks like Anna. He watches her with a certain amount of caution until Mike gives her a nod and the boys offer her a smile, then he thrusts his hand out and gives Freda's a good firm shake as Mike speaks.

'This is Freda, Simon's mother. She runs the local shop, the one Anna used to work at.'

Freda feels her face burn as if owning the corner shop is something to be ashamed of.

'Hi, I'm Toby, Anna's brother. Your son was a massive help yesterday. He gave us all the kick up the backside we needed. We were all in shock, too exhausted and muddled to think straight.'

Freda feels herself go lightheaded. Compliments, whatever form they come in, always take her by surprise and she is never sure of how to react. She nods and gives a tight smile, hoping she doesn't come across as dismissive.

'Thanks. He's a good lad.'

An awkward silence descends as they stand and stare at one another in turn. Freda feels sure the sound of her own heartbeat is audible to everyone else in the room. She takes a long breath and clears her throat. 'I take it there's no news yet?'

Mike shakes his head and she hears the older boy let out a small sigh of resignation.

'I just wanted to call in to say if there's anything at all you need...' She runs out of words, fatigue and sorrow swamping her. As if anything she will say can make it better anyway. Her words would be an insult to these people. Here she is, offering useless platitudes when her friend, their mother, wife and sister is out there somewhere. Silly to come here, really. Like her presence is going to be of any use whatsoever. She turns and stares outside, anger at this situation bubbling up inside of her. How many people will this river claim in her lifetime?

'Too many,' she mutters and feels a dart of ice travel down her spine as the words spill out of her mouth. She didn't mean for that to happen. They were out before she could stop them. A rush of heat covers her face as she sees everyone staring at her.

'I know,' says Mason, who is obviously attuned to her thoughts. 'Mum is the second one. Stupid fucking river.'

'Mind your language!' Mike roars. Toby reaches out and drapes his arm around Mason's shoulders before the reprimand escalates into something totally unnecessary. They don't have the time or energy for arguments. The boy is upset. He needs to vent his anger somehow.

'Third,' Freda says quietly and wishes she had the ability to keep her mouth shut as they all turn to stare at her. She isn't even sure why she said it. It happened such a long time ago. No point bringing it up now. Slowly, she unbuttons her coat and slips it over her shoulders, expecting to see a rush of steam at its re-

moval. She is burning up, misery and crippling embarrassment at her unintended words sending her
blood pressure soaring.

'Third?' Mike has a deep furrow etched across his
forehead. Freda wishes she were elsewhere, anywhere. Just away from this dreadful situation. Why
couldn't she just have stayed home?

'It was years ago,' she whispers as she fiddles with
the fabric of her coat. 'Sorry, I shouldn't have said
anything. Nothing to do with what's happening here.'

'How long ago?' Toby asks, his voice softer than
Mike's, who seems ready to snap at any given
moment.

'Oh, thirty odd years ago. Probably nearer forty,
actually. Too many to remember. Sorry, I've just had it
on my mind recently and it came out before I could
stop it.' Freda looks up from the unravelling fabric of
the hem to see them waiting and watching. 'It's just
with her moving back here. It brought back a lot of
memories. Then Nancy went missing and now
Anna...'

'Who has moved back here?' The groove on
Mike's forehead has deepened even further. Freda
feels sure she could fit her whole fist in there if she
really tried.

'Her over the road.' She nods behind her, the

memory of that time, that day, coming back to her in painful waves. The story that didn't fit, the holes in the timeline, the lack of sorrow at losing her sister. It was never right. Still isn't.

'Phoebe?' says one of the lads. 'Why, what's she got to do with it?'

Freda's voice starts to shake. She shouldn't be saying anything really but what did this Phoebe expect – moving back to where it all happened? She should have known somebody would recognise her, that her presence would stir up a whole load of bad memories. It was bound to happen.

'Rumour had it that she was behind it all. Course nobody could prove anything. Forensics and stuff wasn't what it is now.' Freda sighs as she looks around for a seat. She suddenly feels quite wobbly.

Toby watches this strange little woman, hears her words and feels a stone sink somewhere deep in his abdomen. He drags a chair out and lets her slump into it, then listens as she tells her tale.

33

Tom is standing under the porch when I pull on the drive. Bloody tractors and bloody stupid traffic. I got stuck on the A1(M) after a lorry collided with a car. Then ended up sitting behind some kind of farm vehicle on the narrow, winding country lanes all the way here, unable to see around it to overtake and now I'm late. I loathe being late.

'Sorry,' I gasp as I struggle to get out of the car, my arms caught up in the seatbelt, 'got stuck in traffic.' I pray he doesn't ask where I've been as I don't have an answer at the ready. Fortunately, he doesn't and instead holds out his hands to me.

'What's going on over there?' he asks, nodding towards the crowd of police and people milling about over the road.

'What?' I say glibly, 'Oh, that. Some walker has gone missing apparently. I'm sure they'll turn up. They always do, don't they?'

He shakes his head and sighs loudly. 'Looks like they're searching that path down there.' He points behind my house and I feel a shiver of trepidation run up my spine.

'Well, that's the route most of them take,' I reply quickly. 'Anyway, the bedrooms are all made up. You can take your pick,' I say as he envelops me in his big, strong arms. I had forgotten how tall he is and it does feel good to be embraced. Fighting back the tears, I move away from him and unlock the door, swinging it open to let him in.

He drops his bag in the hallway and looks around. 'Sorry Mum. I'm flying back tonight so it's only a brief visit I'm afraid.'

I stare at him, not knowing whether to feel aghast or elated. 'They don't come much briefer,' I say as I stare up at his handsome face. He has been likened to many good-looking superstars, the usual one being Robert Downey Jr. Many mothers would be proud of such a thing but it doesn't bother me one iota. To me, he is my Tom. Personally, I think he looks just like his father. Or at least a younger version of Martyn. I can understand why he has proved to be so popular with his American colleagues. Tall, charming and good looking.

I stand in the stillness of the room and look around at the bare walls of my home; they are in stark contrast to his warm smile and his charismatic and happy demeanour. Sterile, plain, unwelcoming. Is it any wonder he doesn't want to come back?

'Are you flying from London?' I try to work out the travelling time and feel my stomach knot in apprehension. So little time together.

'Leeds Bradford,' he says smiling, already knowing what's going through my head.

'I'll give you a lift to the airport then. It's only an hour or so's drive away so...'

'Already sorted,' he says cutting in quickly. 'I've booked another taxi from here in precisely two hours.'

'Two hours?' I half shriek. 'That's no time at all and it'll cost you an absolute fortune, Tom!'

He shrugs, unperturbed by my outburst. 'Less than an hour and a half from here. Anyway, I've already paid in advance. Or at least the company has.'

I sigh and scurry through to the living room. He follows me and sits down on the large, leather couch, his legs spread out in front of him. I look at his clothes and shoes – very expensive looking – and with his tan, he does actually look every inch the movie star, not an IT consultant or engineer or whatever it is he does over there on the other side of the ocean. He is obviously doing very well for himself. I tell myself I should be pleased for him. Most mothers would be. But then again, I am not most mothers.

'So how are you doing, Mum?' His eyes bore into me, watching my every move, scrutinising every syllable that comes out of my mouth. I know exactly what his little game is.

'I'm fine, darling. Absolutely fine. Do you like the new house? Isn't that why you came? To have a good look around?' I stand up and push an imaginary lock of hair behind my ears. 'I can show you upstairs if you like?' I stop, aware I am babbling. Tom doesn't get up to follow me. He stays put, his body now rigid.

'Mum, sit down. We need to talk.'

His words send a wave of fear through me. I balance on the edge of the chair, my back ramrod straight, dread tugging at my innards.

'What's going on, Mum? That conversation on the phone yesterday – you made me really worried. You weren't making any sense.'

I am lost for words. I shrug my shoulders and

look down at my hands, willing something to come. I say nothing. The words I want to say remain stubbornly elusive, locked away in the deepest, darkest corners of my brain.

'Have you been remembering to take your medication?'

I stare at him, trying to make sense of what he is saying. His eyes grow dim, haunted, searching mine for answers I cannot give.

'Oh for God's sake, Mother. Have you even bothered to register with a new doctor here?'

I stay silent again, too wary to speak. What exactly is it he wants me to say?

'Okay, well while I'm here, why don't we look up your nearest surgery and get you registered? It won't take too long.'.'

I widen my eyes and start to speak but he puts his hand up to silence me.

'Mum, you need the help. I'm not here to nag you but I am worried about you. Please say you'll do it? Go along with them, yes? And be nice!' He wags his finger playfully but we both know the real meaning behind his words.

I nod mutely. Looks like I have no choice.

'Have you thought about getting out more? What about volunteering somewhere? Lots of National

Trust places are crying out for—'

I almost choke at his words. 'Volunteering? Why on earth would I want to be a volunteer?'

'You're acting as if it's something to be ashamed of and it isn't.' He is almost shouting now, his tone accusatory and sharp. 'I just thought it would get you out of the house. I thought you might be bored with not working.'

And there it is. The unspoken has been voiced out loud. My job. Or rather the fact that I left it. I know what he thinks. That it was my fault. It wasn't. Of course it wasn't. I had gone into teaching when Tom started secondary school, taking my PGCE when he was eleven years old, and I loved it. The workload was immense, sitting night after night marking and planning, but I still enjoyed it. It was my haven. It gave me something to focus on. Until the matter of Tara came along. Lovely, sweet, neglected Tara with her golden curls and pale skin, she was every inch the perfect child. Pity her parents didn't feel the same way about her. I took her under my wing after noticing how thin she was becoming, how sad and forlorn she looked. There were bruises too. On her arms and legs and the odd one on her face. I passed my concerns on to our Child Protection Officer who carried out her own enquiries and called on

Social Services. They did a home visit and assured me that Tara came from a caring, stable family and that she was being looked after properly. That was nonsense. I knew that was most certainly not the case at all. I was with her five days a week, saw her distress first hand and I refused to believe she was anything but okay. So I started bringing her small gifts to cheer her up. Nothing too fancy. Bars of chocolate, little plastic toys, anything I could find that would bring a smile to her face. And it worked. She became animated, enthusiastic about her schoolwork, relaxed in class, a happier child all round. Her world became a damn sight brighter because of me. But then one day, her parents took exception to my 'special interest' in their daughter and complained to Andrew Melberg, the head teacher, who asked that I stop buying her things. I refused, asked him to provide me with evidence that I was doing any harm. He remained calm, composed, but bandied the word 'grooming' around in the hope of scaring me. Gave me veiled threats. So I backed off. For a while anyway.

It was a crisp, snowy day the last time I saw Tara. All the children were out in the playground, sliding around, shrieking with excitement at the powdery white stuff that was falling from the sky and covering everything in sight. It had been quite a few years since we'd had any snow and their excitement was at an all-time high. I was drinking my coffee in the classroom, watching her from a distance, making sure she came to no harm, when it happened. A gang of older children were parading around, cruising the playground, looking for victims. I saw them approach her and shove snow down her back. The teacher on duty didn't see it. But I did. I saw it all. They watched, this gang of bullies, as she squirmed about, trying to empty it out of her clothes. And then came the push. I watched horrified, as one of them roughly nudged her to the floor and shoved snow in her face. Incensed, I dropped everything and raced outside where I grabbed the offender and hauled him inside, refusing to listen to his cries of defence that it was just a game. His screams alerted the staff in the class next door as I let go of his arm and threw him to the floor in disgust.

His parents didn't press charges and Andrew and I came to a mutual agreement that I would take some time off on unpaid leave. I handed my notice in the following day, only too glad to see the back of the place. But of course there was Tara to think about. I missed her terribly and thought about her all the time. So I wrote her letters and sent them to the school in the hope they would be passed onto her but

I got nothing back in return. I doubt she even received them. Her parents and Andrew will have made sure of that.

I spent the following few years drifting in and out of part time jobs in retail, as a receptionist, at the local library, but none of them lasted. It wasn't as if we needed the money anyway. So I ended up staying at home. Nothing wrong with that, is there? Lots of people do it. And now my own son is making it sound like I've committed some awful crime by being a 'housewife.'

Tom is staring at me, putting me under pressure, forcing me to agree to his ridiculous plan.

'I'll give it some thought,' I say quietly. Easier to acquiesce. Or at least give him the impression that I am.

He smiles and claps his hands together lightly. 'Right, let's get some lunch, shall we? While you're preparing it, I'll find out the name of the local surgery and give them a call. Have you got any of that posh cheese you used to buy? I'm starving.'

* * *

His taxi arrives early and I can tell by the look on his face, he is only too relieved to be leaving. This isn't where he belongs any more. I can see that now. And although it upsets me that he lives so far away, I can spend the rest of my life wishing things had turned out differently or I can accept the way things are now and make the best of it. I opt for the latter. After all, I have Suzie now, don't I? I'll drive back and see her soon. I straighten my shoulders, suddenly buoyed up by the thought.

'Don't forget everything we spoke about, Mum,' Tom is saying as he throws his bag in the back of the taxi and gives me a quick hug. 'I'll call you when I get back and I'll also set up the doctor's visit.'

I smile and give him a wave as the taxi crunches its way out of the drive and out onto the lane. Then as soon as I see them disappear out of sight, I grab some essentials, my car keys and close the door with a slam.

34

Suzie is awake when I get there. Her appearance perturbs me. She seems flaccid and her complexion is pasty. I touch her forehead. Her temperature is normal. No fever, no clammy skin. Perhaps this is a good time to explain to her what's going on, while she is less likely to resist. I grasp the opportunity and squat down next to her, placing my hand on her arm tenderly. I'm genuinely upset to see that she flinches and tries to pull away. That hurts. After all I've done for her as well. I keep my voice soft as I speak. I need to win her round, to make her see that this is all for the best.

'Okay, you've probably realised that you've been moved. Don't worry, it's warm and comfortable in here but you see I had no choice. My son was visiting and we needed to talk. Also there's the matter of what you did upstairs, isn't there? We haven't had chance to discuss that yet, have we? Knocking my container over and seeing what was in there. Those papers were private and now... well, now you know all there is to know and now we're stuck together whether you like it or not.'

I wag my finger at her playfully and purse my lips. 'So anyway, this is where you're going to stay now. It's a lovely place actually and once you get used to it, I'm almost certain you won't want to leave.' I smile and shrug my shoulders, trying to appear nonchalant. 'Not that I would let you even if you wanted to. After all,' I whisper as I lean closer into her face, 'we're sisters and sisters are meant to be together, aren't they?'

She remains unresponsive, her eyes glassy as she stares at me. I'm almost certain she can hear me. She is just being typically stubborn.

'Okay,' I say as I stand up, my knees cracking as I do so, 'have it your way. But in time, you'll come round to my way of thinking.' I look around the room and sigh. 'After all, you don't really have any other choice, do you?'

* * *

The sun is setting over the hills as I round the bend back into the village. Suzie is fed and toileted. She will be fine till the morning now. Keeping her there is the obvious thing to do. Tom did me a favour calling unexpectedly. Sometimes the hand of fate is a welcome one. And there's still a fair amount of activity in the village. Better safe than sorry. I just wish they knew that they are all wasting their time, that she is safe with me. Not with me here, but at least she is safe and fed and warm and not dead in the river. Actually, it's probably easier to let them think that. They will give up looking for her pretty soon and wait for the current to wash her up somewhere downstream. I smile, feeling slightly smug about the whole affair. They will have a long wait.

Martyn is still in his study when I get back inside. He is reading, keeping his distance from me. He doesn't question where I've been, which is just as well. I would find it hard to explain it to him. I'm just starting to get my own head around it all. It is a complex issue and not one I am able to unpick and analyse so easily. I just know that it is what it is, and sometimes that is all the explanation that is needed.

I kick my shoes off and flop into an armchair in the living room, overcome with a sudden bout of exhaustion. I mustn't fall asleep. I still have so much to do. Clothes and toiletries to pack. She can't stay in those ragged, grimy trousers indefinitely. And at some point, she is going to need a bath. I lean my head back and let it rest on the back of the chair, mentally counting off the tasks I have to do for Suzie.

Sleep comes quickly, deep and sound full of dreams about water, raging streams pulling people under, swirling riptides and frothing currents that drag everyone away. The continual ringing of the phone wakes me, snapping me out of my deep slumber. I stagger up onto my feet to get it but it stops before I get there. My mind is foggy. Tom. Will he back in New York yet? Or still at the airport? I have no idea of what time it is or how long I've slept for. Furious at having missed his call, I march through to the study to see Martyn. He has his nose stuck into some medical journal or other and ignores me as I stand at the door, anger scratching at me.

'Didn't you hear the phone ringing? Christ, you could have answered it!'

He lowers the book and smiles at me, then shrugs his shoulders and places the book down with a thump, the noise causing me to flinch. A searing pain runs up the back of my scalp and sits behind my eyes, throbbing, insistent.

'I can't answer it, Phoebe. You know I can't.'

'Why on earth not?' I screech, furious at his lack-adaisical attitude. Do I have to do everything round here? I am utterly exhausted by it all.

'You know why not,' he replies. The look on his face scares me. Not sarcasm, not happiness, more a look of helplessness and resignation. I purse my lips and turn away. His voice echoes around the hushed stillness of the house.

'Look at me Phoebe. Just look at me!'

Something in his voice sets my nerves jangling. Not anger. He isn't in one of his raging tempers. He is insistent, despondent. His voiced laced with hope-lessness. I spin back around and stare at him. He looks different, his face lined, his features pinched and shrunken. He stands up and all of a sudden, he has the appearance of somebody much older. A hor-ribly troubled and decrepit old man. One of his shoulders is hanging to one side and his legs wobble about under him as he shuffles out from behind his large, mahogany desk. His skin is colourless and mot-tled and as he begins to walk toward me I can see a trail of something on the floor at his feet. It follows him through the room and as I step closer, I am horri-fied to see a long line of blood seeping out from somewhere on his body, dark and viscous, a huge oil slick pooling at his feet. I want to scream but nothing will come. Has he done it again? Hurt somebody and they are here in the house? Hidden somewhere, dying or dead as we speak? Or are they outside in the dark being dragged away by the intense swell of the river? A huge wall of freezing water lapping over them, pulling them downstream. Something tells me that isn't the case. And I know it isn't Anna's blood. I cleaned that up thoroughly, mopping and sterilising until I could see my face in every inch of floor space. The vice around my head tightens as I try to work out what is going on. And then Martyn turns and I see it: the huge hole at the back of his head from which blood is pulsing in gigantic, rhythmic waves. A deep, cavernous split that runs across the base of his skull and up over the top of his head.

I stagger backwards, struggling to think straight. I am unable to do anything. Words refuse to come as my throat thickens and begins to close up. I slump to the floor, overcome with horror and confusion. When I look up, he is standing over me – Martyn, my Martyn – a shadow of his former self, his leaning body crooked and lifeless, a river of scarlet escaping from the deep hole in his head. Vomit rises and spills out of me. I lift my head and stare at the figure in front of me, the Martyn I no longer recognise. All I can hear are his words clanging and reverberating in my head as everything tilts and blurs. The room spins as he bends down and leans over me, a trail of blood-stained saliva dripping from his mouth as he hollers in my face, 'This is your fault, Phoebe. It's about time you accepted that. Everything that's happened is all because of you!'

35

Apart from one tiny lamp in the corner that is emitting just enough light to allow Anna to make out vague shapes and outlines, she is blanketed in darkness. Somebody's front room. That's where she is. In a stranger's living room. In what street or town is a complete mystery to her. There is no sound. She is pretty sure she is alone but can't be absolutely certain. She has to be careful here. The last thing she wants is for Phoebe to descend on her and pump her full of more drugs.

Despite feeling cold and shivery, her skin is coated with a clammy sheen and the pain in her head hasn't eased up. In fact, it's worse. It feels as if a bullet has ripped through it. The searing pain runs around the back of her neck and up behind her eyes, making her feel woozy and nauseous. She tries to sit up, the throbbing sensation heightening and increasing in force with every movement she takes. Bit by bit, using her hands to rest on, she manages to shuffle herself into a partial upright position and leans back, small clouds of heat puffing out of her nostrils, warming up the air in front of her face. Her cheeks burn as she inhales deeply in an attempt to get more oxygen into her lungs. She stops and listens for any kind of movement nearby. Nothing. No footsteps or creaking floorboards. Just complete silence. She prays she is alone. Dear God, please let her be alone here. The thought of Phoebe making a sudden appearance with her manic expression and psychotic behaviour makes her feel sick.

She blinks and tries to regulate her breathing. Panicking will only exacerbate things. She must stay calm. Saliva builds in her mouth and she has to swallow it back, the tape too tight to allow her to move her lips even the slightest inch. The lower half of her face is starting to turn numb and the top half is in agony. Every time she tries to shuffle her way into another position, the pain behind her eyes intensifies and the rope tying her hands together has rubbed away the thin skin around her wrists, leaving her with weeping sores and blisters. A lump rises in her throat. It sits there, immobile until she squeezes her eyes shut and forces it back down. She will not cry. Under no circumstances will she allow herself to cry. What she needs to do right now is think clearly and gather what little strength she has left to get out of this place and away from the clutches of Phoebe, a woman so unhinged, it is utterly terrifying. How did Anna not see what was right in front of her eyes all along? It's all so clear now. Phoebe's whole life is one huge fabrication. The woman is psychotic. Completely delusional. It makes perfect sense now: ushering Anna out of the house when offering help and asking to see him, claiming he was napping whenever she was in the house. Nobody saw or heard him because he doesn't exist; he's just a figment of her imagination.

Anna emits a low, desperate groan. How could she have been so blind? And worst of all, how could she have been so pathetically naïve? Seeing the newspaper clippings that had fallen out of the wooden box had been like a physical blow. How anybody could lie about such a dreadful thing is beyond her. And more importantly, why would they? That poor man had multiple injuries and stood no chance of surviving. According to the article, he fell over the edge of the cliff and bounced hundreds of feet, almost to the bottom, hitting every boulder and crag on the way down.

There was another cutting about a woman. A missing person. Just like she is now. Anna has no idea who the woman is. Or was. She swallows back a mouthful of vomit. The word 'was' is probably more fitting.

And then the final one, barely legible, tattered and browned with age, about a child drowning in the river and some possible suspicious circumstances surrounding her death. The stuff of nightmares. And as Phoebe said, now Anna knows her secret, she will go to any lengths to make sure she never returns home to tell anybody. Well, that is not going to happen. Not while she has an ounce of strength left in her body. She will fight that horrific woman till the very end if she has to, but come what may, Anna *will* get back home. God knows what Mike and the boys think has happened to her. Her mind races, trying to envisage every possible scenario. Are they racing around, looking for her? Do they think she's dead and are dredging the river at this very minute?

She stops herself. Second guessing is a pointless way to spend her time, which is without doubt at the moment, very precious indeed. Phoebe will be back.

She has no idea when but she will be back. How long has she kept her captive? Anna tries to count it up. Three days? Four? Her family will be in complete meltdown. She is a monster, this Phoebe: unpredictable, deranged. And she could walk in the door at any minute. Anna has to act quickly.

With limited strength, a raging thirst and a head that feels like a grenade exploded in there, she begins to rock. She tilts herself backwards and forwards over and over until she eventually gives a colossal push and manages to stand upright, her hands and ankles still tightly bound. The room swims and her stomach heaves as she staggers to keep her balance. She stops for a minute to right herself and looks around. Still no sound or movement from anywhere in the house. What now?

The vague shapes begin to take on sharper edges as Anna hobbles over to a doorway. She feels her way through it and into another room. Long and dark. A hallway? She trips on a rug which bunches up under her feet and finds herself catapulted forward into the side of a tall cabinet. She hits it with her shoulder, which sends her bouncing back over, but somehow she manages to stay upright. Anna stops for a minute, waiting for the sickness, which is rising in her gut, to abate. After a minute, she staggers on, moving backwards, sidled up against the wall and feeling her way with her fingers behind her back to help keep her upright until she enters a larger room. She drags herself along the wall and immediately recognises the hard, angular edges. A kitchen. She is definitely in a kitchen. Her fingers trace their way over a series of wooden doors, over the long, chrome handles and finally, up to a set of drawers. Shadows gradually take form and in a limited fashion, Anna begins to see her way around.

Opening each drawer with her hands tied behind her back is easier than she anticipated but being able to see the contents of each one proves way more difficult. With a growing rage, she hops around, dragging them open, bending and twisting her body until each top drawer is jutting out, their contents too grainy to discern in the poor light. Except for one.

Anna's heart gallops around her chest. Coiling her way over to it like an upright snake, she peers down at an array of cutlery that gives off a tiny glint, the silver reflected in the smallest sliver of light peeking in from a gap in the blinds. Mismatching teaspoons and forks, butter knives, small scissors. Too tiny to be of any real use. And then something else. *Bingo*. A knife. She has no idea how this is going to work, but it is. She will make it work. She has to. It's her only option. If she stays here and does nothing, she is without a doubt a dead woman.

She inches her way closer to the drawer. Turning sideways on, she lifts her arms and manoeuvres her hands then gently traces them over the blade of a large silver serrated knife, its thin, jagged edges scaring her as she contemplates its capabilities. That blade could either be her key to freedom, or with one wrong movement, her demise. Her wrists ache as she tries to pick it up and with limited dexterity, twist it round to cut at the rope. Even after a few attempts, Anna can see it is a waste of energy. The whole thing is physically impossible. She leans back against the kitchen counter to think, the knife still precariously balanced between her fingers. Slumping down, Anna sits on the floor, her brain ticking over with ideas, many ridiculous and unfeasible, some possible but difficult to execute. Her head thumps, a sickly sensation ever present deep down in her stomach. One idea, however, sticks in her mind, probably the only one that has a chance of working.

Resting the knife beside her on the tiles, she brings her knees up to her chin and bit by bit, forces her bound hands under her bottom. Her knuckles graze against the stone flooring and her shoulders feel as if they are about to pop out of their sockets.

She stops every few seconds to catch her breath, then very slowly, shuffles about, her slim hips gradually working their way through the narrow gap, her arms lodged painfully under her bottom. Her breath is ragged. A hot and sour taste floods her mouth. She swallows to stem the retch that she feels rising in her belly. She cannot allow herself to be sick. The pounding in her head increases while she waits for the feeling to pass. She mustn't stop for too long. She has a fear that she won't be able to muster up the energy to finish this task if she stops for too long. She has to keep the adrenalin flowing, no matter what. A vision of an egg-timer flashes in her head, her energy the grains of sand slowly disappearing, leaving her body until she is completely empty. A vacant vessel with nothing left to give. She has to keep going, pain or no pain, sickness or no sickness.

With one last mighty effort and a loud grunt, Anna loops her hands round her backside in a swift movement and up behind her knees. She stops, her nostrils flaring, her eyes wide as she pants for breath before rolling on her back and squirming about to try to hook her feet through her hands. It's exhausting and difficult and so very, very painful. But not impossible. There is no way she has come this far to give in. Both her hands and feet are tied too tight to wriggle one through the other, but there has to be a way. The knife sits next to her, tempting her with its possibilities. She moves her bottom over to where the knife lay and scrapes her knuckles over the cold, hard floor to pick it up. Holding the handle as tightly as she can, Anna brings her feet up and begins to hack at the twine binding her ankles. She is surprised by how soft it is, its texture more woollen than the coarse fibres of rope she expected to feel. Her hands are slippery and she has to stop every few seconds to keep her fingers clasped around the handle, which keeps wobbling about and sliding out of her grip. Developing a rhythm, Anna saws slowly, dragging her feet backwards and forwards until she feels a soft but definite *ping* beneath her palms as the threads of the rope begin to snap and break. She keeps going, her body now attuned to the delicate feeling each strand makes as it collapses beneath the sharp edge of the blade, until eventually, she feels a sensation that brings tears to her eyes. With a final snap, her legs fall apart, her ankles free of the constraints that have held her prisoner for days.

Gasping with exhilaration and exhaustion, Anna puts the knife down and turns it around so the handle is facing away from her. She leans forward, holding the handle from underneath. It's awkward and possibly dangerous but she is determined to try it. She brings her knees up and rests her elbows on each one to take the weight of her arms and starts the process all over again. With a precision and strength she wasn't aware she possessed, Anna saws, slowly and deliberately, occasionally slipping and cutting the soft skin under her forearms before retrieving the knife and starting all over again. Blood trickles down her arms and over her fingers, greasy and warm. She won't allow it to stop her. What are a few cuts compared with what may lay in store if she doesn't get out of here? Imbued with a sudden burst of energy, Anna clasps the knife tighter and hacks away until she feels the wonderful sensation of material slackening and giving way under the unrelenting friction of the blade as she draws it over the twine time and time again, fibres ripping free and snapping, the feeling so beautiful, she cries. Hot tears roll down her face and drip onto her blood-smeared hands. One last thread to go and she has done it. She drops the knife and pushes her hands apart, until the rope finally rips and her hands spring free. Snot and tears mix as she scrambles up off the floor, sliding around wildly, her ankles numb from being held together for so long. She is overwhelmed with dizziness and euphoria but can't stop to celebrate. Not enough time to stop.

Holding herself steady, Anna brings her hand up to the tape on her mouth and pinches the corner before ripping it back and letting out an almighty howl. She gingerly brings her shaking hand up to her lips, expecting to feel loose flaps of skin after tearing half of her mouth away. Everything feels intact. Hot and wet with blood, but still there.

Staggering over to a wall, Anna feels her way along it until a familiar feeling of plastic comes under her groping fingers. She presses down as firmly as she can and a light comes on overhead. Blinking and squinting against its harsh glare, Anna gives herself a few seconds, then looks around. She is standing at the entrance of a large kitchen that is all but empty. She can see now that the drawers she pulled open contain the bare minimum. Some tea-towels, a few utensils and a couple of yellow dusters. Anna hangs onto the edge of one of the drawers, still lightheaded and nauseous. Suddenly terrified of being seen, she switches the light back off. She cannot risk being caught, not after coming so far. And she can't allow herself any time to hang around. She has got to get out of this place as quickly as possible. She has no idea where Phoebe is. For all she knows, she could be upstairs, in the garage, anywhere nearby, ready to pounce. Blackout blinds cover every window and she finds herself praying that she isn't locked in a remote farmhouse in the back end of beyond, otherwise her Houdini escape act will have been in vain.

Teetering through the house, Anna heads towards the front door. It's locked. Of course it's locked. What did she expect? Her deeply unstable neighbour has been nothing if not precise. Anna rattles at the handle in anger and lets out a frustrated growl, her lips cracking as she does so. Turning on her heel, she stalks from room to room looking for another way out. The house is large and sparsely furnished with no obvious means of escape. Anna tries the back door but isn't surprised to find that locked too. She hunts around for anything remotely resembling a key box but in a house so empty, it quickly becomes obvious that she is well and truly locked in. A prisoner in somebody else's home.

The need to get out swells in her chest and without warning, the walls begin to close in. She feels herself starting to hyperventilate and squeezes her eyes shut to try to control her breathing. Opening them again, she can see that all of the windows are double glazed and she knows breaking them won't be easy. But it's worth a try. It may well be her only way out of here. Anna pulls up the blinds and stares at the top opening windows. She surveys the thickness of the glass, wondering if a chair would be enough to take out the entire pane cleanly or if it would simply bounce back, aggravating her growing sense of claustrophobia. Her eyes sweep over the glass and stop. She blinks and stares hard. She narrows her eyes, wanting to be sure she actually saw it and isn't hallucinating. Her heart speeds up and a rush of adrenalin heats up her freezing skin. It's there. It is actually there. Not a hallucination from the drugs. It is definitely there. She pictures Phoebe's stern face and smiles. Not so careful after all. A small key is sticking out of one of the window locks, tiny and gleaming and very possibly the most alluring thing she has ever seen. She reaches up and carefully pulls at it. It slides out with ease and she wraps her fingers around the tiny metal object, holding it tightly in her hand. It is cold smooth and sits perfectly in the creases of her palm. The key to freedom.

Anna breaks into something resembling a run as she moves from room to room looking for a window that is large enough for her to fit through. She stumbles into the dining room. Two large bay windows with openings far too small for anyone to fit through. No use at all. Upstairs is too far to fall. There's no use even looking there. Room after room proves fruitless. Each and every window is too small. Except for one.

With her breath coming out in rapid, hot blasts and a shaking hand, Anna slips the key into the lock of the perfectly person-sized kitchen window, the room where she managed to hack herself free. The key turns in the lock with a liquid rotation and in one short leap, Anna hauls herself onto the kitchen counter and scrambles out of the open window, gulping in great deep breaths of clean air as she lands in a crumpled heap on a patch of wet grass, a shriek of exhilaration caught in her throat. She lies for a short while, taking in the sounds around her, trying to work out her surroundings. In the distance, she can hear the low drone of car tyres on tarmac. One after another after another. Her pulse quickens. She wants to scream that she is free, to jump up and down and holler and cry, to clap her hands and dance around the garden in the darkness. Instead, she keeps completely still and stares up at the deep blue sky, counting the myriad stars that glitter like diamonds dipped in ink, a sight so beautiful, so breath-taking, it mists her vision. And that's when she hears it. The squeak of a door opening back inside the house, and the clump of footsteps as they make their way across the wooden flooring, accompanied by a low mutter that slowly augments into a fierce screech. It doesn't take long for the noise to register. Anna stills her breathing and with burning limbs and a pounding head, she crawls up onto her knees to listen. Phoebe. It is her neighbour. She has come back. And she is furious. Unhinged and on the hunt for Anna and absolutely bloody furious.

36

'Right, so from what you've told me about Mrs Whitegate, I'm not sure we could count any of this information as evidence.'

The policeman looks at Freda then at Toby, waiting for some sort of response. They are both silent, unsure what to say next.

'I mean I can see that she has mental health issues and had,' he clears his throat before continuing, 'shall we say, a troubled childhood?' The officer taps his pencil on his notepad, a sound that is beginning to grate on Toby. 'But that doesn't make her a suspect.'

Toby shuffles his feet awkwardly and looks at

Freda for inspiration. She lowers her gaze and shakes her head.

'Our current priority is the river path as that was the route Anna took,' the officer states with a certain amount of authority.

'And the river,' Callum adds flatly.

'And the river,' the policeman repeats quietly.

Toby takes in his features, notices his pale skin, the slight tremor in his fingers as he wrote down everything they told him about Phoebe. He is barely more than a teenager. What can he possibly know about people and the inner machinations of a disturbed mind?

'Right, well thank you for listening and taking on board our concerns,' Toby says in his best professional tone. 'We're all getting pretty desperate here as you can probably imagine.'

The young officer nods his head sympathetically and slips the notepad into his top pocket. 'Well, rest assured, we're doing all we can to find her. I'll pass this new information on to my superiors and see what they think.' He straightens up his jacket and heads back outside.

'Waste of time,' Toby mutters. Freda raises her eyebrows in exasperation and turns to look at Mike, who looks exhausted.

'I just saw her leave,' Mason says idly, his voice a whisper in the heavy silence of the room.

'Saw who leave?' Toby asks.

'That Phoebe woman. The one you were just talking about. I was out the front and saw her car pull off the drive.'

'Right. So what?' Toby asks, feeling his pulse quicken. He knows exactly what Mason is getting at but isn't sure how they can do it with so many police officers hanging about.

'Nothing,' Mason shrugs, feeling stung by his uncle's response. He thought Toby had more about him than to let some useless police officer walk all over him.

Toby stretches and rubs at face wearily. 'Right, I'm off out for a bit of a walk. I need some fresh air.'

Freda picks up her jacket and leans forward to hug Mike. 'I'd better be off as well. You know where we are if you need anything.'

Toby and Freda leave the house together, their intentions subliminally clear to one another.

'Wait up!' Mason is at their side as they head over the road towards Phoebe's house.

Toby glances back, relieved that the police haven't noticed their exit. 'You should get back home, laddo. We're about to carry out our own investigation.'

'I know,' he answers quickly, shoving his hands deep in his pockets. 'That's why I'm here.'

Toby stops and faces his nephew, his face made of stone. 'This is between us three, yes?'

The boy nods and they all disappear behind the high hedge that surrounds Phoebe's house.

* * *

'There's no way in,' Mason gasps as he peers through the rear window, 'and the police keep coming along the path. We're gonna be seen if we're not careful.'

'So what?' Toby is fast losing faith in the police and their investigation. His sister is missing and the new neighbour over the road is mentally unbalanced. If they can't connect the dots then he will do it for them.

'Keep looking,' he whispers, 'there has to be some way of getting in. Even the most secure of places have their weak points.'

'And I think I may have just found it,' Freda croons, a small smile starting to spread over her face.

Toby looks to see Freda huddled next to a small window in what appears to be a utility room next to the kitchen. She looks over in his direction and spreads her outstretched palm over the glass. 'Single pane,' she mouths and before he can say or do anything, she uses her elbow as a battering ram and knocks the glass clean out of its frame.

'Rotten and about to fall out anyway,' she whispers as if to justify her actions.

'What now?' Mason hisses, his face devoid of any colour. This is breaking and entering. He thought they would just come and have a nose around, find an open window or something, not smash their way in to somebody else's house. Especially with the police so close by. He feels his heart begin to claw its way up his chest.

'We get inside as fast as we can,' Toby says and before Mason can reply, his uncle hoists himself up onto the wooden windowsill and half clambers, half throws himself through the small space, landing with a clatter on the other side. He watches as Freda, who is surprisingly nimble, does the same. Feeling his throat constrict, Mason begins to back off.

'I'll stay here and keep watch,' Mason says as he feels Toby's eyes on him. Freda and Toby look at one another conspiratorially and nod before moving off into the rest of the house. Mason listens to the sound of their footsteps as they disappear out of sight. He wants to tell them to keep quiet, that they run the risk of being caught, but is unable to find his voice so instead stands mute, fear rooting him to the spot.

'Nothing here,' Freda murmurs as they tread through the huge living room.

'You're right there,' Toby replies as he looks around at the bare, magnolia walls.

'What's in here?' Freda has made her way along the long hallway to a small room that contains one large, mahogany desk.

'Well, I presume it's some kind of study but by the looks of things, she's forgotten to put the rest of the furniture in. Where are all the pictures and books, for God's sake?' Toby visualises his own study, crammed full of journals and hardbacks and paperbacks and general detritus he has gathered over the years. This place is positively clinical.

Toby starts to think this is a pointless exercise when he hears Freda's footsteps thundering upstairs. There is a short silence as he backs out of the study and closes the door behind him. Suddenly, Freda's voice breaks through the quiet, turning his blood cold.

'Up here, Toby!'

He takes the stairs two at a time, genuinely horrified at what he might find when he gets there. Freda is bent over something in the main bedroom at the top of the stairs, her backside swaying as she moves forward to grab a piece of yellowed paper which she brandishes at him, her face flushed with success.

'We've got her, Toby! We've bloody well got her!'

37

I had to leave. It was all too painful for me. Too much to take in. The sight of him. I had to get out, get away from it all, get back to Suzie. My Suzie. You see, I have some wrongs that I need to put right after that day down by the river. A lot to make up for. So I ran, leaving it all behind me and took off in the car, thinking that the faster I drive, the further away I will be.

I take a bend too sharply and hear the blast of a horn from an oncoming vehicle as I swerve back into my own lane, its headlights dazzling me in the gloom of the car. My hands slip on the steering wheel, damp with misery and fear. I rub at my eyes which are sore from crying, and place my hands back on the wheel, gripping it tightly, my knuckles taut with the strain. Tillie scampers about in her cage as it slides from side to side in the back of the car. I had to bring her with me. Leaving her there with him was unthinkable. She's all I have left. Apart from Suzie, obviously. I sniff and a warm glow rises in my chest at the thought of her back at the house, waiting for me.

By my feet I have a flask of juice and some fruit. Not much but better than nothing. Suzie will be starving and ready for a drink. Perhaps I can even untie her hands and allow her more mobility. I'm sure she will appreciate that. I don't want her to hate me. I really don't. The thought of losing her love and trust fills me with dread. It would unhinge me completely. I did what I did because there was no other way. She knows that. Deep down, I'm sure she understands it all, and probably always has.

I turn on the radio to while away the time as I drive. It is full of gravelly voiced whispering presenters working the graveyard shift, reading out inane emails from bored loners who make requests for a stream of morose music. Music for dead people. I turn it off and tap out a light rhythm on the steering wheel, feeling myself loosen up with each consecutive beat. When I get there, I will put some soft music on and Suzie and I can eat together. We can reminisce about the past and then plan for the future. I think about what clothes I can put her in and how stunning she will look when she is clean and fed. It will all work out perfectly. I'll make sure of it.

I turn the corner to the road and slowly pull up on the drive, now energised at the thought of seeing her again. It was a good decision to keep my old house and not rent it out. I wasn't sure at the time, wondering whether I would find it too arduous having to maintain two properties. My plan had been to keep it to use whenever I felt like doing any shopping in York and fancied staying over. Better than any dated hotel or guest house. And now it transpires that it is Suzie's new home. Things have, at long last, worked out perfectly. I couldn't be happier. My heart beats a steady and excited rhythm as I step out of the car and slowly unlock the front door, the memory of Martyn back at the house by the river already slipping far from my mind.

A cool breeze greets me as I tentatively open the door and shuffle inside. A door is open somewhere inside. Or a window. I feel a pressure begin to build inside my head as I flick the light on and walk through the hallway and into the living room. I survey it carefully. No Suzie. The rug has moved and there is a dent on the sofa where she was laid but apart from that, nothing has altered. The kitchen, however, is a different matter. The cool breeze becomes a cold gust as I enter and look around at the state of the place. The window is wide open and on the floor, scattered far and wide are the remains of the tiebacks I used to keep her still. Drawers are open and a large bread knife sits on the floor next to the broken threads and fibres. Pieces of cotton. That's all that remains of her. My Suzie. I can't believe she is gone. I had her here with me, all to myself and now she is gone. Fear claws at me and I hear a small moan becoming louder and louder, shrill and demonic, before I realise it is coming from me. I tear at my arms until I feel blood start to ooze out and I sigh at the immense relief that accompanies it. But it's a temporary release and I have to claw some more to stop the build up or I fear I will go mad. I simply cannot believe she has left me. Another one gone, disappeared out of my life. Vanished without a thought as to how I feel or how I will cope without them. Blackness descends, shrouding me, pinning me down. I am finding it hard to breathe properly. I wrestle with the key in the back door and run outside.

I feel the air leaving my lungs as I am slammed

into the wall and hear the crunch of my right arm as it connects with brick. Pain explodes in my shoulder as she passes me, a slim grey shadow running off into the obscurity of the night. It takes a couple of seconds for my instincts to kick in but when they do, I am as swift as a hawk catching its prey. I bolt after her, watching her shadow as she stumbles and falls ahead of me, scrambling to get up. But I am faster, more able bodied than she is. Still drugged and lacking nourishment, she is weak and easy to catch. My fingers grasp at a chunk of her hair as I drag her back and cover her mouth with my free hand and press down hard. She claws at me but her fingers are still too sore and bloody to be of any real use.

Her feet slip about in the mud as I pull her over the back step and throw her to the floor. I have to think quickly. I have no tape or rope here to restrain her. But I'm stronger and uninjured. That must count for something. Without thinking, I squat over her and press my knees into her stomach. She retches and turns her head to one side to be sick but nothing comes.

'I really wish you would stop fighting me Suzie and see things as they really are.'

A strong breeze blows over my head. The window.

It's still open. And so is the door. I have to think quickly, to act quickly to make this place secure once more. With one swift movement, I bring my hand up to form a fist and bring it down hard onto the side of her face, not enough to cause any real damage but enough to inflict so much pain, she is rendered immobile.

While she is curled up in a tight little ball, moaning and crying, I jump up and lock the door, shoving the key deep in my pocket. It's as I step around her to lock the open window that I feel it. A sharp, pulsating pain in the side of my leg that stops me. I let out a squawk of shock and pain and look down to see something sticking out of my calf. It takes a couple of seconds for it to register. And then it hits me. The knife.

Ignoring the searing pain, I chase after Suzie as she drags herself upright and clambers up onto the kitchen top, her legs buckling under her. She is weak, wobbling about and losing her balance. I can do this. I can bring her back to where she belongs. I grab at her shirt and she starts to fall back on me. My ankle twists under the pressure and I let out a scream as an unbearable line of pain courses its way up my leg. She grasps the opportunity and worms her way free.

But not for long. With a surge of strength I didn't know I possessed, I am upon her again, my arm locked around her neck as we both clamber up onto the kitchen top and fall out of the open window onto the grass below. The pain in my leg is beyond anything I've ever experienced before but as I turn, I can see that Suzie looks in far worse shape than I am. She is completely still, her face down in the wet grass, hair splayed out around her. My breath catches in my chest, tight and unyielding and for one awful minute, I fear she may be dead.

My voice cracks as I lean in close, feeling the heat of her body next to mine. 'Suzie, wake up. Please wake up. I couldn't bear to lose you again!' I shake her gently and am horrified as she turns her head and without missing a beat, sinks her teeth into my arm. I start to scream but a sudden, hard pain to the side of my face stops me, knocking all the strength out of me as her fist connects with my cheekbone. Then she is on top of me, her bloodied, blackened face inches from mine, her eyes bulging in anger.

'Who the fuck are you? And who is Suzie?'

Saliva drips from her mouth and I'm horrified to see the hatred evident in her expression. The wound on her head is bleeding and her hair is once again matted and filthy. I try to speak but she blocks me, her words thick with such obvious loathing, it takes my breath away.

'You killed him, didn't you? Your husband. You're nothing but a fucking murderer. He's dead and it's your fault!'

The sentence cuts me in two. *All my fault*. How could she say such a thing? Martyn is the love of my life. Always will be. She inclines her lithe body even closer in, so close I can smell the blood on her hair, pungent and earthy.

'I'm getting up now, and I am leaving. Don't try to stop me because if you do, Phoebe, if you do, I swear to God I will kill you.'

The pain in my leg suddenly becomes excruciating, sharp lines of pain howling their way up and down my calf muscle. I glance down to see she is holding the knife, moving it about. Driving it further in. I watch, as with one quick, vicious flick of her wrist, she puts all her weight on the handle and pushes hard.

* * *

By the time I finish throwing up and am able to move, she is gone. A shadow disappearing into the gloom of the night. I call after her to return, to not leave me again, to stay with me. I tell her how sorry I am for everything I have put her through, for that day down by the river and beg for her to turn around but as I drag myself round to the back door and slink into a crumpled heap on the doorstep, I know I am doomed. It's over. She's gone and once more, I am left alone.

I have no idea how long I am there for. Hours, probably. No matter how hard I try, I can't seem to summon up the energy or inclination to move, even when I hear the heavy thud of footsteps as they thunder up the driveway and into the house. I stay there, perched on the cold stone of the doorstep as an army of police officers tear through my house, their muddy feet trampling over my polished floors, their harsh, cold voices filling the vacuum of silence behind me. I listen to their boorish behaviour, hear them barking orders and patiently await their approach. I know what comes next. I'm prepared. My arms drip with fresh blood after more scratching. It runs down my hands in snaking rivulets, a creeping lattice of oily scarlet liquid that drips down and covers my bony fingers. I take a deep breath and try to relax as the door behind is barged open and a hand is placed under my elbow. I let myself be manoeuvred about as I'm roughly wrenched to my feet and dragged away.

'I'm ready,' I say as a female officer leads me out of the house and into the back of a car. 'I've been ready for a long time now.'

38

'York?' Mike says incredulously. 'How in God's name did she get to York and why there of all places? It's an hour away. She had no car and no money with her. It doesn't make any sense.'

The police officer shakes his head, bewildered.

'We don't have the full details as yet but we will get them to you as soon as we do. All we know is that a female claiming to be Anna has been found in a street in York by a group of young women. She's been admitted to York District Hospital for injuries that aren't life threatening. She has a head injury and is dehydrated. I'm afraid I don't have any more information for you but as soon as I do, you'll be the first to know.'

His radio crackles into life and Mike feels his blood freeze in his veins. An update, perhaps? He needs to know more. The officer turns away and heads over to his superior where they flock into a corner whispering to one another and talking into radios. Mike pulls on his coat and shouts over to Toby and the boys, who are busy crying and hugging each other after hearing the news that Anna is alive.

'I'm heading off to York to see her. Anyone want to come?'

They stop, too stunned to speak. Callum breaks the silence first. 'Yeah! Course we do.' He turns to Mason, who is already pushing his arms into the sleeves of his jacket, a huge grin spreading across his face.

'We've received more information, if we can just have another few minutes of your time?' The officer is back from the brief meeting and eyes up Callum's coat. He sees the determined look in Mike's face and puts two and two together. 'Before you head off to the hospital.'

Mike nods and sits down, his backside balanced on the edge of the sofa, ready to leave as soon as this is over. He hopes this is important. More important than setting off to the hospital to see his wife. His patience is at an all-time low right now. So this had better be bloody good.

'We've just had word that the police in York have arrested somebody in connection with the disappearance of your wife and have taken them in for questioning.'

Mike feels himself shrink as the words are spoken. A cold finger of dread traces its way up and down his spine and he is overcome with a sense of queasiness. He didn't want to begin to wonder how she had made her way to York. Truth be told, he had convinced himself she had taken herself off there after having a mini breakdown. Stuffed a handful of cash in her pocket and taken a train or a bus or even hitchhiked her way there. But this piece of news changes all that. Mike grits his teeth and thinks about some hideous pervert running his hands over Anna's terrified body, his pulpy fingers tracing their way over the slim contours of his wife's tiny frame. He feels a rage build in his abdomen and brings his fists together, banging them rhythmically on his knees, tapping out the beat of his blood as it pulses round his system, thick and furious.

'Who? I want his name.' Mike stares over at the officer, daring him to refuse his request.

The collective sound of their breathing is all that can be heard as they await his reply.

'I'm sorry. All I can say is that she was taken in for

questioning shortly after Anna was found in the street. If I knew more than that, I would tell you.'

Mike blinks, his vision becoming blurred as he looks to Toby and to the boys then back to the policeman. 'I'm sorry? Who was taken in for questioning? You said, "she".'

'That's right.' The officer lets out a little cough and meets Mike's gaze. 'A woman in her late forties is currently being held in York Police station in connection with the abduction of your wife. I don't have a name as yet but when I do, you will be the first to hear about it.' The officer gives an uncharacteristic smile and stands up.

Toby stares at the officer, who pulls at his collar uncomfortably.

'A woman in her late forties?' Toby barks. 'Would this be the same woman who owns those newspaper clippings I gave you half an hour ago by any chance?'

Mike places a steady hand on Toby's shoulder. 'She's alive, Toby. Let's save the recriminations for later, eh?'

The young officer dips his head and slowly backs out of the room.

39

FOUR MONTHS LATER

The sound of the hammering sends an icy trail down her spine. Standing to one side, out of sight, Anna watches as the *For Sale* sign is erected in the garden, set amongst the rose bushes and dwarf conifers, a splash of colour protruding from the dark-green foliage. Such a welcome sight, that sign. A new chapter, a way of putting the last few months behind her.

'Don't, Anna.' Mike places a hand on her shoulder and tries to move her away. She shrugs him off and continues to stare out. He rubs her back and rolls his eyes. 'Okay, have it your way. But no complaining if you wake up tonight with nightmares.'

'Nonsense,' she whispers and stands on her tiptoes to watch as the estate agent squats on the side of the pavement to take a photograph of the exterior. She feels stronger now, able to deal with it. She refuses to give in to the demons. They're there all right. Always lurking, ready to pounce. But she's stronger than they are.

'I wonder how they will market it?' she says to nobody in particular. 'Will they admit to its past or just brush over it?' She thinks back to when pictures of the house were splashed across the front pages of every tabloid both here and abroad for God knows how many weeks, the ins and outs of the case dissected under the scrutiny of the public eye. Who would want to buy such a house now? She peeks further down into the village. At least the road is now free of reporters and journalists. Their behaviour sickened her, peering through the windows and hammering on their door day and night, wanting a story. Not the real story. Any story. And the more gruesome, the better. Any morsel of gossip that would feed the interest of the masses and sell papers. But the worst is over now. And once the house is sold, it will be an end to it. In theory, anyway.

'There'll be plenty of nosy buggers booking appointments to look round,' Mike says as he comes back in and hands Anna a cup of coffee.

'I'm not sure what they'll expect to find.' Anna

hooks her finger through the handle and stares at swirling froth.

'Whether you like it or not, people are fascinated by murderers and all the grisly details of their victims. Especially female killers. She's the new Rosemary West, according to Sky News. Now, are you going to come away from that window and let the poor estate agent get on with her job without feeling as if she's being spied on?'

Anna shrugs. 'She can't see me.' She continues to watch. She has a right to know what is going on after what she endured. It's cathartic. Her therapy. She was offered counselling but politely declined. Isn't that what families are for? To help each other through stuff like this? She thinks of Phoebe's family and shakes her head. She's been over it time and time again. Has spent too long trying to fathom the workings of that woman's mind and decided she would rather remain ignorant of the mind of a psychopath.

'Me and Toby spoke about this last week. We both think they should demolish it.' Callum slopes past carrying a plateful of sandwiches that threaten to topple at any given moment. His schoolbag is slung over his shoulder, crammed full of textbooks. Things have changed. For both boys. Reading magazines and watching programmes about high-powered, souped-up cars suddenly seems such a pointless way to spend their time. A geography book pokes out of the top of his bag. Anna leans over and surreptitiously pushes it back in place. They've both done a lot of growing up in a short space of time and realised that teachers are not their nemesis. Anna laughs into her coffee. Some good had to come out of this whole sorry mess.

'Apparently, those reporters practically camped on the doorstep of poor Nancy's family after her body was washed up further downstream.' Anna still thinks of her all the time and wishes she had known, wishes she had been able to see Nancy, catch her before she set off down the path and been able to warn her and tell her to turn around and go back home. They still haven't worked out why Phoebe killed her but are now re-opening a missing persons case: a lady who resembles Nancy. A friend of Phoebe's. No surprise there. Anna just can't work it all out and Phoebe isn't forthcoming with any reasons as according to the police, she is still in denial, claiming her husband did it. Anna blinks hard and swallows back the tears. They are there most days now, always present, always ready to spill out with very little provocation. Sometimes deranged killers don't need a reason to kill perfect strangers. That's what makes them deranged.

'Well, I'm with Callum on that one.' Mason is behind her, staring out at the new sign sticking up over the hedge. 'Reckon they should burn the fucker. Raze it to the ground.'

She should correct him, tell him to curb his language, but things have changed in their house just recently. People have altered, their family dynamics transformed and morphed beyond recognition. And she can only think that that is a good thing. Shortly after her release from hospital, Anna considered moving house. It was a short-lived desire but a strong one. She no longer knew herself. But after a while, she began to realise that this is her home. Phoebe was an intruder, a brief interlude in her idyllic life and now she is gone. This is where Anna belongs, in her home next to the river. She lets her gaze wander over to the water, so still now after the heavy rains, so deceptively calm and tranquil. She hasn't walked the river path since it happened. But she will. She refuses to be defeated by it, to be ground down by her ordeal. A cormorant hops its way along the edge of the water before opening its long, black wings and taking off into the haze of the hot, summer sky.

'Tom said he doesn't care how much it sells for.

He just wants rid,' Mason says as he mirrors his mother's stance and stares out at the river. 'He never got on with his mother anyway. She didn't want him to move to New York. Said she never forgave him not becoming a doctor like his dad.'

'And when did he tell you all this?' Anna raises her eyebrows and surveys him carefully. His skin is clearing up and his jaw and neck have thickened. He has had a growth spurt and it shows.

'When he brought the flowers round for but you but you didn't want to see him, remember?'

She nods, feeling her face burn. It was churlish of her to do that but she just couldn't bring herself to look at him. He was a connection to Phoebe and anything to do with her made Anna's skin crawl. Still does. So instead, she went out for a walk. Not by the river but to the shop. Just to prove to herself that she could. And she did. It wasn't half as daunting as she had expected it to be. In fact, it was rather liberating, knowing she would be safe, knowing that her attacker is safely incarcerated many hundreds of miles away in a psychiatric unit awaiting trial. If there ever is one. Rumour has it she isn't fit to stand trial and may just remain there for the rest of her born days. That suits Anna just fine. Court dates and appearances would only whip up more public interest and that's something she can well do without.

Dark clouds the colour of gunmetal scud across the sky, heading east, ominous and heavy, ready to spill their innards. How easily the weather can change. So volatile. So unpredictable. And she should know.

40

Nothing has changed. My life has come full circle. Once again, I'm alone and as always, nobody believes anything I say. I stare up at the ceiling and count the cracks. There's not a lot else to do around here. So I count. Grooves on the floor, cracks in the ceiling, bars on the windows.

They have accused me of some hideous crimes, these people, tried to tell me I murdered my own husband. Ridiculous, I told them. How can I possibly have murdered him when he is still alive? One of them laughed when I said this and the others sat with stern expressions, scribbling away taking notes then looking up to scrutinise my every move. They think I'm mad, you see. Disturbed, psychopathic, call it what you will. They think I am a murderer. Check the house, I told them. You will find him there, in his study reading a newspaper or sitting in his usual position, arms resting behind his head as he stares out of the window watching everything and everyone go by, unable to join in with any of it. A passive onlooker in a mad, mad world.

I have seen a number of doctors while I've been in here. They want to work out what is going on inside my head. How can you work it out when I don't fully understand it myself? I told them just the other day. They don't like it when I come out with that one. They accuse me of being obtuse, trying to hinder their investigation. There is no investigation, I told them. They have accused me of all kinds of atrocities. Kidnapping, assault, a whole host of lies. Apparently, I attacked a woman called Anna and held her captive. I keep telling them I don't know anyone called Anna. Instead, I tell them about Suzie, how we were meant to be together, how her hair twirls lightly in the breeze, how beautiful she is and about how much I have missed her. God, how I have missed her. And to think I had her back and then let her go. I was so close. So close. Such stupidity and carelessness on my part to lose her. Not like me at all.

They tell me they are looking into a number of

other unsolved cases and have given me names to see if I remember them. I shake my head as they ask me about a lady called Nancy who went missing while walking by the river at the back of my house. I tell them they should ask Martyn about that one and listen when they sigh loudly and scratch their pens over their writing pads while they take more notes. They tell me to think back to when Debra went missing and ask where I was when she disappeared. I reply that I can barely remember where I was last week, let alone two years ago. More sighs and head shaking along with cautious, furtive glances to see if I am being deliberately inept or whether or not I am truly mad.

Sometimes, they leave me alone and I am allowed to wander outside with one of the doctors. They are generally kind but I get the feeling they think I'm wasting their time. Just yesterday, I talked to one of them about the day I found my mother. He seemed very interested in that and suggested we talk about it some more when we got back inside. It fuelled his interest further when I mentioned Dr Tavel. There are occasions when I get it right and I think yesterday was perhaps one of those times.

It's fairly comfortable in here and everyone is friendly. I keep thinking I can see Suzie or can hear her voice. Often, I catch the tinkling of her laughter as it floats in on the breeze, or spot the hue of her hair as it glints like liquid gold in the rays of the early-morning sun. And then she disappears, leaving me alone once again.

They have talked about transferring me to a more secure place. I realise I don't have any say over where I am going but have mentioned to them about my love of being near the water. At night, when my mind is free of the clutter they fill it with, I dream of tidal surges and dark currents and swirling eddies and wonder if I will ever get to see the river again. To not see it will be hell on earth. Like living in a cold vacuum and I'm not sure I can handle that.

I find myself wondering how Martyn is managing without me, whether or not he is remembering to take his medication properly and whether he is missing me. That day on the cliff still haunts me: the look of horror on his face as he tumbled downwards, the sound his head made as it hit the boulders below but mainly whether or not it was my fault. He had been having an affair with Debra and I had been furious with him. It wasn't a push, more of an attempt to get him away from me. But that's not how they see it in here. They keep telling me that every action causes a reaction and every action has consequences.

But as I keep telling them, it doesn't count because Martyn isn't dead. He is as alive as you or I. They exchange surreptitious glances when I say this and scribble away with motorised arms, trying to recall everything I say, asking me to backtrack, to repeat and reiterate until I am blue in the face.

There are a few things that worry me. Firstly, I think about Tillie and how she is doing. They have assured me she is happy and is with new owners who are taking good care of her. I don't know how they can be so sure of that but don't want to probe for fear of what I might hear. I just want her to be loved and happy. That's all I ask. Then there is the business of my houses. What will become of them? It's not the money. I have no interest in that kind of thing. That sort of behaviour is for the nouveau riche. But who will look after them? Martyn is in no fit state to maintain a house. He can barely look after himself, let alone a couple of huge, rambling properties.

The final thing that I am worried about – and it does depress me deeply – is the fact that Tom hasn't visited or called me or written. No communication at all. They have spoken to him, you see, and warped his mind. I have no doubts about that. Told him I murdered his father, and for that he can't forgive me. I am now a *persona non grata* as far as my only child is concerned. They have spoken to me about him, making out as if they know him better than I do. The person I brought into the world, the boy I taught to read, the young man I taught to drive. My son. As if they know him better than I do. They reckon he has told the police that I have suffered from mental illness for most of my life. Such nonsense. They said he told them lots of things. All about my life after losing Suzie and my parents, about my life in foster care, about my teaching career. They read all this out to me and wanted to know why I hadn't been taking my medication regularly. I explained over and over that the tablets weren't even mine, that they belong to Martyn but they argued otherwise, saying I had become unstable and dangerous because of it. I laughed long and hard at that comment. Me, dangerous? I sigh and think back to that day down by the river, how I had inadvertently pushed Suzie deeper under the water, accidentally trapped her long, golden hair around my freezing fingers when all I wanted to do was help her. That was all it was. I was just trying to help.

I stare up at the bars on the windows that keep me captive and laugh until I cry. I rub at my nose and wipe my eyes with the back of my sleeve then shake my head until it hurts. Dangerous indeed. For goodness sake. They don't know the half of it.

ACKNOWLEDGMENTS

Although *The Girl in the Water* is one of my later releases with Boldwood Books, in 2017 under the title of *Undercurrent*, this was my first novel and after years of wanting to be a writer, it became my first ever published book, entering the Top 100 within days of release. So with that in mind, I would like to thank my current publishers, Boldwood Books for taking it on and republishing it, and also my previous publisher for giving me a chance after years of submitting to publishers and agents everywhere and receiving a pile of rejection letters that weighed as much as your average house. The book, although initially successful, quickly disappeared and languished at the bottom of the rankings for many years, forgotten and unloved until Boldwood Books breathed life into it with a new title and cover.

Huge thanks to Amanda and her team at Boldwood who work tirelessly to give my books the very best chance of being noticed and read. Thank you to

Emily Ruston, my wonderful editor and to Jenna Houston for her wonderful marketing techniques. Also, thank you to Ben for his timely delivery of paperbacks and his assistance with the audio copies of my books.

Thanks as always, to my family and friends for their continual support and to you, the reader for choosing my book over the millions of others that are out there.

In 2013, my husband and I moved to our current home, a house that backs onto a public walkway and a river. It was totally different to anywhere I had ever lived before and it was this house that gave me the inspiration for this story, so I would like to show some gratitude to my once rundown, but thankfully now pretty bungalow for being the thing that helped kickstart my career as a writer. Well done, Harmony. We got there in the end.

ABOUT THE AUTHOR

J.A. Baker is a successful writer of numerous psychological thrillers. Born and brought up in Middlesbrough, she still lives in the North East, which inspires the settings for her books.

Sign up to J.A. Baker's mailing list here for news, competitions and updates on future books.

Follow J.A. Baker on social media:

f facebook.com/thewriterjude

t twitter.com/thewriterjude

O instagram.com/jabakerauthor

d tiktok.com/@jabaker41

BB bookbub.com/authors/JABaker

ALSO BY J.A. BAKER

Local Girl Missing

The Last Wife

The Woman at Number 19

The Other Mother

The Toxic Friend

The Retreat

The Woman in the Woods

The Stranger

The Intruder

The Girl In The Water The

Quiet One

THE *Murder* LIST

THE MURDER LIST IS A NEWSLETTER
DEDICATED TO ALL THINGS CRIME AND
THRILLER FICTION!

SIGN UP TO MAKE SURE YOU'RE ON OUR
HIT LIST FOR GRIPPING PAGE-TURNERS
AND HEARTSTOPPING READS.

SIGN UP TO OUR NEWSLETTER

BIT.LY/THEMURDERLISTNEWS

Boldwood

Boldwood Books is an award-winning fiction publishing company seeking out the best stories from around the world.

Find out more at www.boldwoodbooks.com

Join our reader community for brilliant books, competitions and offers!

Follow us
@BoldwoodBooks
@TheBoldBookClub

Sign up to our weekly deals newsletter

https://bit.ly/BoldwoodBNewsletter

www.ingramcontent.com/pod-product-compliance
Lightning Source LLC
Chambersburg PA
CBHW010658100726
47900CB00010B/2711